VAGABONDS!

VAGABONDS!

ELOGHOSA OSUNDE

4th ESTATE • *London*

4th Estate
An imprint of HarperCollins*Publishers*
1 London Bridge Street
London SE1 9GF

www.4thestate.co.uk

HarperCollins*Publishers*
1st Floor, Watermarque Building, Ringsend Road
Dublin 4, Ireland

First published in Great Britain in 2022 by 4th Estate
First published in the United States by Riverhead Books,
an imprint of Penguin Random House LLC in 2022

1

Grateful acknowledgment is made for permission to reprint the following:
Selection from "Call," from *Too Much Midnight*. Copyright © 2020 by Krista Franklin.
Published by Haymarket Books. Used with permission.

Book design by Meighan Cavanaugh

A catalogue record for this book is
available from the British Library

ISBN 978-0-00-849801-6 (hardback)
ISBN 978-0-00-849802-3 (trade paperback)

There are *simple* and *good* and *straightforward*
and *well-behaved* people, I'm sure.

But this is not a book about them.

If you find your imagination
cannot stop itself from churning out
the scripts of the Death Machines,
pull its plug. Dismantle it. Reprogram it.
Dream Daylight. Manufacture Daylight.
We are the Magicians.
Make Magic.

KRISTA FRANKLIN

● ● ●

All paradises, all utopias are designed by who is not there,
by the people who are not allowed in.

TONI MORRISON

● ● ●

Definitions belong to the definers, not the defined.

What I think the political correctness debate is really about is the
power to be able to define. The definers want the power to name.
And the defined are now taking that power away from them.

TONI MORRISON

VAGABONDS!

1. Vagabond (n)

Definition:
A person who wanders from place to place without a home

Synonyms: itinerant, wanderer, nomad, wayfarer, traveler, gypsy, rover, vagrant, drifter, transient, migrant, beachcomber, person of no fixed address/abode, knight of the road, bird of passage, rolling stone;

In other words: an outsider, an unbelonger, many.

2. Vagabond (adj)

Definition:
Having no settled home

Synonyms: itinerant, wandering, nomadic, traveling, ambulatory, mobile, on the move, journeying, roving, vagrant, transient, floating, migrant, migratory, refugee, displaced, homeless, rootless, drifting, unsettled, footloose;

In other words: in the city but not of it; i.e., unforgettably unloved by it. In other words: a giant, dumbfounding bulk of the country. In other words: not always by choice.

3. Vagabond (n)

Definition [Nigerian]:
In the states of Bauchi, Gombe, Jigawa, Kaduna, Kano, Katsina, Kebbi, Sokoto, Yobe, and Zamfara, "any male person who dresses or is attired in the fashion of a woman in a public place or who practices sodomy as a means of livelihood or as a profession" is a vagabond.

In the states of Kano and Katsina, "any female person who dresses or is attired in the fashion of a man in a public place" is a vagabond.

In the states of Bauchi, Gombe, Jigawa, Kaduna, Kano, Katsina, Kebbi, Sokoto, Yobe, and Zamfara, an "incorrigible vagabond" is "any person who after being convicted as a vagabond commits any of the offenses which will render him liable to be convicted as such again."

Synonyms: [redacted], [redacted], fucking [redacted], [redacted], bloody [redacted] [redacted].

In other words: hunted. In other words: wanted. In other words: kept secret. In other words: invisible, hypervisible, threat, trouble.

There are punishments for this.

People also search for:

Gross Indecency (n)

Definition [Nigerian]:
. . . a person commits an act of gross indecency by "exposure of nakedness in public and other related acts of a similar nature capable of corrupting public morals."

. . . a person commits an act of gross indecency by way of "kissing in public, exposure of nakedness in public, and other related acts of a similar nature in order to corrupt public morals."

. . . a person commits an act of gross indecency by "committing any sexual offence against the normal or usual standards of behavior."

In other words: common. In other words: everyday. In other words: unseen on purpose, for a purpose. In other words: rot at the root, rot in the head, rot in the highest places.

An added note: "[Some states] do not define gross indecency. Their laws instead say: 'Whoever commits an act of gross indecency upon the person of another or by the use of force or threat compels a person to join with him in the commission of such an act shall be punished.'"

In other words: should be taken seriously. In other words:

should be disincentive.

In fine print: sometimes forgivable.*

* Depending on . . .
and especially if the perpetrator is/has . . .
Or the victim is/has . . .

. . .

. . .

[*So sorry. Pardon the glitch so early in the story. It's getting harder to read; this part of the law is written in invisible ink.*]

A WELCOME NOTE
FROM THE CITY

There is an eye following you and you know. Everywhere you go, e dey look you. The eye is made up of people. The eye does not blink, talk less of sleep. The eye is us, curious. The eye is a city; this eye na Lagos. Èkó. This eye is a gossip, a hypocrite. An eye is naturally unfillable, yes. But this is an overpopulated, opinionated, twenty-one-million-bodied eye. A famished eye. This is an eye full of lies, full of mouths, full of secrets, full of death. And dem no dey take us play, because we plenty inside this eye. So na amebo we be. Busy body. Eye service. Na our spirit be dat. Who wan challenge us? You don see us? Na who born dem?

So, who dey look you? (Na we.)
Who is judging you? (Everyone. Us.)
Who know you pass you? (Na we.)
Who will ask for more even if you give us what we want?
    (Everyone. Us.)
Who go build your safe house? (Ask us again!)

Who will save your child-heart? (Can't you see where
    you are?)
Who knows your real face?
Who can jam the door and make our eye cry? (JAMB
    question!)
Who fit turn and return our eye? (Na you. Na only you.)

(Are you with me?)

So, if you catch us looking at you, if you're lucky enough to see our
eye on your body, if you gauge cutlass swinging in somebody's hand,
tire on another person's shoulder, fire on another one's wood, you better turn your back. Don't look back, don't pass go. Turn your back.
Have mercy on yourself, straighten your steps. Turn your back. Because if you dey wait for us to turn our own back and start to go, then
my dear, na the weight of our eye go surely kill you.

TATAFO

(GENESIS)

—·‹ ● ›·—

Not one person, living or dead, has ever seen Èkó's face. Neither has any single person heard Èkó's voice, because Èkó does not talk to people. (Which masquerade do you know that does?)

So, in the beginning, there was Èkó. Èkó looked around its own sprawling body—where concrete meets lagoons and beaches and bridges and great great noise—and saw that it was good.

"Let there be lives!" Èkó said, and immediately, there were lives.

But also, Èkó could foresee what was coming; the cityspirit knew that if it were to make its children in its own troubled likeness, spitting out flesh-skinned denizens born with masks fastened to their faces, then they, like Èkó, would be troublesome. (Do you know how much you can get away with with a mask on?) Any force worth its weight needs eyes at its front, eyes at its back, eyes in its sides, eyes for a heart, eyes darting in the streets. To stay on top of all things, one must foresee them first. Èkó knew that it would need more than itself to forestall the wahala its children would bring. So, Èkó created and recruited all of us: monitoring spirits, if you like. Ears to do its hearing, heads to do fast thinking, mouthpieces to deliver any message (blessing or punishment, warning or praise), and eyes everywhere to do its watching—of which I am one.

Èkó was right to make us, of course; the city needs all the hands it can get, with how wildly it spins out of control. So we do what we can to help the many-eyed god, the master and minister of excessive enjoyment; the roiling mass of flesh seated on a gold-plated throne made from the trained backs of its children, agbada pouring down in threaded gold, hallowed by thousands of hands.

Èkó has always known what is best for us. So when the city assigned us to our people, based on our personalities, our weaknesses, how much suffering each life could hold and how much each of us could withstand—we took our assignments as praise and accepted them, no questions asked. But I was Èkó's favorite; Èkó was my egbon, my mentor, the one who taught me everything, and I was his aburo, his Little, the right-hand angel after Èkó's heart.

Èkó teased me sometimes for my efficiency—how good I was at gathering facts, at seeing, at executing orders—and that sweet appreciation of my swiftness is where my name was born. One day, he looked at me through one of his eyes after I had completed an assignment with more thoroughness than he had expected of me, and his translator, his speaker, one of his mouths said, "Tatafo! You no go kill person." Tatafo. Blabbermouth. Minder of all business. Gossip. He said the word, my name, in a teasing voice, but I could hear Èkó's pleasure ringing there, sweet dip into warm low.

I can mumu ehn, so me I said, "Ahhh Baba wash me again," and the mouth repeated it, over and over, until I quivered to the floor, cackling with glee.

"How many times did I call you?" the mouth asked, endearment packed into its question like teeth. But I'd lost count of all things. The city had taken my lust for praise and used it to tickle me down to the soul.

Of all Èkó's messengers and host of spirits, I was the youngest but also the most talented; my talent shone like twenty-one million suns. It's true that me I don't know how to mind my own business, but is that not why he made me? Is that not why they hired me? Is that not why you have these stories in the first place? I still carry that name with me now.

What you need to know is this: my name was not a mistake. Whatever Èkó sent me to do, I did. He knew I would do anything for him. And from the moment I was chosen to the moment I was released, I did not answer to another name. My job was one thing, and that thing was to obey; so in those days, there was nowhere in this life that Èkó could have sent me that me I'd say I wouldn't go.

And my god, did I go dark places.

THOMAS

**"Blessed are they that have not seen
and yet have believed."**

—JESUS, IN JOHN 20:29

There's a story Nigerians know and pass on with the conviction reserved for Holy Communion bread. *Here, a slice of our history: we don't lose unless something happens; unless there's foul play. Here: an extra source to cite when defending our collective arrogance.* It's the story of that football match where Nigeria played against India and India scored 99 goals against Nigeria's 1. Most Nigerians remember this match, whether they were born at the time or not; know the story like they know God—with a fervent, fastidious faith. No need to question it, or search for it, or relive it. It's a story that happens to you once and then lives with you forever.

Throughout the full ninety minutes of the match, Nigeria's players did their best, as Nigerians do; sprightly on their feet and quick to react, just as their coach had taught them. But something kept happening: Every time one of the players went near the ball, it morphed into something else. Some say it was a lion that came roaring into the air, all hungry-mouthed and thirsty-eyed; some say it was a snake uncoiling itself from the dead leather; others say it was both inter-changeably. The rest claim that the match was only confusing because the ball kept on doubling, or tripling, and Nigeria's goalkeeper found it impossible to know which one to focus on. The latter was what Thomas's uncle claimed.

"That day? Ha! The whole Nigeria went haywire! The country was vibrating with shock. A whole us? Lose to India? *India?* One of our players even died. I forget his name now. One Samuel, abi Simon something, dropped dead on the field from a heart attack. People had so much anger in them that they poured into the streets and started to fight each other. Strangers who'd never met before in their lives o, lunging at each other, trying to draw blood. But in the end, many people made friends that day."

Thomas could see the streets as his Uncle Anjos spoke, people grappling mercilessly, butting heads like rams, like they had nothing to lose: women on the sidelines picking fights with each other, chil-dren following suit. None of it was done with malice, or direction-lessly. It was for a purpose. Everybody outside was trying to prove the same thing to themselves and everyone else: *We're a strong and talented people; it's not that we were not ready*, they insisted, *it's just that India used juju to confuse our players. They would never have won if they didn't use juju. If one of us beats the other here, we can show each other we're still strong.* They fought to exhaustion, then hugged and shook hands before heading off together, asking: "So what was that your name again?" Some joked about it: "My name is Yusuf. But guy, you beat the hell out of me wallahi," and got placating replies: "Sorry, my brother, you know we did what we had to do." And they did.

After that match, India was banned from playing international football. It's hard to know the year, but it's a fact. It really happened. Everybody saw it. After all, what's the alternative: That an entire coun-try had a choreographed hallucination? A nationwide delusion?

Exactly.

Thomas knew animal stories too. He knew that tortoises had cracked shells as punishment for their unrepentant greed, from when they were dropped from heaven on their backs by a tired God. For all their haste, God had decided to delay them as a lesson. Hyenas sounded the way they did because they were found gossiping among themselves during a meeting in heaven which ended with God turning to them and saying in a bitter voice: *Oh, you want to laugh? You will keep laughing forever.* To Thomas, all this was believable because he had read Genesis, which made it clear how God felt about disobedience. A moment in time could lead to punishments forever. God seemed to love forevers.

But the stories Thomas loved the most were the ones about humans; stories that could still be happening right right now in the world as his uncle spoke. Still just a young teenager in secondary school, there was little else to do, so apart from serving God, Thomas had made it his life's purpose to stack stories, to hunt and squash the fear that came with them.

Every evening, his uncle told him tales by moonlight. A genius with four degrees under his belt, Uncle Anjos wore his belt tightly. Thomas enjoyed horror because it added speed to his breathing and a sheen to his heart. Sometimes he dissolved into the words as Uncle Anjos was talking, fading off in the middle of a sentence, going somewhere new on the wing of a detail with his mouth ajar.

Like Thomas, when Anjos was a boy, he studied old stories from before the country earned its name, from way before the land was taken and way way way before it had to be wrested out of white hands. He filled notebooks with true and frightening realities he'd gathered from his grandparents. His peers couldn't bear them; there had been enough bloodshed, enough loss, too much grief behind, the promise of freedom in front and they were only trying to be young in peace. Anjos, they decided, was the delusional one. He was the one imagining things. And this was what frightened his family about him: *What do you mean*

you want to dig the past? Why are you trying to trouble the ground? If we get
to know what happened then, how will we survive what did or didn't happen
after? Whose child is this? Take this Bible and eat it.

As with Thomas now, the rumor back then was that Anjos had
turned out this way because he took books too seriously, too literally.
They weren't even saying this to be cruel o. They were only worried
for him, because the family tree seemed to grow toward a warning:
madness was wet soil and many people, once they'd stumbled on it,
couldn't help hurtling to the end of a too-dark valley. If Thomas's
parents were around enough to talk a lot, he would have been warned
to take everything his uncle said with a hill of salt, warned about how
some resemblances should be left alone. But even without their talking, Thomas heard them clearly through the parallels and proverbs
they shared in letters; through the roundabouts in their speech. He
knew exactly what they were talking around, but still he loved Uncle
Anjos thickly, specifically because he'd managed to protect his child-
likeness in a way most adults could not, and he wasn't afraid to show
how brightly his eyes could shine with belief, new faiths brewing behind them. Listening to him, Thomas could feel both the danger and
the promise of the world in full, and it thrilled him to the bone.

Uncle Anjos told Thomas about a time when mobile phones had
just come out and jazz caught up with technology. People were warned
not to take phone calls from unknown numbers, but the stubborn
ones did. And you know what happened? Exactly what they had been
warned about. It didn't happen now anymore, but it used to. It really
really used to. People who answered those calls heard something—
godknowswhat; a crackling sound? A threat? An incantation?—that
made their bodies go haywire, bleeding through the ears and nose and
eyes until they died. This story was told to Thomas when he was ten.

After he turned eleven and got his first phone—a Nokia 3310—
a call came in one day from an unknown number. His heart was

pounding in his bladder when he pressed answer. But it was just his
father calling from somewhere in America, where he'd been working
for years.

"How are you, my boy? You're okay?"

"Yes, sir."

"Good. Give the phone to your uncle."

Regular. Boring. Disappointing.

But that rush? That rush from doing something that could have
killed him if he'd just been unfortunate that day? It never left him.
He tried it with chain messages, too, when he started receiving those.
"If you don't forward this in the next ten minutes, you will die within
seven days," the messages read, complete with the full names of people
who'd fallen down in front of their families, foaming at the mouth.
Thomas watched the ten minutes go by, rebellion hissing up his spine.
On the seventh day, he ran laps around the house, rode his bicycle,
and ate vegetable soup with snails and periwinkles—all of this in a
hedonistic chase, a few last hits of joy before reaping a ripe death. He
knew, he always had, that life was about timing and death was always
lurking and all of life was hide-and-seek. Why not enjoy the game?

But it was not yet his time, so night came with its darkblack fur,
and after all those hours of Thomas trying to keep awake, it rolled
over on its back like an excited dog to show Thomas the dawn on its
stomach, the sun at its center, a bright and brilliant navel.

There was another story, too, about not letting people touch your
head because you don't know what spirit they're carrying. "Don't share
your hairbrush with anybody because they can use that to steal your
star."

"What star?" Thomas asked.

Uncle Anjos struggled to explain it. "Your destiny," he said finally.
"You're a boy with a bright future. It's one of the first things people
notice about you. You have a star on you, and sometimes, people can

see that before you do. And they can steal it. They don't give this kind
of advice to just anybody. Many are heading nowhere fast. But you?
You, my boy, the road ahead of you is covered in gold."

Thomas blushed under his skin, pleasure perching on his smile.
"But . . . how do they steal it? And why? What do they use it for?"

"Why? Because the heart of man is desperately wicked. Even the
Bible says so. And what do they use it for? If they can apply your destiny to themselves, their lives can change course. What should have
been your future then becomes theirs—and you will suddenly find
yourself on their own dull road."

Thomas had friends whose hairbrushes he sometimes borrowed at
school to keep the waves rolling in his hair. It was important for all
the cool boys to have, because the girls always checked for them. His
star—whatever that meant—still seemed to be there, what with all
the As he was still getting in most subjects. The only exception was
introtech, but he doubted that that was because someone had stolen
his ability through his hair and stored it in a calabash somewhere. It
was just because he and technology simply didn't agree with each
other. So, even if all these stories were true—and he did believe
them—by some odd magic, he seemed to be cosmically protected
from their dangers.

• • •

What turned Uncle Anjos into who he was? Thomas wanted to know.

Well. Anjos used to have an aunt. His family still lived in Benin
then, and he believed that all the stories his father was telling him
were just stories, because he had the privilege of a strong bubble, and
just enough distance. Like his nephew, Anjos had found the stories
thrilling to hear; but unlike Thomas, had felt that it was only uncivi-
lized people who stretched that fascination into faith by *truly* believing things they could not see, gods who revealed themselves out of

people's mouths, who demanded sacrifices and called for libations to be poured into the ground.

In Benin those days, there was a notorious whirlwind called Eziza. People believed that the gods sent Eziza as an ambassador of their anger. Little Anjos was gifted a story about this whirlwind through an encounter with a rainmaker. Right there in his grandfather's house, he'd watched the man start and stop a furious downpour—complete with streaks of thunder—in the space of ten minutes. When he waved his handkerchief and let out a string of Bini prayers and incantations, the rain immediately ceased. Anjos, seeing this was no coincidence, asked him to do it again. "I don't abuse my power," the man had said in a coiled voice. "I did it for you, because with the life you have ahead, you're going to need faith. You're going to need to root your eyes in places other people can't see." Anjos didn't understand what the man meant then, but he took note of what he felt in his own body, of how witnessing that miracle had put weight in his feet, had scrambled his gut.

When Eziza came, the man explained, it arrived in full force, seizing whole human beings in its body. People could be sitting down in a beer parlor casually drinking and the whirlwind would swoop in suddenly to collect a single person from their midst. The gods were very sure of what they were looking for whenever they sent Eziza, the rainmaker told Anjos, but in the process of trying to find those things and those people, they didn't hesitate to clear anything or anyone that stood in their way. They seemed to be calmer now, though, he said. His theory was that they had probably grown tired of fighting to retain their worshippers, and had resigned themselves to letting people face the Christ they were hellbent on choosing. As Anjos listened to all this, with his elbow in his grandfather's lap, he wondered what factors determined the strength of gods' tempers. He'd heard a theory once that gods lose power if you stop believing in them. It seemed possible.

Anjos's mother knew that story too. When he went home and told her about it, she confirmed it with a shrug. She didn't need a rain-maker to convince her; she already believed. She had lost an old class-mate to Eziza back in the day, so none of this was new. (She wasn't there o. But must she be there to know?) So she pulled her ear as she told Anjos, "Stay away from Eziza, if you like your life; just stay away. If you see strong breeze, run enter house. You hear me?" Little Anjos had questions, but his mother had long decided for him that he would keep liking his life, and that no spirit would come out of nowhere to claim him.

One Saturday, Anjos was in Ring Road market with his cousin Sam. They were looking for cardboard for their school project when a small child looked up and said, *See oh, see*, pointing at the sky. They looked, and true true, somebody was trapped up there inside the wail-ing wind like a small, weightless kite. *Nonsense*, little Anjos thought, *nonsense*, even though he could see it. But people were exclaiming as they deserted the market quick quick, so he followed them, running with his hand in Sam's. Later, when they got back home, his rascal of a neighbor, a ten-year-old boy called Bingo, told him what had hap-pened. He said that Iye Ruth was sitting down in her backyard, wash-ing clothes under the big ebelebo tree, when Eziza encircled her body and took her into a dizzying lightness.

"Which Iye Ruth?" Anjos had asked, still dazed.

"How many do you know?" Bingo asked, a chewing stick dangling out of his mouth.

Anjos never saw his aunt again. That was the invisible putting its hand on him, digging its hand into his shoulder, making a mark on his bones.

So, *what is the difference between truth and myth? Who gets to determine it? Does a lack of faith in something make it unreal? How do unreal things happen? Why do they have witnesses? Is it a parallel world that leaks into ours from time to time, or does one real overlap with others?* Anjos was full of questions then, just as Thomas was now.

You're not the only one who has lost someone, his family used to say. *Do you know what people will say if they hear how she went? Your aunty died, that's it. Just tell them she died.* They showed him Ecclesiastes 1:18: *In much wisdom is much grief; and he that increaseth knowledge increaseth also sorrow with it.* But it was too late. Inside him, Uncle Anjos had grown a compulsion as crucial as a breastbone. No one could break it without breaking him. Uncle Anjos dedicated his life and intelligence to asking these questions and relayracing with other academics toward ever-shifting answers. And this race consumed so much of his strength and mind that he had only a little space left to keep a lasting love.

* * *

For Christmas, Thomas bought Uncle Anjos a harmonica, because as much as his uncle loved playing his old one, its age was starting to show on its body. "Is that so," his uncle said, trying to hide his joy.

"Yes," Thomas said.

"Okay then," his uncle asked, "what would Thomas like in return?"

Instead of the new clothes and new gadgets his friends were asking for, Thomas asked for more stories. He knew they were expensive. They didn't cost money, but they cost a great deal in memory and time, and no one should have to give those without consideration. He knew that his request might be more costly than any harmonica he could have found, even one made of pure gold. Uncle looked at him long and hard. Was this him enabling the boy? Was this him ruining his nephew's life by exposing him to such things? He was already growing an addict glint in his eyes.

"Any story you know, Uncle," Thomas begged. "The scariest ones. But real life." This curiosity was one of the reasons Uncle Anjos agreed to take care of Thomas, to raise him as he would his own son. It was why he'd been saving acres and acres of real estate in his heart for his nephew since before the boy could talk. He was no seer, but he knew even then that the boy was hungry for more than a regular life. And he knew that hunger could mean real trouble.

"Fine," Uncle Anjos said finally. "I'll tell you three."

While Thomas clipped Uncle Anjos's toenails for him, Uncle told Thomas about rainmakers—living people who could hold and start rain by muttering incantations. They held that power in their bodies every waking moment. It didn't matter what the forecast for that day said; if rainmakers came together to say there would be no rain in a certain area that day, there would be none. Did Thomas know this? Thomas rolled the information around in his brain. "No," he said. How was it possible for human beings to reverse God's hand? Wasn't God the only one in charge of weather?

"Who knows," Uncle said. "But it happens. I've seen it with my two eyes. My grandfather was one of them."

Uncle admitted that he wasn't sure if the second story he was going to tell was true, because he'd never seen it, but he'd heard that in Benin, for a new Oba to come into power, he had to eat the old king's heart—so that, whatever the old Oba had not been able to achieve in his lifetime, the new one would have the heart to execute.

Thomas gasped. "His real heart? A human being's heart?"

"Yes. Spiritual things work differently. Like I said, I cannot confirm this one. But this part I'm about to tell you now, I'm sure of. Come, sit down." Thomas sat on the bench next to Uncle and listened as his voice swung low and his eyes went far. "When they are selecting a new Oba, people don't stay out late in Benin. Six p.m. and everybody is at home, because nobody knows who they will choose."

"Choose for what?"

"You see, when the Oba passes, because of all the spiritual authority he carries, even in the dead body, he cannot go to the spirit realm unaccompanied. So, people get taken to, you know, *follow* him."

"Follow him—to the grave?"

"Yes. They are taken from the streets and buried with the Oba."

"What? Why should they kill innocent people?"

"Kill? They're just buried."

"Alive?"

Uncle nodded. These were stories Thomas couldn't test, but he knew they were true from the way the air tightened around them. He imagined those bodies being lowered six feet into the ground with a dead king, terrified men screaming and begging, eyes open as they were baptized in sand. "Some people go like that. You'll hear they went to market and you'll just not see them again. It has happened to many. Anywhere you go in Benin, ask in a low voice into the right ear, and people will tell you."

The story turned Thomas's stomach into sky, twisted *feardelightsad* prickling and darting around like shooting stars. What world was this?

· · ·

Years later, when Thomas was moving to Lagos to study, he had a hard time parting from his uncle. He held onto Anjos, crying on his shoulder as his uncle told him, "It's okay, it's okay." Thomas swore up and down that he would come back. He'd never had to live without Uncle, and honestly, he didn't know how to process a city his uncle's body wasn't breathing in. But he was a man now, a real adult, and UNILAG was calling. He could always come back. He could.

"Be careful when you go," Uncle said. "You're going to a city that eats people. Carry yourself like somebody who knows something. Like somebody who understands. The eyes at your back of your head, eh, keep them open."

Because of this, Thomas was careful not to be in a rush to make friends. He walked with a certain caution, like he understood that he was sharing this world, and that, at any given time, another reality could override his own. It wasn't a matter of whether it was happening or not; it was more about whether you were willing to see it. And, he was still the boy his uncle raised—ever curious, ever believing—so no bad thing had seen him.

But one evening, Thomas met a group of men at a bar arguing about that India-Nigeria match over sixteen bottles of Gulder. Was it 99–0 or 99–1 or 100–0 or 100–1? Was it a lion or snake or was the ball tripling? Their voices deepened; one man stood up and threatened to break a bottle on another's head. It occurred to Thomas for the first time to Google the story behind the game.

The first link that came up was for a BBC story, where Nigerians were stopped in the streets and interviewed about this same match, all giving conflicting accounts. Thomas immediately burst out laughing as he felt a black box of doubt opening in him. It expanded like gathering steam, spreading to touch all the other stories that had made him this person who calculated his every step in advance. The destiny-thieves, the people buried alive, the whirlwind—were any of those things true at all? He didn't know anymore.

"Please, one Heineken," he said to the waiter, feeling too stupid to scroll any further through the Google results. A weakness wrapped around his waist like two loving arms. He was sure that even this, his newly acquired iPhone, was judging him, that Siri was rolling her eyes in her head. But this was Lagos, right? As his parting gift, Uncle *had* told him stories about Lagos.

"Around festive periods in Lagos," said Uncle Anjos, "reports of missing body parts are at an all-time high. People must trade something in to get the money they need to put food on their families' tables, after all. And so we know to avoid the markets during these periods, especially Christmas. Especially night markets. They have them in Benin too. It's not hard: all the person needs to really do is brush past you and your . . . you know, your private part, will be gone."

Thomas tried to imagine the flat quiet that kind of theft would cause. What would his body be without his penis dangling there, saying *I'm here, I'm here* all the time? Really thinking about it, he wasn't sure he'd mind much, to be honest, since the presence of the thing sometimes confused him in the first place. But he had friends who loved theirs, who bragged about them every other breath. He could see how that type of loss could end some.

"And before you ask, yes, of course you can run through the crowd trying to find the person," his uncle continued. "But, I mean, how easy is it to find lost breasts or a lost penis in someone's bag or in their pocket? If they were sharp enough to steal your part, you think they won't become invisible before you can blink twice? You think they won't wear the face of a child or an elder with an untroubled conscience, the kind of innocent look that makes it impossible to question them?" He shrugged. "Some people don't notice at all until they get home, because not everybody stays inside their body when they're walking. Others don't want to believe it; they tell themselves it's all in their heads. You know, we Nigerians, there's nothing we like more than denial. And I guess the rest keep walking, because it's better to lose one part than lose the whole body."

Come to think of it, when he was growing up, Thomas had been watching NTA with his uncle one night when they'd seen a story about a thief who'd been caught trying to shoplift because the jazz he used didn't catch. Just as he was trying to escape, the people nearby gathered around him and started calling out *thief thief thief.* On TV, there was a black bar covering his eyes as he apologized, his mouth a basin of blood. But the man was grateful, because it really could have gone like this: all of a sudden, tire; all of a sudden, fire; all of a sudden, burning; and then voices rising into the air like ash. But the man confessed and surrendered the charm that had helped him. They beat shege out of him, because scapegoat. *It was the devil*, the man kept yelling. *It was the devil.* Thomas remembered watching as they beat him, eyes glued to the television, and thinking even as he flinched:

This is more entertaining than Papa Ajasco. *More than* Super Story. *More than Telemundo.*

* * *

Because doubt arrives like a cool breeze, Thomas went to the market on Christmas Eve, specifically to roam. He'd decided he was going to see Uncle closer to New Year's. Thomas would have called his uncle to spew out his angry thoughts to him directly if it weren't for his home training, but instead he just thought to himself: *It's a lie, everything Uncle told me is a lie.* And it felt like a small victory for him, this new ability to unlock himself from Uncle's faith and author his own unbelief.

But he couldn't stop thinking about those stories. They followed him everywhere, adding weight to his shadow and dragging him down. Still, they couldn't be real. None of these things made sense. How could someone's body part get stolen? And if it was so possible, why was it not happening in other countries? How could a destiny be swapped or overridden? How could people just disappear?

Exactly.

At the market, the air was tight with joy. Live chickens flapped around in a woman's left hand as her right hand held her baby; a bag of rice on someone's head as they breezed by on the back of an okada; towers of tinned tomatoes; a woman's ring glistening on a hill of garri; a man smoking a cigarette with one hand on his hip; two men gossiping in fake designer clothes; people beating down prices. ("Madam abeg now. Reduce your price for Jesus. You never watch *Passion of Christ*? Na Christmas time be dis o. Hour of grace.") Everybody was facing their life. He couldn't imagine any of them having the time.

Thomas roamed around the market with his phone in hand, his body on him and him inside it. He was waiting for someone to do something dramatic—steal his phone, steal his penis—but nothing happened. He was testing something, daring whatever force was in charge of misfortunes: If someone stole his part, then he'd believe the stories. All of them. But for now? Everything was nonsense to him. Nigerians and their theatrics. Same people who would later claim that snakes ate eight million naira. Or that witches sometimes turn into birds. Or that one baby was born in a white nylon bag, and another with a rosary around their neck. On the pavement, Thomas saw a tattered one-hundred-naira note and decided to pick it up. Would he turn into yam? Because that was a story too. But he put it in his pocket and his body remained itself.

Already, Thomas could feel his love for Uncle turning into a ghost. He was about to turn around and leave when he realized that— wait!—he was already in the market, and in thirty minutes the sun would be done setting, so he might as well test out the story Uncle told him about nights. Uncle Anjos had told him that markets don't just exist one way at night. There is the market you see—right side up—but underneath it there is another world. That's why, even if you drop something in the market, you must always look straight ahead of you—never between your legs—when you bend to pick it up. You should not try to look behind you with your face upside down. People lived whole lives without ever trying it, because they'd heard of those who got sucked out of this realm, never to be found again. Uncle Anjos had told Thomas, with tears in his eyes, about one man he used to love who got lost in that exact way. But now all of it felt questionable. When the dark started to settle, Thomas bent in half from his waist, his legs spread wide apart, palms wrapped around their respective ankles, head upside down. Then he opened his eyes and looked.

· · ·

Now, when Jesus came into the Upper Room, his disciple Thomas did not believe it was him, so he put his finger in the holes in Jesus's hands and sides. To hear and see were not enough for his stubborn spirit; he needed to touch, he needed to feel the assurance of death. A name leads the head, you know? So, noting the way he came into the world—all eager to cry, already suspicious about food and water, rejecting his mother's breast—they should have known better than to name this boy that trap.

In between his legs, Thomas saw people scurrying toward him. Blood rushed to his head and everything in his line of sight turned gray. He saw bodies fading, skeletons walking on their palms, hawkers headstanding, hawking food with their feet. Two men strolling idly. Two women in a looped one-second hug. His vision began to spin until it looked like a hurricane inhaling. Before he could blink twice, a furious gust of wind grabbed him by the head and pulled him inside with the force of a godhand.

Well.

You must know what happens when a vortex gets hungry like that, no?

Aw baby! Somebody should have taught you.

[Last Seen: 12/24/201X]

TATAFO

(DEMOCRAZY!)

What did we not do in this Lagos, in Money's name? We arrested innocent citizens, we gave petty thieves to jungle justice in the streets—ended their lives with fire because they stole chickens, goats, common ten thousand naira. We slammed people's heads against iron and teargassed their faces because they upset one police officer or soldier. We called it the wage of disrespect. War against indiscipline. The ones we didn't kill on the streets, we threw behind high maximum-security walls and sentenced them without clause.

The truth is, we needed them there. There were prisoners in there for this reason: to replace those with greater crimes. We needed the ones whose families didn't have the hands or mouth to return our hand. We knew that even if they were to try to find justice, they'd be discouraged by their position in the queue, so far back that it'd take them years to touch the hem of the law's garment. It's not every day that a rich person gets arrested in Lagos. When it happens, it's because the noise around their crime has gotten too tall. So we do it, put them behind bars sometimes, but it's really to shut the protesters up. All that one is for show. Have the right phone number, and what is a little embezzlement? A little looting? A little murder case? Serial killings?

Anything in this country is one phone call away from being settled. We can sweep anything under the rug if you just pay the right person the right amount. So the ones who are arrested are out in no time. We let them walk out into the sun with flesh-colored face and body masks; we make them change their names and promise never to be seen in public again. If the criminal is lucky—and a lot of them are—he'll still have enough money to have a new face sculpted, a new life drafted, to build a tiny country for himself on some stolen land. Because, as for our Excepts, our VIPs, our Vagabonds In Power? We'll give up our lives, we'll bite hot bullets with our ribcages to protect them. We accept bribes with our chests, we auction our pity without flinching, we hawk our consciences in broad daylight. Here, morality has never been the issue. Every city demands its own sacrifices.

Èkó doesn't demand goodness, you see; it never has. What it does demand is luxury, beauty, boastful excesses, loud colors—as long as you keep your mask on in public. Kill a person if you want and sweep up the body, tucking it sweet and flat under gravel; fuck your brother if you want; eat a forbidden fruit and choke on it—just not in public. You'll ruin the aesthetics. And everybody who knows, knows that that's what drives the cityspirit mad. There's nothing Èkó loves more than packaging. And nothing he hates more than jagajaga movement.

* * *

Èkó is competitive. Ruthlessly so. I was there when he almost threw the whole city on its head because hawkers were hawking in the streets and women were setting up stalls on the sides of the roads and okada riders were doing their job. *I just want to know,* he said, crossing his eyes in rage, *does this happen in Miami? Are there beggars on the road just touching people's brand-new Range Rovers and Rolls-Royces? Does this happen in Dubai? New York? Do you see people on the roads selling mirrors and mattresses and gala and groceries on their heads in the sun? The cityspirits that manage to keep their rot off the streets, do they have two heads?*

Well, I said. *We don't have the same blood or history or family tree as the places you just mentioned. But your family has what your family has. Miami and New York have a different bloodline. America is not Nigeria. Our own is different.*

He didn't find that funny. *They may be my blood, but none of the others can say they're my mate! Even they know it. Never compare me. I make Nigeria what it is!* With the way Èkó looked down on the rest, I often wondered if he hated them, but who born me to ask that kind of question? It was left to me to transcribe the new rule to the others: *We've already warned those people. If you find them still selling, scatter their wares and do with them as you like. You have Èkó's permission to make them disappear.*

We went for it. And I'll say this now: more people than can be counted suffered for this.

People are still being searched for because of it.

• • •

We mobilized units like SARS, the Special Anti-Robbery Squad, and KAI, Kick Against Indiscipline. We arrested people, asked them to remain silent until they reached the station. We told them, pointing to our records: *From today, your name is this.* If they tried to say no, if they tried to fight or argue too much, we knocked off their knee-caps, sliced their thighs, or put a boiling ring where they didn't expect it. Soon enough, we didn't need to tell them to shut up anymore. They told themselves. When we had them where we needed them, we skinned both criminal and scapegoat and then swapped their faces. We were thorough. We had skinmakers on the ground for when we needed extra. It was so that just in case anybody had the audacity to come and check our records to see if a certain person was still there, we would have a body to show. We'd say: *This is him, the scapegoat we caught, look at the wounds on his body, look at him quarter-to-dying, yes, he is suffering well*—and we'd go back to our days and they'd go back with their news, because you can trust people not to look past faces.

"We will free you," our favorite police officer would always say, tribal marks fanning out of the side of his mouth like mad rays, "but you have to promise to die first." Criminals love a good deal, so of course they said yes. What was a common face when they didn't have to serve time? It worked out well for everybody anyway. What other way was there to extinguish people with no money? That was the only true crime in the end.

Having nothing, in a place where others had more than everything, was blasphemy against Èkó's spirit, an accusatory finger pointing. So we let the *good* sinners out into the streets, forgetting and forgiving, but always at a price. It was religious, this concept: if you repent and humble yourself, your old life could pass away and you—your life, your body, your self—could become new. Depending on where you were looking from, criminals could be sinners, policemen could be God.

Some days, we would go to communities of people making what they could of their lives from the crumbs and grains Èkó offered them once every four years—we'd go to their homes, where they were raising their children, and uproot them from the ground, flinging them on to the main road like stray blades of grass. We'd pack them and take them wailing to our master. Èkó, hating their ugliness, would swish them around in his mouth before spitting them out. They'd wake up in other cities not knowing how they got there. But that part was their own business.

We would be prettier for it.

• • •

Nobody is better at anything than us—not even corruption. We're the best, and you know it. Talk true, you sef know. Here, we don't see people unless they're big, and to get big you need to eat money, breathe money, piss money, shit money. We see opportunity. We see the megacity; Èkó's vision. When you're enrolled as one of Èkó's core workers, you don't see anything but the promise of the city transforming. You can see it becoming a point of envy, somewhere to call your own, a place to be proud of, that you can beat your chest and say you contributed to building. You see it and that's why you carry your machete and go to the intended site when the city says go. What to do with all this mess you find there? All the families and their petty trading lives? You clear them like the disturbances you've been told they are. And then you build something fancy on top of their wails. All of this for beauty's sake, because you've been told that beauty matters. Beauty matters more than life. And you believe it, of course. You believe it.

Every day, we had a new person to update, a new chip to install, a new zombie to make. Bad things happened to children, too, that I saw, but I don't need to show you that. You have eyes of your own. And besides, their collective rage has written its own justice, a holy book from a fair future that's on its way already. Since I can't go back and change anything, all I can do is point you truthward. I can only try my best to be open.

• • •

Why didn't I leave, abi? Why did I go that far, shey? Because I believed Èkó. I believed his manifesto. And I knew more than anything that he didn't belong to himself. Everybody must call somebody sir, that is life; even the person you look up to answers to somebody. Even your boss has a boss. Powerful as it is, Èkó has its god, Èkó has its government, Èkó knows who it must obey, who it must answer to. Here, the only one above the city, the only one that matters, is money—kudi, cash, Owo—because money makes beauty possible. Owo is the jagaban, the old soldier, the agbalagba. If Èkó is a spirit, Owo is a legion, a battalion, a pantheon. Infinite, uncountable notes, spraying from seven heavens like rain. When Owo calls for Èkó, the city goes, and when it reaches there, it prostrates. Èkó knows that Owo's children are in the city, but not of it. They can't be roughhandled the way other citizens can, because they're made of butter and you know how easy butter is to injure. To touch Money's anointed is to touch Owo in the eye, and that spells big trouble, kasala, insurmountable gbege.

Money answers all things. And money is the root of all evil. Both things are true. Laws exist, yes, but laws are for the poor. Laws are for the masses. Laws are for those who answer only to the city. Laws are for those who don't have master keys. Know this: for every law made, there are always people who are under it and people who are above it. At a certain point, the city no longer has absolute power; can no longer fight for you. That point is where Èkó's children reach a certain level of wealth, when they serve two gods with equal devotion. Anything is possible then. And because nothing in this life is free, especially freedom, some will be able to afford it, many will not. Some will let this go. But there are those who will gladly pay through their teeth, or don't mind paying with all thirty-two of yours.

Owo insists on similar things—like appearances; like performance; like pretense.

Once, when Owo called a meeting, I followed Èkó there to his house. Èkó entered on his head, with his spiritstance. As soon as we appeared, Owo stoned Èkó with a vault.

"I'm not your mate in that realm!" he bellowed. What he said in

Yoruba can be translated as, "Don't you ever come to me that way. You don't go to visit the king with a crown on your own head."

Èkó apologized immediately and shapeshifted again. I'd never seen him that humble before, that plain, that unadorned. That day, everything unchaosed. Èkó lay down flat in his resplendent agbada, his head bowed in respect, until Owo allowed him stand up. Owo cleared his throat before he spoke. His voice was thick with requests, with small and big needs.

"Let my people go," he said, finally, stretching his hand forward with a scroll in it.

The next day, Èkó released a flock of pastors and politicians and VIPs from jail—ears still spilling with cries, hands still caked with fresh blood—and replaced them with doubles who'd serve their time. All this to say, I've seen times when Èkó made a law and Owo revoked or rewrote it. I've seen money make fools out of people. I've seen it take their heads. I pitied Èkó because I understand this. Worshippers find it hard to remember, but even gods have an Almighty. Èkó wasn't up against his mate.

Believe me, the cityspirit tries to be good when it can. Sometimes, it deliberately misses great opportunities for cruelty. On a good day, it gives people things to rejoice over just so it can watch them dance. It hooks friends up on the streets. It gifts lovers to lonely hearts. It spits up new dance floors on random street corners. It does these good things too, let me be clear. But more than wanting to be good, Èkó wants to be seen, to be revered, to be worshipped, to be peerless. He needs to be called beautiful, needs to feel secure. This is his thinking: Let them call us the poverty capital of the world if they want. How can that harm us if, when they visit us, they can see no proof of that? What does it matter if we can show them the best parts of my body, our ostentatious real estate, our new Link Bridge? What does it matter if we host their favorite megalomaniacs? What does it matter if we're the greatest dancers? If they still export our music? If we can still find oil in our soil? How can it matter, when we know that they try and try and try in their private rooms to replicate our spirit, that they secretly want to be us?

Forget what you know. It doesn't matter what's underneath, Èkó used to say. *What matters is what it looks like. Appearance over truth. Perception over actuality. Do what it takes to keep your master's mask on. That's your job: to show them we can wear invisibility better than ghosts themselves. We can make the problems disappear. We're the magicians the world's been waiting for.*

Yes sah, I'd say, because na me efficient pass. *Yes sah,* because me I'm Tatafo, first of my name. *Yes sah yes sah,* to keep being loved.

I don't know you like that, but ask yourself: If it were you, and you had the chance I had, wouldn't you have done the same?

JOHNNY JUST COME

The things Johnny used his eyes to see in Lagos ehn, his mouth could not say out loud. Literally. Before he arrived in Lagos from the Raffia City, by GIGM night bus, his cousin Clement—the one he finally swallowed his pride and asked to connect him to real wealth in Lagos—had told him this: "This job you are going for, they reserve it for mute people. You go get money well well, you go fit take care of your whole family with zero qualms. But once your leg touch Lagos, forget your voice o."

"Which kain job be dat?" Johnny asked.

"Driver."

Johnny chuckled. He could drive well, sure. But, "Ah ah, wetin concyn driver with silence again? How will I now reply if they give me instruction?"

"You see? You're already talking too much." Clement hissed. "You're not ready." It gave him great pleasure to flaunt the out-of-reachness of his bright city life every time he visited home. He felt a twisted knot of pleasure at the bottom of his stomach each time someone's eyes softened with pleas. He liked knowing that people wanted what he had, that they would wear his life quickly if he took it off and offered it to them. And why not? Who doesn't like good things?

Fine, Johnny said back with his own eyes.

The first thing Clement had given up when he left Uyo years ago was his name. He'd left Uyo as Enieffiong—his given name—and returned as Clement. Nobody at home questioned him because he re-turned as a new man with arrogant cologne that could lift you by your collar and pin you to the wall. What he didn't bother explaining was that this was simply the sensible thing to do, because which filthy-rich boss had more than two seconds to be pronouncing your difficult name in a fast city like Lagos? Everything in Lagos moves at stagger-ing speed, and the first thing to know about the rich is this: they hate stress. Clement had learned this from his friend Alamieyeseigha, whose boss had said, "Your name is what?" when he introduced himself, and then rechristened him on the spot before Alamieyeseigha could even say Allah. "From now on, you answer to James. Do you understand?" Of course, he did. This was the first lesson Clement gave his cousin too: "Nobody has time to be calling you Aniekan, un'sten? I think you should be answering John. Well, John for short, or as the oyinbos like to say it: *Johnny*. It fits you."

"Okay," Johnny had said. That night, alone in his room, he tried the name on over and over again. It didn't feel too tight. "Not An-iekan anymore, do you hear me? Johnny. Johnny. Johnny." He was eager to learn, especially from someone like Clement, who seemed to have mastered the ways of the city.

So, "Explain na," Johnny said, half-begging Clement the next day. "About the job."

Again, that sweet knot. "Well," Clement said. "To work in Lagos, you have to give up something. Everybody does—even the high and mighty. Some give up their language, some their names, some their sanity, some their conscience, some their ears, their eyes, and so forth. Me, for instance, in my place of work, I don't speak all this pidgin. I speak only the Queen's English. If they find out I use broken at home, they can fire me for that alone, because the man doesn't want his children to be speaking nonsense. And my boss is not as strict as some." He paused for effect.

"Now," he continued, "this job I'm talking about for you, I say you will be *rolling* in money, get that right. You go get pass anybody wey you know. But even if they curse you, curse your family, curse your whole generation, no make mistake open mouth o. Anything wey you see, you no go fit talk. Because na kill dem go kill you once. Dem go just put bullet for your body, and you go close eye."

Johnny's heart hiccupped. Ha. A whole kill? Who was he going to be driving? The president? The thought jarred him, but he replaced that fear with a bright curiosity to keep Clement's irritation at bay. "So I go need deaf too?"

Clement shook his head. "Okay, so if you're also deaf, how will you hear instructions? Ehn, young man. Ezacly. Think! They need you to hear, but they don't need your reply."

"Ahhh," Johnny said. "Okay, I get now. Is that the one you're doing, too, in Lagos?"

Clement laughed. "I resemble person wey mute? They offered me that job, but me I say I no do. I don't have the liver for that sor' of a thing." Johnny had never craved a different accent than the one he had, but when Clement spoke, rolling his tongue over syllables the way he did, Johnny sometimes found himself eager to train his tongue too— though it was unclear what exactly the accent was.

"No be driver work? Wetin concyn driver with liver?"

"If your mouth dey sharp like that, go try am now?"

Johnny sighed. "But bros, hook me up to the one wey you dey do now? Since na that one better pass. Me I don't know if I can give up my voice."

Clement chuckled. In all his years working in Lagos, Clement had never said what his actual work was. But every two Christmases when

he visited home, he arrived in a new car with a trunk full of months'
worth of provisions for his parents, so nobody bothered to ask him, in
case he read it as an insult. Because what would they do then? What
if he stopped coming home out of vex?

Johnny knew this too. But now that they were having a frank conversation, Johnny wanted to make his envy clear, and he knew that it
flattered Clement to see it shining out of his voice like a new kobo.

"If to say I fit," Clement said, "I for don hook you up since. You
know you're my brother. But I ken' lie to you, there's no vacancy there.
And besides, the kind of work I do, you can't, you *cannot*, do it."

Johnny knew better than to push. Clement was older than him by
five whole years and it was by God's grace that he chose him out of all
the other cousins to sit next to. When Johnny asked him, Clement said
he chose him as his right hand because he wasn't like the rest—"you're
cool-headed," he said—and it was the first time Johnny felt proud of
his temperament. Johnny thought hard about it and decided that he'd
take what was on offer. He could make a good driver. What was there
to it? He could drive and drive well. And he loved cars—but the good
kinds, not the yeye V-boot he'd been towing around for years. He loved
feeling the cool of the air conditioning on his face whenever Clement
let him drive his Toyota, both of them keeping their eyes straight
ahead, ignoring people trekking by in the next lane. On rough days, he
made sure he made eye contact with them. It felt good to be comfortable, simple, and he wanted people to know.

When Johnny first moved to Uyo from the Raffia City, he was still
shiny-eyed. But Lagos could run circles around Uyo. Everything was
better in Lagos. If all he had to do was obey, he already knew enough
about that. Growing up, his father had done the necessary work of eating his rebellion with koboko and canes and belt buckles. There was
not even a single crumb of resistance remaining in him. If it was his
younger brother now, ehehn, he'd hesitate to send him, because by the
time that one was born, all the violence in their father's hands had

fallen to a quivering hush—and it showed. You could provoke that boy just by breathing next to him; he had anger that could boil yam. He'd make a terrible employee. But Johnny wasn't like that. He was different.

Johnny was the kind of person life would have rewarded well by now if things were fair. But life was not fair—which is why, even with his first-class degree in physics, Johnny ended up a lesson teacher earning forty thousand naira per month for teaching spoiled children science on their parents' Italian dining tables; tables that were worth enough to pay his rent for six years. He was over it. He'd done everything right. He'd waited on God—what again? Sure, Uyo was cleaner and saner and quieter than Lagos, but who sane and quiet and clean help, when there was no money to match it?

• • •

When Johnny arrived Lagos at 6:02 a.m., he off-loaded his single suitcase from the bus and signed his thanks to the driver who'd offered him some plantain chips on the way. By then, his tongue was already heavy and flat. After close to a month practicing—moving around without using his words, nodding instead of talking, shrugging instead of answering—he'd forgotten the sound of his own voice and didn't miss it as much as he thought he would. To be fair, at first he *did* feel himself edging toward madness. But it happens. When you stop talking suddenly, the first few days, the words try to find somewhere to go; when they can't, they dart between bones, echoing around, gbim gbim gbim. You hear everything and you're not able to filter it. It takes some getting used to, but everything eventually falls quiet.

Because of all this, the first thing Johnny noticed when he arrived in the city was the jarring volume—horns and voices and curses and catcalls and buildings and children and dogs and hawkers and chants and speakers and fabrics and music and preachers and billboards and posters—the tallness of all that sound. When an okada sped by him and splashed muddy water on the new black jeans he'd bought from a happening kiosk called Flayvours, he spread his fingers wide. *Waka. E no go better for you.* Had this been his old life, he'd have been able to yell that curse aloud, but he reminded himself that he'd done the hard inside work of replacing that old frustration with the kind of hope the okada man couldn't even imagine. He could see a future in front of himself, his eye speeding down a great horizon into the promise of a rich life. He needed new composure for that, as Clement told him: "Rich people don't do gra gra, they move slow, with intention, because they're confident that the world will wait for them." In only a few weeks, what had started as a seed of patience had already become a small tree inside him. Soon, he assured himself, it would be an entire tangled forest, powerful enough to swallow grievances both small and large. It was only a matter of time.

"Within the first hour of landing, somebody will come and meet you at the park," Clement said. "Before you get there, clear your thoughts, so that the only thing on your mind is what you're there for. The people who come for you will come from behind, blindfold you and take you to the house where you'll be working. Don't be afraid; it's all part of it. They're not kidnappers. Well, not really. It's for security reasons, so that if the person you're to work for doesn't like you and decides not to hire you, you won't know road to their house." This made sense to Johnny. "But make sure they like you," Clement added, a soft warning spiking between words. "You didn't leave your home behind to come and hear *no*."

The next thing Johnny thought was that people who enjoy Lagos must have mute buttons installed in their ears. Eye filters too. They couldn't possibly be taking in the city as he had when he first arrived, unless they really wanted to, unless they deliberately turned the sound on or slipped their lenses out. Lagos was not pleasant to hear or see, except from behind tinted car windows (from where anything could happen), dark sunglasses, headphones, even armed men with guns—

real buffers in real places to protect them from the raw insanity. There was clean wealth here, obviously, as with any other country. But there was also filthy richness, as with any other country. That must also count for something.

*   *   *

"Swear that the tongue in your mouth does not move, whether your oga is there or not," a huge voice said when Johnny arrived at the house. Kneeling on what felt like interlocking stones, he couldn't see a thing, but the voice carried the weight of a life handled roughly. Johnny knew, just from him saying one sentence, that a man like that knew exactly where in the body to put a bullet to achieve excellent results. If not for Clement, Johnny would have said, *I swear to God who made me I can't talk*, and immediately gotten thrown out of the city and sent back home to his old life. But despite the fear, he remembered Clement's warnings, and touched his index finger to his tongue before raising it to the sky. "Good," the voice said. "Because we have ears everywhere and no be joke be dat. Even if you move your tongue in your bedroom, we will hear you." Johnny nodded quickly. The man continued. "Even when you leave this place, our ears will follow you. And if you're found wanting then, well . . ." Johnny showed his understanding, then he heard whispers and the blindfold came off.

When Johnny thought of the man he was going to work for in Lagos, he had imagined a man around forty-five, with a distended belly, who wore his wealth around his waist in love handles. But Mr. H was a thin man in his sixties who wore Ralph Lauren and Lacoste and Tom Ford with shorts or trousers and went everywhere in simple sandals with understated designer logos. "Welcome," he said calmly.

The big man stood aside, chest like a vault, and he winked a glass eye.

In the two years Johnny would work for Mr. H, he never once heard him shout. Mr. H didn't believe in that. He delegated his anger to Samson, his MOPOL, the big man with the big voice and the scar that mapped his cheek toward his ear. Samson was Mr. H's unrighteous right hand, stretching out to touch his offenders, meting out orders at the speed of light because he just didn't have time to waste.

Mr. H was a dealer, a harvester, though this was not what it said on the business cards he kept by the dozen in his trouser pocket. He'd long outgrown the Lagos Big Man uniform, the strictly ironed and starched trad with a Montblanc pen in the breast pocket and a car key in his hand. Now his business card read simply *businessman*, but that was just a modest way to put it. Mr. H didn't run a business; he ran a beastly conglomerate with four of his brothers. For decades, he'd headed this untouchable monopoly, selling spare human parts to private hospitals for people who needed them urgently, at black market rate. Beyond that, he had two other target audiences: For conscience sake, he anonymously sponsored a number of poor Nigerians who couldn't afford their medical bills, securing necessary organs for them in record time. But he made the most cash from providing organs at a premium for registered Nigerian criminals hiding in Èkó's underarms, who had to do medical procedures at home because they were not to be seen elsewhere.

Before Mr. H became himself, he had lost his mother in a hospital due to Nigeria being Nigeria. A doctor had operated on her using a torchlight because there was no light, and she had died because there was no blood. He was still a teenager then, but that day mattered in the way the end of the world tends to. All the motivation in his life came from that fury, from the anger he felt toward the country's unrelenting negligence. He decided there and then to do what he could to reduce the number of hospital deaths. If he made some extra cash along the way, there was no harm in that. So, he had one underground network for sourcing individuals who wanted to donate their organs, another for sourcing fresh cadavers as they hit the ground all around the city, and a third for making sure the bodies were available in the first place.

Johnny looked around the house in awe. The size alone was staggering, before he saw the infinity pool at the back of the house. The matte black cars, all lined up in two garages: Rolls-Royce Phantom. Bentley. Range Rover Sport. Range Rover Evoque. Land Rover Classic. Hummer. G-Wagon. Maserati. Ford. Porsche. For his work to go smoothly, he explained, he needed a trusted driver to take him around, but also to do the required transporting. In exchange, he was offering a starting salary of four hundred thousand naira. Johnny's mates were making thirty to ninety thousand. "I'm an easy man," Mr. H said. "You do what I tell you to do and before you know it, you'll be settled for life. People who work in banks don't even earn as much as you." Johnny could see his future gleaming.

Inside the nine-bedroom house, there were fourteen Filipino women working on rotation, chosen and dressed to look like photocopies of one another: tiny women, none over five feet in height, all with small feet, all wearing the same uniform, hair packed up in neat ponytails. Johnny watched them scurry about the house, carrying towels and oils in bowls. Later he would learn their routines: Appearing out of nowhere with bleach for the toilets, cloths to catch and remove dust just as it was landing, offering massages to Mr. H's guests. One of them was hired just to kill mosquitoes. One to stand all day looking pretty, welcoming visitors. Another to buy fresh flowers daily. Another to pour the wine.

Johnny learned all this not because he ever entered the house but because Oga's twin daughters talked about the house all the time, like even they'd never get used to it—and he took them everywhere. Because of them, Johnny had used his mind to enter their indoor cinema; he'd enjoyed an imaginary massage in their spa, he'd eaten fresh fish on the kitchen's island. They let his imagination enter the concert hall when they hired the biggest Afrobeats musicians to perform for them, because why go to an overpacked Eko Hotel when they could bring the concert home? They had a room lined with pure gold, where Mr. H hosted his VVVIP guests; an all-black darkroom for when Mrs. H needed to turn the world off. It was from their mouths Johnny heard all this. When they talked in the car, it was as if they forgot altogether that someone else was there. The cars could be self-driving, for all they cared; he was just a fixture in front.

Once, Johnny picked the girls up from a nightclub at 3:00 a.m. There was silence at the back of the car, and Johnny saw one of them shine her phone light over the other one's hands as she rolled a blunt. Then the car filled with smoke.

"Ays, you," the more disrespectful one said, "turn up the music." Johnny did as he was told, without asking or turning. From under the music, the other twin started talking in her high-pitched voice. "Look, there's normal weed, which *regular* people smoke. Then there's loud. Then there's *deafening*!" And then they'd both collapsed into a heap of laughter at the dead joke. "I told you. This guy's shit is insane. My head is getting loOoOose."

Johnny was responsible for picking up drugs for them. They'd never met their dealer (and why would they need to?). They'd call the number in the car, giggling to each other, and a man would say out of the speaker, "Yes. You may send your driver. Baba will see him." Then the twins would say, "Johnny, you heard him," and so he'd drive them to the pickup place—a house that was only ever there at night and completely disappeared in daylight. The protocol for pickup was the same every time: the gateman squinted at Johnny, asked him to open the trunk, used a bomb detector to scan the car before letting him drive in.

Their drug dealer was a man everybody called Baba. A man with vision, he had his head in the future. He was driving a Tesla in Lagos when it was still an idea forming in Elon Musk's head. The car updated itself with every new draft without Baba having to move a muscle. Whichever drug dealer one knew in Lagos—even the ones who get offended when asked for weed, because they *only sell white products*—he's their daddy. In fact, he's their daddy's father. In Baba's house, the instruction was clear: you're not allowed to look at his face or you'll drop down and die. If he needed to adjust his neck in your direction, the wise thing to do was to bow your head or prostrate at once.

That night, as usual, Johnny picked up four bags of dark green and took it to the girls. It was curiosity that made him steal what was left of their blunt after they got out of the car. He made a mental note to smoke it at home. Let's put it this way: He misplaced his eyes and mind that whole next day. Rookie mistake. He wasn't carrying the secrets those girls had—secrets that build the stomach and tolerance required—so of course he buckled under the influence. If he knew half the things the girls had to hide under their upbeat personas, he, too, would only be able to function by leaning on drugs from a higher realm, drugs that could bend his eyes all the way in.

* * *

Johnny was driving the girls one evening when a childhood friend asked how their mum was these days. "A lot better than in her first life," one said. "A lot happier." And then they laughed: *Haha! Hahaha! Haha! Yeah, dark, I know.* Johnny didn't know what that meant at first, but with time the pieces fell into place.

Mr. H's wife had been a subject of widespread scorn: "Barren woman," they used to say about her. "Witch! Stone!" But then, in the year he turned forty-five, she died, and two months later he remarried. There were whispers about this until his mistress-turned-wife gave him what people thought he had always deserved—children, and two at that. That was the public story.

What had happened with his wife, it turned out, was part of a ploy to deflect attention from what Mr. H was really doing. What was more scandalous to womb-watching Nigerians than a barren wife? Not much. Except, when the rumors started about Mr. H's sexuality veering off in suspicious directions, they had to make another story. To prove you love women, introduce a mistress. And how to do that without actually dealing with another woman? Easy. End this life and start another. In the months after Madam stopped making public appearances, before her death was announced, her new face and new body were being sculpted by expat doctors flown in from all over the world. People went under the knife so often in Lagos, acquiring new asses, flat stomachs, new breasts. How was this different? For Mr. H, it was a no-brainer. Home to him was always Madam, and it would continue to be for the rest of their lives. She was his nearest and dearest friend; she knew his life under their marriage, she knew about his men and he knew about her women. But Lagosians didn't need to know about any of that. She could lose a face and body for him, easy. For her, none of it mattered as long as she still got to be herself inside.

The body they made for her was an oppressive hourglass made in a doll's image, and her new skin was butter-smooth. It took some getting used to, but the death story was an efficient mask that turned hungry eyes away. Everything was a front; a surrogate had been hired to make the twins real.

When Johnny found all of this out, first he wondered where they stowed that woman, what they paid her, where she was. Then he wished he was still in a position to gossip. All he wanted was to be able to call someone—his brother, or even Clement—and say, *See wetin my eye see o!*

Fine, he thought. *The wealthy have their own restaurants, their own spas, their own clubs, their own beaches, their own hospitals, sure.* But this one? This one was beyond him.

Before Johnny started working for his boss, he'd heard of Clifford

Oji, of Evans the kidnapper, of the cult of men who ate human flesh and drank blood out of people's skulls for rituals. Yes, Mr. H was nothing like them; he did what he did for a cause—to save important lives. He was kind to people who were loyal to him: his oldest worker had a five-bedroom home in Obalende, and Mr. H had put all his children through school. How many could boast of improving lives in that way? But Mr. H was also the kind of man who let no breach go unpunished. Johnny had seen this with his eyes. When Mr. H learned that a former cook had forgotten the code of conduct he'd sworn his life to and started running his mouth all over town to bloggers for money, it went like this: Mr. H sent for him. When he arrived, Mr. H sat in front of a truck, smoking a cigarette, as the gateman tied the man to the back of the truck before opening the gate. Then Mr. H told Johnny to put his foot on it until the man stopped shouting. It was the wildest ride of his life. Everything in Johnny's body was rising up with nausea as he drove; he could have sworn he was an exact second away from chewing his own heart. But everything made sense: the salary, the time Clement had taken to warn him. He knew then that if he wasn't careful, Mr. H would eat his conscience on a gold plate.

That one was bad, but what *ruined* Johnny was what happened to the PA Livinus in the Boys' Quarters—a place more beautiful than many main houses, with bathtubs and showers, endless toiletry supplies, and strong air conditioners that made the rooms feel like winter. Johnny and Livinus became close quickly. They ate together, looking each other in the eye as they licked ogbono and okro soup off their fingers. They played Ludo together and drank stout in the evening. One night, Johnny mistakenly opened the door while Livinus was showering. *Come*, Livinus said, using just his finger. Johnny entered, dropping his towel, faster than fast. Then they shared the bed in Johnny's room, holding hands and tracing shapes on each other's palms in the dark,

writing closeness into their skins. For months it was like this, innocent and consistent, until the day Livinus opened his mouth and told
Johnny with his real voice to come closer.

They could have kept touching for years, using their mouths to
draw the rawest pleasure out of each other, and that wouldn't even be
the crime or sin, as long as they did their jobs. But then, Livinus
added in the lowest whisper, "There's something I want to tell you."
His voice creaked like what it was—out of practice; unused for years;
unoiled at the hinge—and Johnny's ears opened, waiting, receptive.
He knew, just from the grip on his waist, what that something was
going to be. He wanted that truth, that *yes*, that *I'm here*, that *it's you*
in his ear, Livinus's feelings blooming open. But before Livinus could
form another word, a cutlass sliced through the dark and into his
neck. Johnny watched as the head fell to the ground by the bed with
Livinus's mouth still open, the gist gestating inside. The next day,
when Johnny was eating the isi ewu the chef prepared for lunch, his
teeth encountered some cartilage, the crunch of an ear, a biscuit bone.
"I hope you know that that's your friend," said the MOPOL seated
across from him, in a voice colder than a knife's blade. And that was
the end of that warning.

It did the job. Before that, the staff used to laugh at Black, Mr. H's
accountant, a guy in his late twenties who lost his mind just from dealing with Mr. H's finances. He'd taken one look at the accounts and his
marbles fell out. Now he mostly stared into space and wrote equations
on the wall, banging his head against the numbers intermittently. He
was still a genius; he still produced results. He only suffered because he
couldn't talk. He'd tried to run away enough times but always ended
up being bundled back and put behind the desk that was assigned to
him. A mad person was a threat, absolutely frightening, and do you
even want to know what a powerful Nigerian can do to you with their
fear? Not to speak of when they'd warned you already. Johnny knew,
after Livinus, that the man was going to die there.

• • • •

He could quell his own fear with sex, Johnny thought. The acceptable kind. He could find a willing woman to leave his sticky secrets with, then zip up his jeans and go. But he barely had the time to cultivate that, what with the demands of his job, working Monday to Saturday. Sundays, the family drove themselves to church. And where would he even find a woman who would look at him twice in another man's Lagos? All the girls he saw in his day to day were made of butter. They were leagues ahead of him.

He hadn't even been on Tinder for a month before the twins found him there, posing with their father's G-Wagon. "Ah ah, you dey find wife?" they teased. "We like that your bio o." Then they'd read it out, to his eternal embarrassment: *No hookups plz. Am jus a simple guy ready to change yr lyf*, and of course he couldn't say *stop*.

Perhaps he could just leave, he thought now and then, and become an Uber driver, collecting stories with his job. By now, he was earning 500,000 naira every month. He had a car; he had an apartment. He could afford whatever he wanted whenever he wanted. He sent money home often, so that they could still feel his hand. He even built a new house for his mother. How many drivers in Lagos could boast of that? Not many, even the ones working for politicians. Still, Johnny had learned already that even money had levels—that there was money and then there was stupid money. Bastard money that could not tell you where it was born or when or how or in which generation it was going to die. People who thought neighborhoods like Banana Island and Eko Atlantic and co. were the biggest real estate triumphs in the country were just falling their own hands. He'd been like them, too, once; back when he hadn't seen the city fold itself open to reveal sparkling streets, a trafficless life, smooth sailing, yachts on pristine waters, good roads with no potholes, clean beaches with no plastic or pollution. There were people who never used Third Mainland Bridge because they had their own bridges to get where they needed to go. They had jets—their city inside the city, Lagos inside Lagos. People lived fully fleshed lives in the pockets, under the ground.

Even if he wanted to leave, where would he start from? Even if this wasn't risky for him, what would he say? That because of money, he'd been the one responsible for carrying a dead body in Oga's silver Jeep after the crucial organs had been taken out? That he stupidly took the gutted body to the spot in [redacted] where they sell the best suya meat in Lagos? That he sometimes went there during the day, like a sick animal, to watch people come and buy and lick their fingers as they eat? Or that he'd once delivered another man's skull in the front seat of the car in a black waterproof bag to a known politician? What was there to say: That money had eaten his whole conscience? It had been a year now since he'd spoken to anybody outside. He'd eaten his SIM card when Clement wouldn't stop calling, because everybody knows a tongue is as good as useless if you can die from using it.

· · ·

They'd all traveled for summer so Johnny went home. He was alone in there and couldn't shake the image of Livinus's head on the floor, his mouth ajar, a soft confession dead in his mouth. It followed him everywhere, that memory in his body. He knew, he just knew, that regardless of the fact that he'd puked right in front of the people who had laughed at him, there was a part of that man still in his body. Livinus's voice breathed inside him and he was never going to go away. At his apartment, Johnny kept on thinking: *They got me. They got me. I got the money, but I've lost everything.*

At 2:00 a.m., Johnny was scrolling through Twitter when he saw the Nairaland link. A man had found a quarter of a finger in his suya. *I asked for tozo*, he wrote. *And I got this. How did this happen? Nigerians help me!* Comments were flooding in. Already, a hashtag was trending: *Boycott {redacted}! Boycott {redacted}! NigeriaNaWa.*

Johnny left his apartment and went to the suya spot, where the queue was even longer than usual. People weren't just watching, they were buying. He stayed in his car and lay low as the mallam lifted his head in a subtle greeting. Johnny waved and reclined his seat even more. What had they done with the rest of Livinus's body? What if that was the body they'd made him carry in that body bag? Had he even checked to see? The thought of that alone made him want to throw up his whole life.

"Rosa Rosa!" the mallam said to the thick woman with red hair. "Wey that your yeye boyfriend?"

"Abeg leave me. Seun dey where Seun dey." Johnny couldn't stand Seun for anything; he was afraid of him. A man with a blunt in his hand at all times and not a single speck of care left in his eye. In Lagos? Danger, danger.

"How much own?"

"Make we make am four k. Gizzard, one k, kidney one k, tozo two k."

"Ah ah, Rosa Rosa, cash money Rosa!" the mallam hailed. Rosa bounced on her feet as he praised her, with both hands up in fists. "Anytin for you o," he said.

Rosa giggled to herself, wrapping her index finger in her pleated skirt. "Oya now." Johnny focused on her shin.

What have I done? Johnny thought, as he watched the man wrap the suya for Rosa. He adjusted his seat. *What have I done?* The whole ride to the Third Mainland Bridge, Johnny heard Livinus's voice growing louder in his ear. *Come closer. Come closer.* The timbre of those words stalked his whole frame.

Anybody who has tried it before will tell you this: silence is a dangerous thing to give yourself to, especially if you were born to speak. Livinus's voice in his ear was all that was keeping Johnny sane. He was working on forgetting Clement, forgetting Mr. H and his family, forgetting Black and co., forgetting home and the Raffia City, forgetting

Uyo, forgetting the money he'd earned, forgetting Lagos. *Come closer, Come closer.* The only voice that mattered. A new life was waiting, and there it was again—a reassurance. All of this will end. All of this will end. He was going somewhere.

With all the resolve he could muster, he parked the car before the bridge, got out, climbed the road's shoulder, and threw himself off the railing, down down down down into relief. His thoughts whorled as he went. *I'm gone from this body. What's everything if I can't stand myself, if I'm rotting already from the inside? What's the point of continuing my story if they've taken my mouth?*

They can take everything if they want, Johnny thought as he met the water. *I don't want any of it. I just want you.*

OVERHEARD:
A CONVERSATION

Location: Under Third
Mainland Bridge

M r. Adams entered the congregation on a sweltering afternoon after a truck fell off Ojuelegba Bridge and crushed his car into a rumpled sheet of metal. He'd been scrolling through Twitter on his BlackBerry, cackling at yet another trending topic just the second before. He was confused when he first left himself, because what silence was this? It filled him madly. Now here he was, under a bridge on the island, when his last memory was on another side of town entirely. Who could explain it?

"Welcome," the guard said, large black wings fluttering behind him, interrupting Mr. Adams's thoughts. "Sit down." The guard's entire face was charcoal. It was clear he had eyes of some sort, that he could see Mr. Adams, because his head followed when Adams moved. He had teeth, too, it was obvious from the roundedness of his speech. But it was the kind of face that depended on your imagination to be complete; there was no way to make sense of it without getting close enough to be rude. It wasn't an ugly face, or frightening really, it was just . . . unclear.

"Introduce yourself," said the guard. "Tell us how you got here."

Mr. Adams cleared his throat. "I'm Adams," he said. The guard's eyes stayed on him.

"Yes? And why are you here?"

"Oh . . ." He would have laughed if there was room for that. "I'm still trying to figure it out myself, you know? You know the randomness with which chaos and disaster happen in this country. I find it kind of funny, actually. It still feels like a dream." The congregation blinked back at him curiously, and he continued. "I'm not sure how it happened. There was go-slow and I was bored, so I was looking at my phone when something heavy landed on my car. I lost feeling and then I thought: *What?* And now I'm here." He furrowed his eyebrows and cleared his throat. "It didn't take as long as I'd expect something like that to. Getting here . . . didn't feel like how I thought it would. I don't know if it's that I didn't suffer much, or that I don't remember it, but it was, um . . . quick." A brief silence followed, and he cleared his throat again, trying not to meet all their eyes. The guard started a slow applause and his wings heaved behind him as the rest joined in. "So yeah," Mr. Adams said shyly, "that's me."

They were a cohort, the guard explained a bit later, so it was best for Mr. Adams to warm up to the rest as soon as he could. They'd all been assigned to this unit for a reason. There were more all over Lagos.

"Wait, so like Youth Service?" Mr. Adams asked, realizing how ridiculous he sounded.

If the guard found that funny, he didn't show it. "That," he said, "but for dead people."

After that conversation, it was clear he wasn't going anywhere, so Mr. Adams figured he might as well listen to the rest of their stories. There was a man named Kayode who'd died on what he told his wife was a business trip (heart attack while fucking his mistress); a woman named Mercy who described the cause of her death as "my foolish husband!" and left it there; a man named Bayo who only said, "Stress, I guess; my heart had clearly had enough"; a woman whose name Adams didn't hear, who died because the hospital she was rushed to had no extra beds; a man named Johnny who didn't use his words and had to be spoken for by a friend ("He brought himself here! He was looking for someone."); another person who died during the Ikeja Cantonment bomb blast (her body was complete, it wasn't a bomb that killed her; she was running for her life, she said, and fell into a canal); finally, there were four incomplete women, all naked, who walked everywhere with their arms linked and had matching throat wounds. Two of them had their breasts cut off.

Adams was sure he'd be nauseated by now if that were still possible. "Do . . . did you all know each other?" he asked.

"No, we met here," one of the women said. "But we have a killer in common."

"What?" Adams exclaimed, jarred by her casual tone.

Another saw the shock on his face and shrugged. "Awww," she said, baring her condescension. And then the woman beside her said, "People don't know how many serial killers there are in Nigeria. Even me I used to think it's an oyinbo thing, but that's because we don't keep statistics. There are enough of us here to show that it's untrue. They exist, and they're out free in the world. Do you know how wild that is?" Then they blinked in sync and turned around, leaving the awkwardness behind.

The small circle of people he'd been standing with fizzled and they each drifted elsewhere, so Adams moved to another group in the middle of a conversation. Social interactions had always been easy for him, in the sense that people relaxed around him. He carried that grace even after death.

"Hello. I, uh—I go by Adams," he said.

"Yeah, we heard you up there," one of the men there said.

"Oh."

"My story was similar to yours, you know," a woman said after a beat. "The first thing I did when I realized I was dead was laugh. I had to laugh. A trailer with no headlights and no brakes. It's not as if I was drunk. I was seeing clearly, or so I thought. So stupid. If I could do it again, I'd pick a different story. But anyway." She stretched out her hand. "Nice to meet you. My name is Peace."

Adams chuckled and heard a bitter residue in the sound. It matched the one Peace had been holding in her mouth. "It's hilarious, isn't it," he said, "how this country fails us? Me, I spent so much time, day after day, trying not to give in to the voice in my head telling me that everything was pointless, that I should just ram my car into the curb. *One more day*, I told myself, *one more day*, and that's how I'd tricked my brain since the fucking stock market crashed and I lost everything—"

A man in a pinstripe suit showed up behind Adams. "Ah," he said, "one of us." He was still holding his briefcase tightly, as though afraid he might forget what he once was. "Welcome to the club," he said. "That makes seven of us. You'll meet the others at some point. Stock market is how I ended up here. BP hit the roof after that crash. It was a fucking disaster." Adams knew the man wasn't the type to swear frequently, and that it was only because of his frustration that the word clawed its way out. It didn't suit his mouth, but he didn't care. "Shares that were valued at N25 dropped to 25 kobo. How?! Overnight? All the money I'd gathered over the years just ran through a sieve in the space of one fucking night? I lost everything. It was back to square one. This country: You will hustle and almost kill yourself with work only for that to happen? I know the crash was not just a Nigeria thing, and nobody saw it coming, but we can't pretend this country works. Nigeria is the worst place to restart a life. I thought I had it. I did. I was fantastic at trading, everybody knew. Do you know what that can do to a man?"

"I do," Adams said honestly. "It humbles you."

"No," the man said, shaking his head, "it loots you from you. It rockbottoms you. At least you can stand up from humility. But there are lower points than that."

Adams did know what it felt like: the overwhelming regret, the debt crawling quickly up his knee and just rising, faster than he could reach or stop it. He knew what it meant to feel absolutely irresponsible, like someone who hadn't even planned his life. People telling you: *Look, is it not you, my brother? Money comes and money goes for everybody, but is it not you? It's not your fault. You will make it back.* Because they couldn't see the economy laughing in your face. Adams *did* know what the man was talking about; he still felt the memory of that feeling in the left side of his chest. He'd only picked a softer word just to be gentle, but there was no need to prove that now.

The man continued. "My wife told me, *Diversify! Shares are volatile!* But I thought she was talking nonsense, because, I mean . . . *women.* I regret that. Imagine it: just as I was looking forward to retirement— where was the time to start building a new future? I'm not ashamed to say that I could not take it. I couldn't continue life like that."

Adams wanted to say more, but being himself, he was aware of all the others who might not be able to relate. He could feel their attention to the conversation floating off like bored clouds. "I feel you, my brother," Adams said. "We'll talk ehn? Now that I know someone here gets it, we'll talk. You hear? We'll talk." And the man shrugged and walked away. His pain was still raw. That much was obvious.

"How about you?" Adams asked a woman with a quarter of her face melted. She was busy with a wound in her leg that she was obsessed with sewing and unstitching, but she didn't need to meet his face to know that he was talking to her.

"Acid," she said without looking up.

"Me, my family think I'm missing," a woman next to her said. She wore years on her face, but her voice sounded like it was trapped in pre-puberty; you could hear the child in her loud and clear. "They're still sharing my photo in hope that someone will find me one day. It won't happen, but I'm glad they've held on to that hope; it makes me feel at least a little . . . alive? No pun intended, of course. Ha. Ha ha ha." She looked around at their fixed faces. "No? Okay."

The guard appeared behind them. He clapped twice to get their attention. "Okay! Enough with the morbid talk. At least you no longer have bills and you've gotten your deaths over with. There, two blessings; count the rest in your spare time. Now, where are you all going tonight?"

He turned to Adams and explained: "Lesson two: Nobody gets to squat here for free. You need to keep your hands busy or you'll start to fade. Once the sun starts to set, I need you up on your feet. I like to know that you're all doing something." He scanned Mr. Adams's face. "Obviously, you came here because you wanted more time, whether you want to admit that or not, is that not so? You were unhappy to die so you were redirected here. But you must earn it. Thankfully, time doesn't work like money, so no one is here to fight you for a cut. It's all yours, I just need to see you trying. Capiche?"

Adams nodded. The guard continued. "Good. Now, some of them go to the night market, some of them help people park their cars in busy areas, some of them are bouncers, some of them are masseuses and masseurs, some of them find . . . you know, *clients*, for night work. Bankole here is our dreamweaver." The guard pointed to a tall man working behind a loom with brilliant eyes and a slouched back.

Bankole waved from behind his loom. "If you have anyone you need to send a nightmare to, I'm your guy," he said, and winked. "But of course, you'll need a good reason for that." He had earned that power, the guard explained, by being struck by lightning while on an okada. Did Adams know the statistics for lightning accidents? Twenty-four thousand people around the world get struck every year; some estimates put the number of deaths as high as six thousand. "He's special because of it. Everyone has their gifts. So, anything creative you can find to do with your time and your hands, you do it. Capiche? And of course, it's best if it's something you love or can grow to love."

"Yes, sir," Adams said. Now he was wondering: Did everyone here have superpowers? He felt as normal as he did alive. As regular.

"And no," the guard said, pointing at Adams's closed mouth. "I'm not going to tell you what my story is or answer any personal questions to put you at ease. As for your gift? Don't worry, you don't have to figure it out now. All you have is time." The guard shrugged wryly and his eyelashes butterflew. He could be beautiful when he wanted to be—that much was clear. "I'll pick a few of them to take you to one of the clubs on the island tonight for your welcome party. Don't say I never did anything for you."

"Thank you?" Adams said, half-questioning the guard's already-turned back. As Adams watched, the guard's wings flexed out majestically. Spread out like that against the setting sun, Adams thought that the backdrop could have been a heaven forming.

"Now," the guard said, "the rest of you rascals, registration time. Oya, after me!"

TATAFO

(MANUAL)

H ere is what you need to know now about the city you're dealing with:

1. They call it Lagos.
2. It's a city, but not. To say: the city is not what you think a city is.
3. There is city and there is spirit and the two coincide. Yes, this is about the texture of the bridge, the smell in the air, the thick noise everywhere, the inimitable attitude. But there is who the city is at the core: a glow-in-the-dark something, a luminant orb at night, a maelstrom, quicksand spinning. (Not a place, an idea. Not a place, an energy.) There's the spirit named in its mother tongue; ruthless, faceless whirlwind dancing between land and sky. No others come close. Ruled by a treacherous trinity: Èkó, the senior trickster, the melting pot in the sun, the overseer of all, the one who watches the underside of night; Lagos, the plain-mad, plain-fun, plain-loved; and LasGidi, the one with arrogance in its gait, who glimmers under strobe lights, who throws open

the loudest nights. Together they are godhead, three in one. All join. But also, all divides. See the cityspirit as a simulation glitching, mutating into hundreds of selves gathering in a sideways crowd.

4. The cityspirit has uncountable parallels, is something different to every person, its spiritface a mirror. Under the glass is someone (he) and something (it). If he answers to many names, if even it cannot define itself, then just as we will never agree on the color of God's iris, we cannot agree on who or what the someonesomething is. To look at it closely is to look at yourself, to watch your own face, to meet who you are when there's no witness and only you can see you. So, as there are twenty-one million of us, there are twenty-one million of it.

5. Èkó is not the largest of his father's thirty-six children—not in size, at least. But thick-skinned and loud-selved as he is, he is the most powerful, most vibrant, most loved, most wealthy, the one with the business sense; the corporate head of the clan. Together, they're called Nigeria. But Èkó is the child with the anointed head, the prideful distance, a sharp and complex destiny impossible to unsee. It is its own lawmaker, his own parent, the child who raised itself by himself. When Èkó moves into the wider world, or appears notoriously in another country, other cityspirits bow. You name it: Accra, Casablanca, New York, Nairobi, Harare, Cape Town, Jozi, Los Angeles, Dakar, Kuala Lumpur, Kigali. Cities and spirits—celebrated as they may be—aren't deluded or stupid; they know which ones can floor them.

6. People move from all over the world to be near it, to be in it, and it's all these visits, these move-ins, that make the mixture, that make the seething broth. The reputation of a place-but-not, no matter how it is used, cannot die. And, believe this: That arrogance you know the city and its children for? It is earned.

7. This is a city for all. You're not more important because you're alive or because you see this way up or because you walk with your legs and breathe from your face. That it's the only way you know does not mean it's the only way there is. You share this place with flesh and *not*-flesh; it's just as much their city as it is yours. Don't think that just because they forgive you all the time—for running into them, for bumping against them, for slamming their fingers into doors, for not answering when they call you, for stepping on them as they're sunbathing on the road's shoulder—they no longer exist, that their lives will not still touch your life. They are merely forgiving you. All that is mercy; they are only giving you chance.

8. Get money. And in all thy getting, get disrespectful audacity.

9. Be careful, keep a few eyes at your back, and have respect.

10. This is the only commandment with a promise: that if you do anyhow, you will also see anyhow.

NIGHT WIND

The devil was already inside Amenze when she walked past Goodies on Awolowo Road. At first it squatted inside her small stomach, leaning against the walls and eating ground-up groundnut from the day before. Then she felt it becoming a fuller presence from her waist, expanding through the width of her chest.

"You're hungry," the devil told her. She ignored it.

It tried again. "Cross the road."

But stubborn girl that she was, she kept walking toward her boyfriend Olu's house. Since the devil's last visit, she had become born-again, complete with a choirmaster boyfriend who wanted to marry her. She wasn't ready to backslide into those unholy days, so she quickened her steps forward because she could hear the devil's voice differently now—not from far down in the gut anymore but pressing its blurriness against the inside of her throat.

The devil becomes in increments, in spurts, until it has taken over the whole form. Amenze knew this, anticipated it, but hoped that if she moved quickly and steadily enough, it wouldn't be able to spread itself.

"Okay, fine then. Keep going," the devil said.

Amenze stopped and stomped her foot. "That's enough." She couldn't stand its tone; her shoulders tensed at the mocking patience of it. "Just go. Leave!"

The devil sniggered. Amenze was trying what Pastor Pius and the Bible had taught her: *Resist the devil*, they said, *and it will flee*. What she wasn't told was that the devil's entrance into anything is almost always entire. As Amenze seethed, the devil stretched its limbs inside the case of her flesh—legs lengthening inside her own, one then the other and after that, arms, until her flesh fit snug like a jumpsuit. Then it marched her reluctant body toward Chicken Republic.

When she reached the door, she stopped.

"Are you coming in, ma?" the doorman asked, confused.

"Yes," the devil said, straightening Amenze's blouse. "Yes, sorry."

Inside, the devil headed straight to the counter. It had felt Amenze's hunger earlier, but she'd refused to eat anything because, of course, now that she was a Bible-believing, saved-by-grace-through-faith Christian, she fasted with her church at the slightest opportunity.

"Please be fast, ma. Fried rice or jollof rice?" the waitress asked, impatient.

The devil looked at her through the eyes in Amenze's head, considering ways to deal with her curtness; then decided that she wasn't worth the work. "You choose for me."

The waitress—CHIOMA read her nametag—shrugged and ordered one fried rice with chicken. The devil stood aside. The man behind Amenze was a UBA driver and the waitress attended to him better, which assured the devil of her problem: Chioma was one of the desperate ones, leaving all windows in conversation open for any potential husband to creep in. Bored by her predicament, the devil snatched the tray from her hand and left.

Just as the devil was sinking Amenze's teeth into the drumstick, Tunde walked in with his daughter. The devil did not need to look up, having smelled him as they walked past the air conditioner. It straightened Amenze's back as Tunde sat down by a yellow playground slide nearby and bent to untie his daughter's shoelaces. From the corner of Amenze's eye, the devil watched the daughter disappear into the playground as Tunde moved toward the till.

The devil was sat next to a man sitting alone. He was watching Soundcity on the TV above his head—body tilting toward the music, neck craned upward, Adam's apple floating under a sheet of skin as he ate. His kind was easy to discern just by looking at him—thirsty, predictable, would do anything for a gorgeous woman—and between forkfuls of fried rice, the devil dismissed a dull desire to ruin his life. The devil did not take Amenze's eyes off the man as it cleared her throat and then undid the first two buttons of her blouse. It was a way to test the fit, to use the man as one would use a mirror. The man let his neck fall gently, eyes resting on her cleavage. He looked pleased—not even slightly disturbed, aroused even—so the devil, sure now that it had worn her body well, looked away from the man, redid one of the buttons, and returned to the food, opening Amenze's face in a smile.

Tunde passed by with two dishes and glanced in Amenze's direction. The devil met his gaze, already knowing what he had to lose. For one, his relationship with his daughter. With that, a solid business reputation he curated ruthlessly. But the devil was after neither. From this encounter, and with this available body, the devil just wanted sex, simple. It pushed the tray of fried rice away and walked toward Tunde, avoiding Chioma's judging eyes from behind the counter.

They talked for just over ten minutes before exchanging numbers. The devil dazzled the man so well that for the first time in years he got the heady feeling that everything but the woman in front of him was blurring into a stunning irrelevance. In that short time, the core details became clear: Tunde, real estate developer and single father, trying to figure out how to tend to a needy daughter. They were just stopping to get the girl a sandwich en route to a family friend's house, he said.

"Not a sandwich, dad. A chickwizz. That's what it's called." The little girl reappeared out of nowhere, startling them.

For the first time, the devil noticed her properly. It smiled at her with Amenze's full teeth. "Hay. Feisty."

"I know," Tunde said. "She's serious wahala."

The girl ignored them, focusing on her food.

· · ·

Tunde called that evening, and then the next.

"Of course," the devil said in Amenze's voice on a phone call to Tunde. "But let's be clear, I'm not here to be your friend."

"Who said—"

"Or for that love crap."

The devil liked being a woman because in a woman's body, it could feel the truth. The things the body did when no one was watching, the way it could swallow things, drown parts whole, hide and house people. In a woman's body, it could feel the weight of her kindness, the restraint it takes to know exactly how to raze a man's life to the ground but still choose not to. There was something delicious about being that close to being good. But its patience was running thin.

"So, are we doing this or not?" the devil asked him.

They met at his house. His daughter wasn't there. He had dropped her off with his cousin David, who sometimes babysat her. It wasn't the first time, he said, so it was fine.

"This time, I told him it was business," Tunde said, laughing a short, rash laugh. He knelt on the bed behind her and kissed her shoulders gently. Already, his whole mouth was starving for something.

"It is," the devil said, already peeling Amenze's dress off her back. "It's business."

When Amenze returned into herself, naked under the clingy arm of the stranger, she knew what the devil had done. All she could hear in her head was: *What exactly is your life becoming? A Chicken Republic stranger? Chicken Republic? Stranger?* Her mother's voice, reliably judgmental even in death. How would she explain herself—explain that though she might not be above making foolish decisions, she would never have gone *this* far with *this* man if she'd been in her right mind? Which mouth would she use to say that she was walking on her own jeje only to be shrugged aside and ejected from her body? It wouldn't make sense.

Amenze wriggled out from under Tunde's arm and told him not to call her again. She knew he'd try regardless—because he looked like he would never recover from what happened—so she blocked his number to save them both the stress. Whatever happened in that bed wasn't her own skill anyway.

· · ·

The devil had been drawn to Tunde's daughter from the moment it saw her. At the time, she just was not the focus—she could not be because, forget whatever they say, the devil can only enter a house through an adult. But the devil had eyes on her because she looked far too sad for a girl her age, a type it had always enjoyed. Later that afternoon, after she returned from her uncle's, the devil—now restless, aching for a new entrance—entered her room as her father tucked her into bed. "Goodnight, Daddy," she said, and after kissing her forehead, he said "Goodnight, Telema." The devil loved her name: Telema.

The devil lay down on her pillow next to her just as her father turned off the lights. Then it entered the unzipped part of Telema's teddy bear's back, where the batteries sleep, and hummed a small, sweet song from inside: *Sleep, baby, sleep, baby, sleep.* The devil is sexless near a child, so the voice came out sounding like nothing Telema had heard before—not quite male, not quite female, not quite cartoon. Still, being a mere six years old, she wasn't shocked, only grateful to be met halfway with more aliveness.

The devil had sensed the secret chittering under the girl's skin as it introduced itself through Amenze, but it was too desperate for Tunde to give it much thought. Now that it was trying to enter the girl's life for the first time, it sang in that mellifluous tone. The girl hugged the teddy closer to her body so that she could hear the music better. She wanted it desperately, it was obvious, so the devil perched on her shoulder. *Sleep baby sleep baby sleep*—the voice was fluid in Telema's ear, reaching close to her brain, spilling onto the pillow. It called sleep quickly.

When the devil was sure she was asleep, it entered her head, found a space against her skull, and stood there, watching her dream. It made warm, purring sounds, trying to help her sleep unbothered. But things kept falling into each other. Inside her dream, there was a man coming close to her body to touch it. The devil kept trying to ward him off, *Go away!*, but he refused, so the devil smelled the rottenness on the stranger and knew. When the girl woke up, her heart was pounding. The devil, unmoored by her body's stutter, slid into her chest and found chaos.

It took three good nights of the devil whispering, "Tell me. What happened, tell me?" for Telema to say, "God, please kill Uncle David. Please make him go away."

The devil flinched at her mistake but forgave her immediately. Children have a hard time naming their spirits, you see; they make mistakes, interchange them sometimes. But since no request prayed into its ear is ever met with silence—questions are met with fast answers, desperation with sharp release—the devil asked Telema, "Why? What did he do?"

"He has . . . he has bad, painful hands," Telema said, starting to cry.

Tunde came in just then, but when he opened the door, the girl pretended to still be asleep. So he kissed her forehead and left. Something about that simple deceit made the devil like her even more. What a cunning child! If any prayer ever deserved to go unanswered, it wasn't hers.

The devil sang her to sleep again. Before morning, it had left through her left ear.

*   *   *

The devil stood at the edge of Tunde's bed as he slept. His vest had ridden up to show smooth skin above his boxers, so the devil chose his navel as the door, and then stretched itself out until the body was his, closing Tunde's eyes tighter. Then it conjured David, raising Telema's dress and touching her in a senseless place. The devil rolled the scene out in Tunde's head in the texture of a dream, an unraveled story, a secret flowering open, full and fat in the mind's eye.

In the dream, Telema was wearing the same dress she wore the day Tunde slept with the devil. The devil brought the vision closer so that Tunde could see Telema squirm as she watched her uncle pant and sweat and shake and morph into a grotesque thing. The devil was still interested in showing Tunde mercy, so at the part when David took off his belt, coiled it around his knuckles, and hung its tail over Telema like a dangling threat, instructing her to lie down, the devil let the dream cut. When Tunde's body tried to rouse itself, it felt heavy. The devil had left his flesh and was sitting on his stomach, pushing his head into the pillow, holding his hands to the sheets, pinning his feet to the bed. He tried to scream but nothing came out. When the devil let him go, he sat up, muttering, "Jesus! God forbid. God forbid." He knew Telema wouldn't be awake, but he walked to her bedroom with anointing oil in his hands, just to be near her. She looked like such a holy, unharmable thing, upheld and hallowed by clouds of duvet.

Next, of course, Tunde did the most senseless thing. He prayed. He sat by his daughter's sleeping body and prayed. His logic was this: a dark thing revealed was an act of mercy from God, an invitation to cancel something in the spirit realm before it leaked into your flesh life. This amused the devil because if it had been a good dream, Tunde would have done the opposite: he would have received it with both hands, trapped it with an *amen* and held it in his body, the sheen of a revelation lighting him up from inside. But you can't blame a father; it's easier to take bad news as a warning than as a fact.

When the child woke up, he held her close and said, "You know you can tell me if anyone does anything to you that you don't like, right? Anything . . . bad." Things only ever grow power when you call their names.

"Yes. Yes, Daddy," the child said.

"I'm here. Daddy is always here. You know that, right?"

"Yes, Daddy." Since Tunde clearly wouldn't be the one to do the necessary, the devil left him.

• • •

Soon enough, the devil was gawking out of David's wife Funke's eyes as they argued.

"The worst part is that you show no fucking remorse," David said, raising his voice. But as he kept shouting, the devil kept Funke's mouth tight-shut, so that no words could come out. *You're not sorry*, the devil thought into her ear, *you're not*. It had no patience for her guilt, for how hungry she was for forgiveness, so it took the rest of her over in seconds.

So, the devil was the one who bent Funke's knees and took David in her mouth, teasing his eyes to the back of his head so that he forgot everything. It was the devil who faked her orgasm, gyrating on the bed as David parted her thighs and moved his tongue where it mattered. It was the devil inside Funke's body afterward, stroking his arm repeatedly, saying, "I love you. Please believe me. It's you I love," until David was soothed and finally able to sleep.

And it was the devil that jolted David out of bed at 3:22 a.m. and made him unable to fall back asleep—so that he'd decide to put in his earphones and go for a run to clear his head. It was the devil that kept his blood awake and made him sprint up Bourdillon Road so that he'd have to slow down just as he was approaching the Lekki-Ikoyi Bridge.

It was the devil that left him there alone.

. . .

Seun, conductor by day and agbero by night, knows the devil well. He knows when it is coming, and he never says no. What for? His own desires are simple: Seun likes action and reactions and shekpe and blood.

That night, since the road was dead, Seun was dragging his feet, sipping Orijin and smoking a blunt, looking at his ex-girlfriend Rosa's picture on his BlackBerry. Then the devil perched on his shoulder. Its entrance came as a simple suggestion in Seun's head: to walk up to the man who had just stopped to breathe. Seun welcomed it lazily, because he felt it, flat as a fact in his chest: that it would be good to just shake him up. Just small, nothing too deep. The man looked like he could use a little surprise in his life.

So, as David was panting, trying to recover his breath, Seun strolled across the road toward him, hands in his pockets, bathroom slippers slapping against gravel.

"Bros!" he called. When David did not respond, not even by turn- ing around to ask what he wanted, Seun chuckled. "Ah! Bros, den no dey ignore me o. Especially now, as my eye don red."

As he moved, the devil climbed into a pore at the back of Seun's neck and descended his spine, using each layer of bone as rung.

"Fuck him," the devil instructed, from the bottom of Seun's back.

Seun didn't want to do that. He didn't want to ram himself into a man's body in a moment of random hunger. He wanted instead—all of a sudden—to draw blood. And on this particular occasion, that was equally fine with the devil.

So, Seun tapped David on the shoulder, and before the man could turn around fully, he collected David's jaw in a sharp punch. David could feel the tip of his tongue dangling in a tiny blood pool in his mouth. Seun wanted to be sorry now that he could see that David had earphones in his ears, but that vague remorse he felt was silenced by the way blood sang through his veins. When he stretched his fingers, his whole palm was a chorus. It was pleasure enough and he was ready to stop—he was—when he heard the dry voice in his ear, asking, "Ah ah, is that all?" And Seun was not the type to resist a challenge.

The devil wanted all of David's blood to spill away and waste on the road. It wanted a mess so severe that David's face would no longer be a face by the time the sky cracked with new light. So he rose from Seun's waistline.

You see, spirits are like liquid; they take the shape of their container. The devil poured itself into every part, every bulge, every muscle—filling the whole of Seun.

"Easy o," Seun said before he left himself. The devil replied, "Ah ahn. You no trust me?"

Seun didn't trust the devil. But it was too late because now he was a wordless, dangling thing, and all the devil could hear, loud in Seun's ears, was Telema saying, "Please kill Uncle David . . . he has bad, painful hands."

It was easy. All it took was a series of belt whippings and a small, eager knife.

When it was done, the devil shrank and shrank and shrank inside Seun until it was small enough to go back to just his waist. Then it climbed back up the spine and out into the night.

Now, the devil had already done many things for itself from Seun's body, but killing a random man was not one of them. So when Seun came back to meet his own body on its knees, bent over David's corpse, he didn't believe it at first. He shook the body, pushed it on its back, and saw his knife still deep in David's stomach. Seun pressed his head against the chest, just to make sure. He heard music, still thud-thud-thudding out of the earphones, but David's body was noiseless, facing the sky, streetlight pouring coolly on his only intact eye.

He's not dead, he's not dead, he cannot be dead, he isn't, Seun told himself as he ran the whole curve of bridge, the breeze parachuting his loose shirt. But not even the sound of a necessary lie can match the night wind, growing dark in your ear like the devil's last laugh.

OVERHEARD:
FAIRYGODGIRLS

O h shit, come close. This one's in trouble."

"Who's behind it this time?"

"This one's wahala is with both parents. The girl is a rascal and unfortunately, they don't know what to do with her. They wanted well-behaved."

One of the girls hissed. She was fed up with all this saving. "Why do people think they can order children like takeout? One good one, please! One successful one! One quiet one! And who keeps giving precious children to undeserving people? Are we going to spend eternity doing damage control?" She wouldn't be the first to feel this way. Some other girls—allowing boredom to creep into them—had chosen instead to rest in peace.

"So what do we do?" another asked, squinting at the new girl projected on the wall. The girl was sobbing to herself, her father resting coolly against their living room wall, asking for more frog jumps. Now in the middle of a scold, he was saying something about distractions, about how she'd learn to concentrate by force because why all the school fees if not? Her siblings watched transfixed, and her mother went on whistling a gospel song as she made banga soup.

One of the fairygodgirls sighed, an old memory breezing through her. "She's going to need an out. Obviously. They'll keep insisting until she turns into something else. She's going to need a break from home so that she doesn't lose her whole self."

"Well, she's almost sixteen. She has the strength in her legs, but I don't think she understands that wanting to be free is not the same as being demonic, being stubborn; it's not the same as wanting to ruin your life and fuck up your family. It's not the same at all."

"Yeah, but how many of us understood that at her age? Isn't that why we send them help? Because we wished someone had told us, or had seen our worry and offered a solution? Like a book, a dream, a look, some advice. Look, the alarm wouldn't be going off on her if she didn't need our help, would it? She needs us."

"Oversabi. She wasn't saying that in a judgmental voice," the stubborn one said, "but that's true, I guess."

One of the girls gasped from the back of the garden. It was the quiet one, the one they called the brain of the group. "I think I know the book for her," she said.

"Of course you do. What's it called? Who's it by?"

"The author's name is Jamaica Kincaid. And the book is called *Annie John*."

This was her favorite thing to do: find the book that would work. Just the week before, she'd helped a girl called Tolu by putting Akwaeke Emezi's *Pet* in her best friend Tani's schoolbag, because some stories won't come directly to you; they go through someone who loves you. Tani still didn't know who had blessed her with the book, but as soon as she opened it, she didn't need to. What mattered was that she saw that world and solved for what needed to be hunted in Tolu's life, a thing she didn't want to believe was possible. Her stomach fell with Redemption's in that library scene because she understood. *Look at*

Jam and Redemption, the book had said, *look at who they are to each other. Look at how you don't have to be perfect. If you love someone and something bad is happening to them, you have to look at that thing.* Tani cried hard reading that book because *Pet* was right about calling the painful thing what it was, about choosing truth and being less obedient to fear. This wasn't Lucille, but the world of that book showed how braided together love was with justice, how inseparable the two were.

Another girl had dropped a blade she thought she needed to use because of Jessamy Harrison in Helen Oyeyemi's *The Icarus Girl*. Out of love, out of seeingship. All that had taken was a book passed from one friend to another under a table in Yoruba class, and the fairygod-girls watched those sentence-seeds save her life right before their eyes. They had to trust this tiny, smart girl. If nothing else, she had the gift of choosing books, of selecting salvations.

The sharp-mouth folded her arms across her chest and raised an eyebrow. "Oh yeah?" There was an edge to her voice. Dead and alive, she couldn't sit with a book to save her life. One page and she'd be yawning already. Sometimes she wondered if they'd grouped her with the wrong set of girls, since all of them here were clearly efikos who wanted to know everything and save the whole world. She'd be better with a group who loved Ten Ten and made new games often. "Why do you think it will work?" she asked, not because she cared but because it was the kind of question a smart girl would have asked.

She'd studied them enough. She knew it was important work they were doing, even though sometimes she couldn't help her own petti-ness. But really, this team worked best when everybody did the part they were actually good at. Together, they took care of thousands of girls across the city every single week. They were unstoppable when they focused—some of them on comforting, some on havoc-wreaking, some on nightmare-causing, some on trouble-ensuring, depending on the problem at hand. They all worked for the living girls, stayed for the living girls, lived for the living girls: girls with gaslighting parents, girls who see black more often than is safe, girls who hide pills under their tongues, girls who need to flush their bodies at night, girls who fly over their own heads while sitting down, girls who run far while standing still, girls who don't cry anymore and get beaten harder for it, girls who cry way too much but only at night in private, girls with lethal lonelinesses growing under their skins, girls with incomprehensible weather in their brains. The statistics had always been frightening: too many of them, too often. It was the fairygodgirls' job to climb fast and cut where it hurt. No time to spend wallowing.

The city would keep eating girls at wild speed after all, but their rescuers are who their rescuers are: all-the-way-gone girls, already-dead girls, and so, untouchable girls. Can't be stopped in the way still-here girls can, because they can't be seen by people who cause damage. They understand better than anybody the way some still-there girls hurt, because they themselves were girls whose hearts used to beat hard against their chests. Girls who know how it feels. The only difference being that they left the world early enough to become girls with powers, girls with speed in their wings—calculating cherubs. And it was their responsibility, each of them, to stay grounded in the world, because who better than some furious girls to save girls no one gets angry enough for? Love is, after all, what fights for us so that we can hold our peace.

The quiet girl made her usual face. "Well," she explained, "I picked this one because Annie John understands freedom, and not only does she understand it, she fights for it. She loves untidily, not just with her heart but with her head, her mouth, her feet, her teeth. She allows herself to hate and resent things without requiring too much justification from herself. She understands, she really understands, that it's okay to choose yourself. And that you can—and maybe should—leave home, if all home knows how to do is kill you."

"Sounds fair," the bully said, dropping her hands in theatrical defeat. "I think she could start there."

"Trust me," the quiet girl said. "In my other life, I was like her."

"So where do we plant the book?" another girl asked, red beads dangling off her braids. She was quick on her feet, the one who often asked for practical solutions.

"Mm. She doesn't go to the library much anymore, because stupid boys stand by the door and make fun of girls who are just trying to go somewhere. So, putting it in the library won't work. Besides, how would she even find it there? That library is huge!"

They fell quiet as they scanned her life for who might have it. They found it finally in the house where the girl's mother worked as a cleaner. That day, when the woman came to clean, the boss's daughter snuck the book into the woman's handbag. She didn't know why she did it or who she was gifting it to. She just knew she had to.

"Okay, but what if it doesn't get to her?" the first girl asked. "I mean, her mother can be terrifying. How do we know the girl will dare to look inside and find it?"

The oldest and tallest of them said, "Remember. Our job is one thing and one thing alone. Put the book, or the door or the road or the manual, in their hands and step away. What they do with it is not our business. All you need to do is get the book to them. Haven't we seen this before?"

When the woman got home and set her bag on the chair before rushing into the shower, her daughter felt an odd compulsion to reach for that bag. She didn't know why, but she knew there was something inside her pulling her to it. Maybe she was searching for sweets, or maybe she was hoping to find something that would explain why everything was more important to her mother than she was. But she opened that bag and she found the book.

The girls rejoiced when they saw her find it, holding hands and spinning in a dizzying circle. On days like this, they felt their true importance. And they were right about it.

Have you ever seen furious girls gather and become unstoppable?

Together, they make the holiest God you've seen—the kind young girls have deserved all along. They offer the kind of friendship cynics call madness, that adults call *imaginary*. They make friendly planets of your mind, touch your afternoons with goodness, slide a chuckle into your belly, plant a kiss behind your ear. They tell you: look, in front of you, that's what it looks like to be free. They are the lifesavers. Fairygodgirls with the most magical hue of skin.

Scared girls believe the girls who find them in their dreams, believe the friend they wish they had in real life. Girls like this one needed girls like them, girls who would fly the whole breadth of the city with solutions for happiness, with formulas for joy despite, with a hunger for justice and freedom, justice and freedom, justice and freedom.

Books mattered, because girls who are at their most real in book pages are sometimes the only reason alive girls get through their years at all. Gone girls shifting the world to help keep here girls alive; gone girls there to say: *I'm seeing you, you're not the one who needs a new mind, it's them.*

"You will be strange," they were saying, "but you won't be strange alone."

They were doing their jobs correctly and it pleased them.

"Wait, wait, wait!" one of the fairygodgirls said. "Let's see how it ends." The quiet girl joined them after a final cartwheel and they stood still and watched, still giddy with glee.

"Annie John," the girl said, turning the book around to read its back cover before hiding it under her shirt and zipping her mother's bag back up. Already, she sounded like a friend.

GRIEF IS THE GIFT THAT
BREAKS THE SPIRIT OPEN

Before Toju met Agbon, she'd been loved more times than she cared to count. She had spanned the breadth of the country, moving between cities, loving and leaving people with an equal, jarring swiftness. Just like that, she was fleshed one day and dust the next.

Of course, as with most abandonments, it started in the heart first, an involuntary reflex. Hoverers are this way, because if you lose a body and people surround it as breath leaves it, watch as it bloats with death, then certain rules apply if you choose to find and wear it again. There is an inexhaustible amount of anywheres you can occupy, but you cannot be seen where you were mourned, you cannot live where you already left.

Toju was to pick the body back up as she'd left it, long-limbed and lithe, just fifteen. She'd been lying on an operating table the morning it happened, with a gloved hand loosening a knot in her intestines, when she felt a sudden slowing down inside, followed by distant sounds of people panicking on the outside. Voices. "We're losing her! Get Dr. Njideka in!" Toju knew there was something to be afraid of—of course, voices didn't sound that way when there wasn't—and she thought briefly of her mother sitting in the waiting area, most likely praying and "believing God," as she liked to say. But then Toju noticed something else: a small partition between the body flayed open on a table and the her that hung gaseous on the body's interior—a fleshless divide, suffused with light. She stood at the clouded eye of a small tunnel, staring into its endlessness, and found herself liking the pink haze spreading inside it. "Suction!" The hands moved with a tighter speed inside the body, as blood slowed to an almost-halt. Toju found her inside self being lifted up and forward, floating quickly into the haze. It was such a freedom that at first she didn't resist it; everything was weightless.

When she finally realized where she was going, she tried to turn around, but the body continued to recede as she sped forward. *My mother's going to kill me!* she thought, trying to look back—which was a joke in itself if you think about it, considering that the woman really had warned her in those words. "Toritseju, they said there is risk involved o! I take God beg you o, don't die. If you die during this surgery, know that me, as your mother, I will find you and kill you!" They'd laughed and she promised. "Don't worry, okay?" her mother had said, with a glazed assurance. "You are covered with the blood of Jesus."

But none of that mattered now, because dead people were, among other reliefs, largely exempt from their mother's wahala. When Toju slipped out of herself, it was with the doctor's hand still pressed against her head. That was before the *I'm sorry, we tried everything*, before Toju's mother's wail ripped through the hospital walls in wild waves, before her voice shouted, "You people have killed me, she was all I had, you have killed me ooooo! Jesus, come and see. I put her in your hands ooooh, now come and see!"

Now, on this side, where time was a smooth and silvered nothing, she didn't know how much of it had passed. All she knew was that after the leaving, she (the one who did the leaving from the inside) had—instead of grinding to some sort of existential halt as she'd expected—felt merely . . . unplugged. So she had that panicked thought about not knowing what to do with herself: how to move disembodied, and where to go; whether she was even supposed to still be awake in the mind, thinking and feeling anything at all. And now here she was, facing familiar yards of flesh, laid down and folded neatly, clearly for her.

Toju hesitated before she reached for the body and slid it back on. Everything was a spinning newness. She closed her eyes and steadied herself, to let the dizzy feeling fall to a flat calm. When she opened her eyes, she was standing at the entrance of CJ & Babalola Secondary School, dressed in a blue-and-white pinafore with a black backpack to match. She took a few steps inside the compound (No security? What kind of school was this?), looking around, wondering if she jutted out awkwardly in this place, which was a loud and bustling contrast to the old town with its slow spirit and red sand—the unnameable town with the mad mourning and a too-young dead body in the ground.

And it was here, in the crowd of student bodies, that she met Ikenna.

* * *

It was lunchtime. Ikenna found Toju by her usual hiding spot behind the library, sitting in the shade with her hair woven all-back in eight neat cornrows, reading *The Philosopher's Stone*. He stood in front of her and held out a meat pie and Gold Spot between them. "For you o. Since you no dey like to chop."

She dog-eared her page and looked up at him. "Thank you."

"No yawa. One more thing sha." He reached into his pocket and handed her a folded piece of paper with a heart on it. It was drawn with a glittery gel pen.

By then, they'd only known each other for a week. That is, for as long as Toju had been successfully camouflaging. She dodged the teachers, looked nervous when other students tried to speak to her, until everyone concluded she was one of the odd new ones, one of the outsiders who were just too slow in the thoughts to belong anywhere. Not the cute kind you eventually accepted, but the kind it wasn't worth making friends with at all because they were too slow for their own good, for their own youth. Most of them left her alone for that reason, assuming that since they'd never heard her speak, she was mute. But when Ikenna found her, he pulled her first words out. He was one of the strange kids, too, cut out of *special* cloth, and when he first found her, he pulled the first words out of her. He didn't seem to pose much of a risk—who could he run his mouth to, since people hardly spoke to him too?—and they'd spent their free time playing games and reading together every day since.

"What's inside?" she asked him.

"There's actually a way people usually find out these things, you know? By unfolding it."

Toju laughed, even as streaks of panic congregated in her chest. She was hoping he hadn't gone and found her out, or that he wasn't going to ask anything she couldn't answer, because what then? She hadn't been there long at all, but already she'd have to leave. It was common sense, really. Being a Hoverer meant staying as free as driftwood, foot-loose, nobody's. This was the rule.

Wait, she thought back at her own head, reminding her of this. *But what if I jus—*

Which is how she knew she was in trouble.

She unfolded the letter, trying to keep a steady hand as Ikenna peered over her shoulder. *Please, please, please,* she thought, *don't say anything heavy.*

"Just read it," he said, as if he could hear inside her head. "It's nothing bad."

She read the first line, *Dear Girl-With-No-Name,* and she held her breath for the remaining six lines. He liked her (everything about her, but especially the recklessness of her laugh); he couldn't wait to get to know her more; and if she liked him too—which he thought she must, since they hung out so much—then could she at least tell him her name? He wouldn't tell anyone.

His handwriting moved in reeling whorls and she jammed her teeth together to stay encased. What should she say? It hadn't even occurred to her that he could tell anyone, but now that he mentioned it, why wouldn't he? This was their school, their city, these were his people. She wasn't real in the ways they were, she was nothing.

"Yo, babe. Are you okay?"

"Um. Yeah . . ."

"Are you sure? Your face went all weird just now."

"Like how?"

"I don't know. . . . Like your mind was far. You're sure you're fine?"

Toju smiled at him and wound an arm around his back, finding his side. "Yes. I'll find you after."

He shrugged and left, disappointment spreading a slight slouch over his walk.

Ikenna was kind, she knew this much, and she didn't want to hurt him. Of all the students, she'd chosen him for the texture of his affection, the general softness of his ways, the generosity of his friendship, and the quality of his ears. But now, something in her needed to gather both strength and sense, despite all that. Exhausted from trying to resist the pull, she slipped a note through the metal slit of his locker. *I'm sorry. I don't think I can do this anymore.*

He found her after school, holding the note up to her face, her handwriting a blue-biroed mess. "What do you mean? Did I do something wrong? What did I do to you? You can't do what? I'm not even—" He was angry and tears were rising tall in his eyes, but he saw how upset she was, too, how she refused to meet his eye, so he softened his voice to an almost-whisper.

"Is something happening at home? Did something bad happen to you? If there's anything, you can tell me. I'm your friend, remember? I don't just want to be your guy, I'm your friend."

But she didn't remember—couldn't afford to, really—and nothing he did to remind her helped. In fact, the harder he tried, the more urgently she needed to move. So, she left him, left the school, left the city. How could she stop all of it and take off this entire *thing*, in fact? When she tugged at the arm or thigh, it didn't feel optional like an outfit. It felt stuck to her and it was frightening. She closed her eyes and focused on the steam multiplying inside her head. She'd gathered from experience that whatever was in there, controlling this and her, didn't talk. It answered by taking her places, by moving her around. *Please*, she thought, *show me how to remove it.*

She opened her eyes to noise in an average white bus, heading out of Lagos. When the driver parked by the toll gate to let people ease themselves, Toju watched them rush out in small droves, scurrying to private corners to do their business. She wondered why she'd been put on the bus. She hadn't even been told where it was heading. Nobody could hurt her, right? Since, essentially, she wasn't real? But still, she was wearing a body. Bodies could always get hurt, no matter who was wearing them.

She was still thinking through this when a thought diffused through her with a sudden sourceless assurance: *Come down and walk straight.* She knew this feeling, knew how sometimes the voice of peace was simply loosened tension in the chest. Toju found the deepest part of the bush and squatted. The body budged at the crotch for the first time since she'd worn it and Toju sighed, relieved at the weight of skin and bone sliding off. She stepped out of the body—left it there on soaked grass—and soared back into an unmoored freedom. She'd left before, obviously, but this time there was less guilt in the transition;

at least now she wasn't ripping her own bloodline to shreds, blowing a wound open where her life had been. She was only setting a young boy back who would get over it eventually. She imagined it getting easier.

· · ·

She would have been around nineteen in alive years when she took the body again. It had been molded differently: more fullness, more assuredness, and she felt like a woman in it. Looked like one too.

This time she met Ejiro, a fifty-year-old physics lecturer at the University of Nigeria, Nsukka. She was in a small canteen called Iya Peperempe, eating nkwobi, when he walked in and found her sitting alone, listening to music on her Walkman. Toju was wearing red lipstick, which remained largely unperturbed even as she dealt with the meat. He hesitated by the door, scanning the room, then took a few steps in her direction. "Mind if I join you?"

She was still wearing her headphones, so she didn't actually hear him, but what he was saying was obvious really, from how he gestured toward the chair. She shrugged: *If you like.* What people chose to do or not do had little bearing on her for the most part. She'd always been able to retreat into herself completely, to take noise, places, people and collapse them into an unrealness; as she would soon learn, this indifference would be exactly what endeared her to people.

When he sat down, Ejiro tried to make conversation (of course), but she had decided against seeing him, so she focused her eyes on her food instead, and he became all the way invisible.

"You don't attend this school, do you?" he said. "I've never seen you around." Nothing. "Hello? Hello?" He tried and tried, and she ignored him. When she was done with her food, she got up, paid the bill, and left. Ejiro watched her in embarrassed surprise.

They met again two months later, when she showed up to his class. Her hair was shaved and dyed red now, her cheekbones pretty much yelling. Before her, he'd never met anyone whose features were so distinctly theirs that they couldn't look like anybody else if they tried. When she picked a seat all the way at the back, he found himself hoping she would come and say something to him after class. She left in a hurry instead, disregarding the crucial tail of his lecture. When she finally spoke to him, it was weeks into the semester, and for no other reason but the sport of it.

She'd tried on her voice on different occasions and decided she liked herself best when it was direct and unsentimental, leaning vaguely toward what most people would call rudeness. It was fine, she realized; she wasn't a child anymore. She was nobody's daughter, so she could do as she liked.

"What are your office hours?" she asked Ejiro.

"Good afternoon to you too," he said, thickening his voice to hide his eagerness. Toju stared at him, scoffing inwardly at how predictable he was. When it became clear to him that not only did she not intend to greet, she was also about to turn around and leave, he cleared his throat. "Mm, twelve to four on most days. But you can send an email if you want to book an appointment outside of those hours. That said, it won't kill you to be respectful."

"Thanks," she said, making her way out.

"What's your name?"

She stopped, but with her back to him. It was a good opportunity to look at her ass, but something he couldn't quite name kept his neck straight.

"Uh . . . ," he continued, warning his eyes, "so that I can, you know, be on the lookout."

She decided on the first one that crossed her mind and turned around. "Steph," she said. "I'll be there."

It was the first time he realized he was afraid of her. Small girl like this, making him fidget in his own lecture hall! A whole him? The thought of her bringing questions to his office made him question if he even knew enough about anything at all. Imagine: In the first three decades of his life alone, he'd conquered three degrees and two grave losses and gone on to do so much more since. Who the hell was she to stand on top of all that? Who was she to make a mountain of herself? And in how long of knowing her? Running all this through his head, he felt angry, then embarrassed, then hopeful.

She didn't show up that week, which was fine with Ejiro; he could use the time to brush up on what he'd been teaching. When he got home, he tried to look her up on the university's portal. He typed the name Steph, then Stephanie. Both times, an infinite scroll of names fell before him. He should have known; how silly of him not to have asked her last name.

He should also have stopped there.

But when she eventually showed up, Ejiro couldn't hide his relief. They sat in his office talking for two hours, and then went to dinner after. He had no kids, he told her. His wife was at NYU, doing her PhD, but they were basically separated anyway. These facts were useful for Toju; an affair meant a secret, and a secret meant she didn't have to worry. It was a plus, too, to see how good he was at taking care of everything. He never let her lift a finger when she visited—not that she would have volunteered in any case, but still. He fed her, read to her in bed, explained topics using the most useful analogies, offered to help her study for other subjects, too, which she accepted because she genuinely enjoyed this life she was trying on.

"So, when can I come and see your place?" he asked once, as they lay naked in bed cuddling. He was smoking a cigarette, a habit it had never occurred to him to pick up in five decades until he met her. But she always smoked after sex, and if you could *see* this girl right now, you'd understand. She made you want to pirouette on the edge of danger. *I want to get there*, he thought often, when they were together. *I want to hack this game; give me the cheat code; get me to the level of freedom you're in.*

"Your place is bigger," she said, then kissed him, pulling a tripled curl of smoke from his mouth into hers. She wriggled out from under him, rolling him over on his back; then she straddled him, leaning into him. "There's just . . . so much more room here."

"That's fair. But . . ."

"But nothing then." He didn't ask again. When her voice grew clipped like that, the rest of the conversation fell off without question, like split ends, disappearing.

Another time, they were cooking jollof rice in his kitchen. Well, he was doing the cooking really, as usual, and she was sitting on the marble counter. "You're always by yourself," he pointed out, concern folding the skin between his eyebrows. "You eat by yourself, go out by yourself. When you're not with me or studying, what do you do? Don't you have friends?"

"No need for all that. I'm perfectly happy with you. I don't really need anything else."

"Well . . . I asked because I was going to tell my friend about you, and I wondered if—" It was right there on the counter that Toju felt it: her heart standing to its feet, climbing out from behind her rib cage, steadying itself on the ground, then finding its way out the door, as if to say *Oya oh, meet me when you're ready.* There are so many things a body can do heartless, so she still let the weight of him press her back into the spine of his scant mattress, night after night, until he woke one morning to find her gone. At his big age, she had him writing letters (he didn't even know where to address them), looking for her through lecture halls, asking around for her (though nobody knew her well enough to guess where she could be). Her leaving wasn't to say that she didn't pity him, because that was not necessarily true. It wasn't about him. She'd made this choice for herself, knowing the possible difficulties involved. In that sense, every damage caused was incidental, simple collateral harm—the kind people can cause when they're swerving between lanes at breakneck speed.

． ． ．

In Edo, she met Tinubu, a six-foot-one football player who trained at Samuel Ogbemudia Stadium every Saturday. He'd been watching her for a while. When she finally caught his eye, she held his gaze until he looked away. When he looked back—which was inevitable, really, seeing as nobody ever looked at Toju only once—she got up and walked to the deserted back of the stadium, where she simply stood and waited for him to arrive. It was an unuttered instruction. When he arrived, she held him against the brick wall and kissed him. He didn't need to think about it.

"Tell me if you want me to stop," she said, tongue pacing the rim of his ear. "I will if you want me to."

"Oh no. Please."

"Please what?" she asked, finding the inside of his shorts. Her voice was erect with authority.

He hesitated, then begged. "Don't stop. Abeg."

She made her way to her knees and held her palms against his hips, keeping him in the warm dark of her mouth, until he yelped, "Oh God, oh God," and unraveled with such force he lost track of his breath.

"What is your name, sef?" he asked afterward, embarrassed, to which she replied, "Does it matter?" He shouldn't have insisted, but he did, so she told him Etin, which was a random name from the Old Town, meaning strength—a name she decided to keep for the rest. She knew from the way he held her and from the saccharine pride with which he showed her to all his friends that Tinubu's mind was going to follow her when she left him. But he was not the first, and he wouldn't be the last either.

After Tinubu there was MuryDee, the musician in Benue with whom she hibernated for a week straight. Then Vincent from Port Harcourt, a manager at Zenith Bank who, unable to tell his colleagues why he couldn't function at work, lied that his sister had died suddenly.

Then Yasmin in Kano, the guitarist, to whom the entire thing felt like a long hallucination. Emem suffered the least after she left, but only because they'd both been high through all the public sex and night walks anyway. Toju sifted through them with more ease as she went, shrugging off their desperation, moving quietly and quickly, leaving a trail of pleas in her wake.

But you know how they say it: just as water must find its level, wahala sef must find its mate. So in a way, this is what God must have intended when he sent Agbon to Toju that night, perched atop a barstool in a dank nightclub in Rivers State, black velvet romper with a deep cut speeding down her sternum, dark rum on the rocks, a small forest full of thick, dark curls for hair.

Toju had started on the dancefloor with her eyes closed, throwing her body back into the bass. As usual, the club shifted its collective eye in her direction, replete with desire as she moved, bodies hovering around in clusters, trying to touch, wanting to watch, as she moved marvelously alone. Someone had told her before—who knows which of them now—that she danced like the music was internal, like she herself was a soundsource, a body with a boombox at the chest, shooting her limbs out in perfect sync. It was true. Between the dancing and the mere fact that Toju knew herself and trusted her body's epic proportions, nights out were predictable. She danced with uninterrupted focus, until sweat started leaking in stray lines, and by the time she made her way to the bar, there would be a short queue of men asking, "Please, what would you like to drink? Just name it," and she would pick the one she found most bearable.

Women usually moved differently, with a more calculated intensity, but so far she had been able to trust that whoever she wanted in the club would find her by the end of the night, or at the very least have a *Yes* in their gaze that made it easy for her to close in on them.

A certain pride had grown in Toju because of this, the kind particular to those who've always refused to stand at attention inside their own beauty. She relaxed her shoulders inside herself, put her feet up on the center table, put all her luggage down. She was at home there. She didn't approach people, really, because she didn't need to; people came to her, the world moved to find her with shame in its eyes, begging for her attention. It knew also what it was like to be left by her, to be shrugged off and swatted like a perching fly.

She arrived at the bar to order her double shot of Hennessy, neat in the glass, and she was right, of course, there were three men behind her. But when she looked to her left and saw Agbon there, she stood still for some time, watching the woman as she watched herself in the mirror, bobbing her head to the music. Despite the desire drooling through Toju's body, she decided against approaching her. Instead she bet with herself that—based on rough estimations and past experience—it would take two hours at most for the woman to make her move.

By the eighth shot that night, Toju's skin was glazed with sweat. Agbon, on the other hand, had gotten up no more than twice to sway from side to side to songs she enjoyed. When she moved, she seemed to bend the mood of the room. When she walked across the room to take a phone call outside, the sweating crowd on the dance floor gasped apart to give way to her, as if there were an invisible barbed-wire fence around her that warned them with its spikes, *donttouchme, donttouchme*. When she walked back into the bar, Toju tried to resist but she found herself glancing back in Agbon's direction, trying to win her own bet. *I bet she'll stand up*, Toju thought, because she was fond of saying that she couldn't trust anyone who could sit still through good music, and it was fucking Gyptian playing. Who could resist his voice doing that thing it does over a beat, on a night like this? It was an order, an instruction to touch somebody. *She's going to get up and walk up to me.* But two hours had passed already and Toju was mostly wrong.

One thing had changed, though: where before Agbon had looked at her with the same calculated curiosity with which she regarded the rest of the club, now she watched Toju with a stubborn unshifting focus as she wound suggestively against a stunned man. But that was it. When Toju tried to make her get up by beckoning to her, she held the same divine posture, politely resisting, wearing that refusal in her squared shoulders, holding Toju at a distance. Toju was afraid of Agbon because it was clear that she was the type who made people discard their pride, those quasi-cruel kinds who were used to devotion. She knew this because even now, only with Agbon's eyes on her, Toju found herself wanting to say yes to questions that hadn't even been asked.

Toju walked into the bathroom with two results in mind: Either Agbon would walk in there to find her, or Toju would come out and walk straight to her. It was that time of night when the shots had built an extra brave bone in her body and unhinged her at the mouth; she could do as she pleased in Jack Daniel's name. But when she returned, Agbon was gone with her bag. Panic slithered through Toju as she left the club, looking around, regretting every moment she'd extended her dumb game for.

She found Agbon outside, leaning against the wall, a beat-up phone in her hand. Toju walked up quickly, muttering thank-yous to god-knowswho under her breath. Just then, Agbon turned in her direction.

"Ah," Toju said, "you're going already?" She knew this was a stupid thing to say to someone she'd never uttered a word to. She sounded like the men she was often amused by.

"I wasn't leaving just yet. Just came out for a cigarette."

"Oh," Toju said, unsure what to say now that she'd brought herself outside. Inside had been so much less intimidating. If she'd waited, she would have had the strobe lights to lean on. She of all people knew how useful they were for casting shadows and swallowing the razored edges between people. "Okay." *Where had her words gone?*

Agbon held out the pack of cigarettes to her. "Want one?"

She nodded, then took one and held it to her mouth. "Lighter, please?" Agbon leaned forward and lit the cigarette for her, then they leaned back against the wall together, in silence.

"So, you're a dancer, huh?"

Toju was thankful for the question. She'd gone through a thousand icebreakers in her head, but they'd all gotten caught in her throat like tiny cold stones. "Well, I wouldn't say that. But I do love to dance."

"That much is clear. You're a pleasure to watch. But you knew that already."

"I like the way you watched me." Toju said this before she could stop herself.

Agbon turned to face her, looking at her intensely now. "Yeah? How did I watch you?"

Toju averted her eyes, suddenly hyperaware of her own face. "I don't know, it was just very . . . sure? I don't know if that's the word I'm looking for. But, um, yeah."

"Well, does it make you uncomfortable?"

"No, I told you—I like it."

"It can't be both?"

"Well, maybe. I guess it could be, yeah."

Agbon looked away, watching the road ahead of them. "Where are you heading after here?"

"Nowhere planned," Toju said, quicker than she would have liked. "Where do you live?"

Amused by something Toju wasn't quite certain of, Agbon giggled and then said, "I guess you'll have to find out."

They walked for ten minutes and arrived at a road, which bent left into a soft darkness. Toju looked up at the building, unclear about its color (*was it white? off-white? a light yellow?*) but she didn't care. She wouldn't have cared if Agbon had taken her to a matchbox at that point, she just wanted to be where she was.

The door opened to a small flat, empty save for two black sofas, a center table, and one plasma television. "Here," Agbon said, throwing her bag onto the sofa. "Make yourself comfortable."

Toju looked around, trying to figure out what it was about the place. "Your house is so . . . clean," she said, finally, though that was putting it mildly. The house looked unlived-in. "It must be new space, right? Because I know that me, I could never keep a place so clean, except I just mo—"

"Would you like some water?" Agbon asked as if she hadn't heard Toju talking at all. "So you're not hung over in the morning. Getting some."

"No, thank you." Then, "Actually, yes."

"Okay, well, I'll go get some and then we can go to my room. Unless you want to sit and watch some tele—"

"No, no, no, not at all," Toju said hurriedly. "I think it's best to go inside. It's late anyway."

Agbon kissed Toju as soon as they entered, with the lights still off. They kept their eyes closed, both starving at the hands, feeling for each other blindly until there was a flurry of clothes on the ground.

Toju woke up to a lightspill on the tile and collected herself quickly, remembering herself in pieces: *I am in the body, I am safe, and I'm with her; I didn't imagine it, it was real.* And it was real, because Agbon's arms were still around her. "Good morning, you," she said, kissing Toju's neck. "I've been waiting for you to wake up because my arm has low-key been numb for like an hour. But I didn't want to wake you. You look fine anyhow when you sleep."

Toju laughed. "Oh God, sorry. Was I asleep long?" She shifted. "I'll leave now, don't worry."

Agbon kept her grip in place. "Who asked you to do that one now? Oversabi." Toju found herself feeling flattered that she wanted her to stay. "Except you want to go, of course. Do you have somewhere to be?"

"No, no. I just thought you'd, you know, want your space back or something." It was also then she realized how ridiculous it was that they hadn't asked each other's names. She figured it might be less awkward if she flitted through her own collection of names and decided on the first one in mind.

"Etin, by the way. My name is Etin." For a moment, she regretted lying. Nothing about this woman called for it, but it's not as if she knew anything about her either. Agbon made to get out of bed and Toju watched a sunray climb down her back.

"Right. Etin. They don't do breakfast where you're from?" She looked back at Toju from the edge of the bed and caught her staring. She smiled and shook her head, and Toju's face refused to close. "I'll go make some."

The full English breakfast was made with so much love it had Toju forgetting she still didn't know her name. She remembered again the next morning, the second time in a row they'd woken together. They'd had dinner, made out, eaten, had sex, watched films, eaten, slept, and woken up, suspending the world outside for each other, and still. "You never told me your name," Toju pointed out as she lay against her on the sofa.

Agbon looked at her. "Well," she said, holding Toju in her arms, "you never asked."

"True. But I just thought you'd—"

"You can just ask now, if you really want to know, you know?"

"Okay, what's your name?"

"Agbon."

"Wait, so Agbon means . . ."

"*Life.*"

"What's the full name?"

"Agbontaen. *Life is long.*" And responding to the look on Toju's face, "I know . . . it's not very common. But that's my name sha."

She stroked the side of Toju's head. "Etin," she said, weighing the name in her mouth. "I like yours too." Toju found herself wishing it was her real name that was being pronounced with that much kindness, so before she could stop herself, she said, "Actually, it's Toju." Agbon repeated it, "Toju," without asking why she'd lied about her name in the first place.

A fear yawned in Toju, lodging there and stretching larger in her chest the more time she spent with Agbon. She was in an apartment with hardly anything to look at, with someone for whom she had no references, whose bedroom was literally a mattress on the ground. Who was Agbon? What did she do? What did she like?

Agbon instructed Toju to lie down and massaged her shoulders and back with oil. "You're so restless. You remind me of a younger me. If you calm down and stop looking for the meaning of things all the time, you'll enjoy them more. You can actually just relax. That's an option too."

Toju looked back at her and smirked. Her body was already stupefied by Agbon's weight on her; she knew her voice would be shaky. "I have no idea what you're talking about. I'm just curious. But okay, I'll stop."

Three nights later, they were eating dinner when Toju started again. "Tell me, what about your family? Where do they live? Do you have friends? Don't you like art?"

Agbon let the discomfort show then, a warning skipping through her face. "Are you sure you want to spend all the time we have together asking all these things? What do they have to do with anything?"

Toju was on her fourth glass of wine and raising her voice now. "What's the matter naw? What's wrong with what I'm asking? I just want to know. That's all. Why the hell won't you let me know you?"

Right then, Agbon felt it: her heart ejecting itself, then making its way out of the room: *Oya oh, meet me outside when you're ready.* She got up and looked at Toju, saying with a new and detached calm, "Listen, find me in the room when you're ready to just be here with me." She shut the bedroom door behind her, trying with everything left to stand still and have mercy.

Toju found her some minutes later, apologetic, though that didn't stop her from wanting to check around, from snooping. Until it was being withheld from her, she hadn't realized how much she depended on knowing, how much the predictability of others helped her map out herself. What could she do with a person she didn't know at all, someone who didn't care to know her past or future, who asked no intrusive questions, giving her an excuse to disappear? How was she to love someone who clearly knew how to leave and be left, who loved with her palms open instead of bundled up in a fist? Toju didn't know what to do with these easy mornings, with this safety.

The next morning, Agbon needed to get groceries. Toju pretended to be asleep. Agbon kissed her forehead and whispered, "I love you" into her ear before walking out the door. Toju wanted to wake from her pretend sleep to tell her that this was mutual, that her heart had never felt this way for anyone before, that this was a threat, that she had never planned to fall into a love that grounded her in her body, that made her want to abandon all the leaving. She wanted to tell her to please stay and hold her instead. She even wanted to confess, to tell her about the hovering, about how she'd left the body before and was only now wearing it again, how ungrounded she was, how gone. But the longer she thought about this, the more she wondered what else might come out, if Agbon might freak and throw her out instead. After all, when Toju asked, "So, what if I leave?" Agbon had responded with a crushing indifference: "Then you leave."

"You won't cry? That's it?"

"I probably would, but the universe is expansive, you know? We never run out of possible loves. Everything is about choice, then. I'm here now, you're here now. This is good. It's enough."

This was too close. A person this disconnected from everything, untethered from the world and its expectations, unbothered by the possibility of grief, could do damage. All this reminded her too much of herself.

When she heard the door click smooth into its lock, Toju jumped out of bed quickly and began pacing the apartment, looking for clues. She was right: Agbon had no favorite objects lying around, no letters, no photos, nothing. Everything there was simply functional: sofa, table, knives, bed. With anxiety shooting through her like a din of live sparks, Toju banged her fist against the table, frustrated now, afraid. *Maybe I should just calm down*, she thought, *maybe I should just relax*. But she had started the search already, troubling the house for answers, and now it answered by ejecting a tiny brown chest into the room, right by the center table.

Toju blinked twice and moved forward. Inside there was a note in black ink, written by a steady hand in perfect calligraphy:

Oh, love, but I warned you. I told you
what your questions could do.
Now look what you've done.

RAIN

Wura Blackson was determined to rest in peace.

To make sure of this, she was going to die alone. She wasn't going to go the traditional way, surrounded on her deathbed by family members who would hold her hand, smile weakly into her face and pray for her, singing worship songs as her body crossed over. Wura was not that kind of believer.

As clearly as some people remembered the day they gave their lives to Christ, she remembered the day she took hers back: a dull Sunday evening over a plate of pounded yam and efo riro when she realized she no longer wanted to cover her food with the blood of Jesus. She had spent all her life praying this prayer, and then quite suddenly decided that Jesus, by now, had already lost enough blood and she didn't need to be part of the millions of people summoning more. With just as much clarity, Wura decided, two years after that Sunday, on her new faith.

When Wura still believed in heaven and hell, she (of course) wanted heaven with all the cells in her body. She wanted to be right, so badly to be right, to be ushered into the afterlife by a warm, holy light and told *well done*. But now? She couldn't imagine an eternity—no matter its promises of golden streets and manymansions—that didn't feel like punishment. She'd done a lot of living and she was thankful for it, sure, but what she wanted at the end was for the room she died in to be still enough for her to hear her own body go quiet, to hear her heart stagger toward its final punctuation. For that moment to feel correct, she knew she had to be the one to think that final thought, *It is done*, as she slid past the slippery threshold into nirvana, into nothingness. After that thought came, what she wanted to follow was silence. No wailing, no mourning, no dramatic grieving, no swollen sighs. A quiet movement away.

Wura knew how she wanted to die way before the cancer, way before the coming of her daughter, Rain. Still, because she was Nigerian and part of a sprawling family tree, she knew that despite her desire to be cremated, her body might still be forced into a shiny casket and then into the ground, because what did large families love more than the opportunity to perform the grief they'd been storing? It's a comfort for people, sometimes, depending on who has gone—the world turning toward them with tenderness, faces softening, offering condolences. Wura had relatives who lived their whole lives for the relief of that moment—just them, finally, in the eyeline of compassion. So she decided not to tell her family about her cancer. It was a way to hold control.

She didn't get there alone, though. It was Rain who confronted her once, in a concerned voice, "You've lived your entire life for other people. All these years and you've convinced yourself that you want what they want you to want. But do you?"

"What do you mean?" Wura had asked her.

"You hate events, but you go to them. You hate geles, but you still wear them to parties. You didn't want children, and yet you summoned me. If you'd found someone to marry, I don't doubt that you'd have gotten married too, even though you hate weddings, even though you don't even want to belong to someone else. Where does it end?"

"This is Nigeria," Wura said weakly. "You won't understand how it is. Wise as you are, you're still a child. You literally came out of nowhere. I live here."

"And so? It's Nigeria, but this is also *your* life. What do *you* want?"

So Wura thought hard about it. Alive, she wanted nothing more than she wanted her work. It was her safety, her sanity, the place where she went to become her real self. But Rain was asking about an ultimate want. The answer couldn't be work. Wura searched herself for a way to explain what she'd always known. What would that be called in summary? How to break it down to a child? "Peace," she told Rain, finally. "Some silence. Something for myself after giving to everyone else. Freedom from, you know . . . all this."

· · ·

Throughout the country, Wura's name was sacred among upper-class women who, despite (and because of) the terrible secrets in their lives, needed to look arresting at parties. Wura founded her brand on this realization: gossipers were easily distracted. If you arrived confidently, looking like you had no skeleton, people would forget any scandal until they got home and had the thinking space to breathe. It was a tried and tested theory that Wura knew from her own life. She'd started out by making dresses for herself and her best friends, after all; all of them from families whose names grew loud in the spotlight, whose fathers were corrupt leaders who'd robbed the country insane. The dresses she made were a healing, in that they were tailored for specific problems. The sharper the pain, the more dramatic the fabric; the deeper the cuts, the louder the sleeves; the weightier the story, the more precise the tail. Soon enough, people started to ask where she and her friends got their clothes from. "I make them," she'd tell curious women in the thumping heart of an owambe, bodies flowing past. And they'd gasp and beg her to take their measurements right there and then. So, "Call me," she started to say. "Here's my card." And two turned to ten to hundreds.

Wura's work stood out because her creativity was bottomless. She was the only designer in Lagos who wouldn't take repeat orders, who never made one outfit twice. She left her job and opened a large store on Admiralty Road as a way to leap into the dream, yes, but only because she could. Her old job was with the family business—what were they going to do? Cane her? Women swarmed in, showing her photos of other outfits she'd made in *City People* and *Ovation*, saying *Just like this.* Men with hefty names came, too, hunting for Valentine's Day presents, Mother's Day presents, I'm Sorry I Cheated Again presents, but her answer was always the same: "I don't repeat my designs."

When Wura hit a block and had nothing in her she could pull for original material, she closed her store for however long she needed to and disconnected the phone. In her twenty-year career, she'd done this only twice: the year she almost ran mad and the year Rain appeared. Both times, she'd returned to the store foaming at the door with bodies. When wearing a Wura Blackson piece, women found themselves feeling taller, bigger, unquestionable. The actor Ifechi Adams said in an interview that wearing Wura Blackson was the closest she'd ever felt to being God. Wura knew the city like the palm of her hand— beyond its skin and blaring heart rate. She knew what Lagos demanded and what it took to appease it. What did it take to divert poisonous attention? Beauty. Sinful amounts of it. Silk pouring from women's elbows, jewelry resting on their clavicles, hips like small hills, expensive scents, air kiss one, air kiss two—meticulous masks.

Wura took only two hundred clients a year. Each client was assigned an hour where they could tell Wura anything they wanted to, and Wura would respond not with advice or apology but with a sketch. *A seventieth birthday? All right, wear this*, she'd say, putting HB pencil to A4 paper. *Your sugar daddy's funeral? Oh, then this. Your husband's nth mistress will be there? Definitely this.* It wasn't very often that a woman in distress would argue with her sketch, because Wura was attentive and thus rarely wrong.

The women who came to Wura knew that she had grief of her own, too, but they never dared confront her about it. Once, a woman tried it. "Was your father *the* Chief Blackson?" she asked. By *the* Chief Blackson, she meant the one whose assassination had been ordered by the government. His car had been shot three times a year prior to his death, and he'd lost all function in one arm as a result. But that wasn't enough, so they sent a letter bomb just to finish off the job. His wife ran away before all this, to Godknowswhere. When it happened, Wura knew why. She found out about her father's other life the year she turned ten—planting boys in the streets to kidnap white expatriates, demanding hefty ransoms in pounds and euros only—but try as she did, she couldn't hate him. By the time they traced it all to him, he'd looted enough to sustain two generations and stowed it all away in a Swiss Bank. It was his way of saying: My daughter, I have taken care of you.

Chief Blackson was a notoriously busy mogul and politician, but still he made time. And her parents together? Whew, a fortress. A powerhouse. The year her father was first detained, a riot broke out; area boys demanding his immediate release. Her parents were thieves, in the truest sense, yes, but which billionaire was not? At least they *did something* for the people; they had veins in the streets—they could feel every need. Chief always told Wura, "It's only someone you feel you need that you have to listen to as they insult you. When you need nobody, you can show everybody the door—even the commander in chief of your entire country. And how do you need nobody? Through money, which is freedom. Strive for that." It wasn't the kind of thing one should tell a child, but her parents knew that their time alive was limited. They had to give what wisdom they could, and quick. They had always known.

So Wura simply shook her head and told the woman, "No, that is another Blackson." When the woman was done talking about her issues, Wura said she had no dress for her, which was worse than seizing her jaw in an uppercut. The woman pleaded. She asked to be permitted to look around, but Wura insisted that the dresses were all taken, that this was high grief season and the woman wasn't the only one with a problem. Wura had the power to have the woman taken out by security when she began being dramatic, but it was punishment enough for her to watch her melt into hysterics instead, her legs softening until she fell to her knees. Wura stood tall over her with no visible remorse in her eyes, thinking, *Serves her right.*

"I'll soon leave," the woman said, desperation peaking in her voice, when she realized Wura's mind was unchangeable. "But please, let me just gather myself. My driver is outside."

"Take her to the crying room," Wura said to her assistant, losing interest.

The crying room was a well-ventilated, thickly dark room with rows of lounge chairs flown in from Italy, each sectioned off with room dividers. Wura gave anyone who entered noise cancellation headphones, so that they wouldn't have to hear other women wailing. Some women had spent entire workdays in there. When women left the room, they often asked, "How do you keep that room so dark? It's almost like it breathes black smoke. Blinds alone can't do that." She'd laugh, pat them on the back, and see them off.

Inside the room, this woman didn't wail. She sighed one million times, tears rolling down her cheeks, until she was ready.

Outside the door and behind the woman's back, Wura turned to her assistant, who read the look without needing words—*If you like yourself, don't ever let me see her here again.* Experience could do that.

"Yes, ma," she said aloud, meaning it with all the bones she had.

• • •

Success was a drug on its own, but Wura still had outside voices in her head, so she asked herself one day: *What's life without love?* She took stock of her life and realized that, yes, she had the longest waiting list of VVVIP clients in the country, but—well, that was it. She was okay with that, until she wasn't. She thought to herself: *I need a person of my own. I need a person who comes from my body, who is a citizen of me, who I can teach about life. I need a child.*

Then she got pregnant. Then she decided that she was going to name her daughter Esther. She also decided that her daughter was going to be one of the most beautiful children in Lagos, that she was going to be a person no one with a heart could ignore. Wura could already see into the future: clients pouring into the store, *ooh*ing and *aah*ing, saying, *What a wonderful mother you are, she looks just like you.* Her whole life, she'd lived on the rim of normalcy; maybe a child would be the cure; maybe this decision would finally shift her in. Wura was strong, yes, and she had unconventional beliefs, also yes, but she was still in a bleedable body. She was still a human being— which meant that, as much as she hated to admit it, she was still malleable. She still said yes to many things she wanted to say no to.

Funerals and weddings, for instance. Rain was right. Wura hated both for their excesses, and each time she showed up to one, she swore to herself that it would be the last time. *I'm never doing this again*, she would think as the bride walked down the aisle or the choir croaked their hymns or the professional mourners burst into the tears they'd been hired to cry. *Never.* And still, when she entered her house and Sanusi, her gateman, handed her yet another invitation from a loyal client, she did the same thing every time: she took off her shoes at the door, put down her bag, sighed, and then began sketching a dress. When done, she'd get on the phone to her tailors. "Afternoon. Yes. Another black boubou. You know the style. You have my measurements. Yes, cut it. I'll be there to do the finishing myself." She couldn't get herself to stop. She was Wura Blackson, after all, a household name— the name always spoken exactly that way, always Wura Blackson, never Wura, never Ms. Blackson. Who else could Lagosians point to that had

become bigger every single year for decades since she started her brand?
No one. At least not in fashion, with its volatile affections.

Wura understood exactly why these women depended on her in
that way—why she was a relevant witness in the first place. They'd all
told her too much about their lives. She had listened. And in turn
they came back again and again, checkbooks ready in their bags. Even
in the deepest recession, when other brands experienced a nosedive in
demand, Wura's profits grew skyscrapingly high. She needed her clients just as much as they needed her; their secrets were endless fod-
der, and Wura enjoyed peeling their layers open, her best work made
under their influence. She knew what problems it would cause if clients who'd spent millions of naira on her clothes invited her to come
to their husband/boyfriend/girlfriend/child's wedding or funeral and
she said no. All that calcified malice would be all over the papers.
Plus, wouldn't a *no* multiply her clients' grief? Wouldn't it be cruel?

"No," her daughter had told her what felt like a million times, her
voice more impatient each time. "Being obsessed with what people
think will kill you one day. You need to be careful. You can say no.
You have cancer, for God's sake! Even if you didn't, so what? Are they
going to beat you? So they'll talk about you. They talk about everyone! Everyone talks about people, including you—and you don't see
the people you judge dropping dead."

Wura shrugged. She had no way of knowing that she wouldn't
drop dead. Wasn't she disintegrating already? Who knew how much
life was left in her.

"Try it," Rain said. "Try to say the word."

"What word?"

"You know the one I mean."

Wura closed her eyes and called on courage. "No," she said finally.
The word sounded like a plant withering.

"Good," Rain said, smiling honestly. "That's a start. We'll strengthen
it together."

Rain arrived out of nowhere—irritable, fully formed, complete with a voice and full of defiance. Not a baby. Her first words were, "I can't believe you wanted to name me after your horror film of a mother. I could never have allowed that."

"My mother was not a horror film," Wura retorted, shocked by this barrage of a presence in her room but too tired to process the bizarreness of it. She'd seen enough strange things in her life. Earlier that week, she'd gone to the doctor to complain about dizzy spells on what would have been her child's due date had it stayed, only to receive news some days later that she was going to die. And then to come back home to meet this? She was exhausted.

"Got it," Rain said. "If you say so. But good luck convincing me of that. Also, just so you know: I will never show myself to any of your relatives. If you try to force me, you will never see me again."

Before Rain, *horror* was not a word Wura would ever have associated with her mother. Strict, she often called her, or disciplinarian, but she wasn't about to start defending herself. She did notice her heart racing, though. Who knew—with the pills on pills on pills, she could be hallucinating. But what did that matter? It felt good to talk to someone.

"Stop looking around like that," Rain said. "She's not here. It's just me."

Wura took a deep breath, realizing her own fear. "So what do you want to be called?"

"It's not about what I want to be called. It's about what my actual name is. It's Rain."

"Rain," Wura repeated, and the girl smiled like the world made sense. With her lips pulled back like that, Wura recognized her—they had the same teeth, the same half-inch gap in their smiles. This was her daughter and she knew it. It didn't make sense, but it did.

"What?" Rain asked.

"Of course, my daughter would have a sharp mouth," Wura said, shaking her head. Rain cackled in response, which made Wura smile.

When Wura got pregnant, she'd expected to have at least a few years to adjust to this part: when the child could talk and ask questions. She'd thought she'd have time to figure out what to do in case of rudeness or rebellion, since she didn't plan to hit her child. But now that the daughter was here and rude, all Wura could do was stare at her.

"Just a warning," Rain said. "I don't come with a mask. Or a filter. I say what I actually think."

"Okay," Wura said again, too full of joy to hear both the words and the warning tone inside them. She wasn't alone anymore. She could deal with anything, including this blade of a child.

"Well," Rain said, swinging her feet from the edge of the bed. "You asked for a daughter. I'm here. Aren't you?"

* * *

Rain had no time to waste. For a person who was above and beyond time itself, there wasn't much to fear. Whatever society wanted her to be was what she refused to become, and she proved that from the beginning. She had existed before and she would do it again and again, if provoked. Her other mothers had barely survived her, but Wura was strong enough for it. She knew that. So Rain had started their relationship by refusing to be born. When Wura was six months pregnant with her, sewing a boubou for the first lady, Rain purged herself out of her body on the storeroom floor, clot by clot, only to arrive by herself at the nine-month mark—already tall and wordy.

She wasn't all mean. Or rather, she wasn't mean at all. She just was not interested in being seen.

"How old are you, even?" Wura asked.

"As old as you want me to be."

So Wura sent Rain to YHS, an expensive school on the more enviable side of the bridge. Every year, she paid her fees and no questions were asked, because it was a school after all and what did it matter if she owed nothing. Wura attended all PTA meetings, a quiet presence at the back of the hall, and because she always showed up with her face all dark and sunglassed, no one dared approach her and ask, *Which one is your child?* Questions like that were for smiling women. She could see Rain, and Rain could see her clearly, and Wura had learned to make that all that mattered. Cancer could do that. So could *this* daughter. Besides, who cared which student matched which parent, if not for gist sake?

Rain was nothing like Wura had been as a child, a student. She loved school, she loved learning, she loved teaching Wura new things. She talked about how all the young girls were just so obsessed with boys and getting their attention, when boys were nothing special at all. She didn't like girls either, really, but if she had to choose someone to kiss, she would pick a girl.

"Your mouth ehn," Wura teased. "This your mouth will put you into trouble one of these days."

"With who?" Rain asked back, her neck a curious arc. She waited a few seconds and then said, "Let me go and change." Wura couldn't think of a quick retort, a fact that she agonized over all night, turning from side to back to belly in bed. What kind of child was this, so unafraid of the world?

"It's okay," Rain said the next morning, her voice gone all toddlered, curling in on itself. This was one of the endless wonders of her: she could switch between ages, between genders, between temperaments whenever she so pleased. Sometimes she become thunderous for no reason at all; other times, she was gentle as a drizzle. She could be a cruel girl or the sweetest boy ever, a son it had never occurred to Wura to pray for, with a dark storm of hair tumbling down his back. "I'll let you win next time, okay?"

When Wura imagined having a child, Rain was the furthest thing from her mind. But now that this was what she got, she didn't hide Rain either. She told the clients she was close to, like Ms. Kolawole, her longest-standing customer, all about her.

"When will we finally meet this daughter of yours, ehn, my sister? Na so so hear we dey hear of the girl, when will we see her?"

"When we're ready," Wura said, even though she knew Rain would never agree.

The only other person Rain had ever showed her true self to was Wura's heaven—a former lover named Adura.

After all the old friends had fallen off like dead leaves, after work had swallowed Wura completely, Adura was the only person who had ever heard Wura's real words out of her real mouth. When Adura met Rain, she didn't try to tell her to brush her hair or that her skirt was too short. She didn't think it either, or Rain would've been able to tell. She also didn't think Rain was *pretty*; she thought she was brilliant and self-assured, which pleased the girl. The three of them lay down on the floor, rolling around in the duvet together until they were perfectly wrapped like three sausage rolls, and watched a film that way. The only way to explain the way Rain felt around them was using the word *glee*. Wura liked seeing Rain like that, so she tried to invite Adura to the house more, but Adura had both a secret wife of her own and a multinational to head. There was only so much time.

"It's okay," Rain told Wura as she cried over the end. All that missing weighed too much at times. "It's okay if your heart is breaking. Maybe you'll get over it or maybe you won't, but you'll still be you and you're a crucial person to be. You still have your work, which makes you so, so bright. Put it all into your work."

· · ·

Rain and her razor mouth stayed away while Wura worked. Wura locked herself away for two weeks and made her final collection called

The Hundred, which rearranged every ache in her body by the time she was done. She sent messages to her favorite clients and asked them not to spread the word, then fell asleep in her office overnight to Rain singing to her. By the time she woke up, there was a queue the length of two anacondas outside. Customers fought each other at the door, yelling. There were men, women, children. Wura kept the door locked and refused to serve anyone.

"I'm proud of you," Rain said, as Wura played Miles Davis's *Kind of Blue*.

"For?"

"For not opening the door. Your *no*s are getting stronger."

"Yeah," Wura said. Then after some time, she asked, "What will happen to you when I die?"

Rain didn't flinch. "I'll just go back to where I came from."

"Where did you come from?" Wura couldn't believe how long it'd taken her to ask this.

Rain laughed a shaky laugh that made her eyes a dark kind of wet. Her voice stiffened. "Where are *you* going when you die?"

"To nothing. Me, I'm fading to black."

"Exactly."

"Fair enough. Are you scared? Of losing me, I mean." Wura sometimes worried that she wasn't doing enough, that motherhood was not supposed to be this easy. But Rain appeared without that need to be cared for. Too much softness suffocated her. She reacted violently to being touched out of the blue, to being held.

Rain chortled and shook her head *no*. Then she asked, "Are *you* scared of losing yourself?"

Wura thought about it. "Hardly. I just didn't expect it to come so soon, you know? The pain, the treatments, all that? Those things are exhausting. Sometimes, I feel like I'm vanishing."

"Blue in Green" entered the room and Wura sat up, playing her fingers in the air. Her song.

"It makes sense," Rain said, seeing Wura's attempt at lightness. There wasn't that much time left for hints, though; she knew. So, "What do you want to happen? What kind of death do you want? How would you like to go?"

Wura put her hands down and sighed. "A silent one," she said, before she could stop herself. And then, "Sorry."

"Why are you sorry?"

"I don't know. Isn't that an odd thing to say to a daughter? That I don't want anyone there?"

"Not when that daughter is me. I won't wilt because you chose to die alone if that's what you're asking. I'm me and you're you. Have a silent death, Mummy. You deserve what you want."

It was the first time Wura had ever heard Rain direct the *M* word at her with such inescapable gentleness. "Are you sure?" she asked. Rain nudged her, and suddenly Wura knew what she had to do.

· · ·

Wura needed herself more than she needed any more secrets, so she shut down the store. Instead, she decided, they would deliver items in the final collection to the hundred clients she'd made them for, each with a personalized note. All gifts.

To Ms. Kolawole she wrote: *I've always admired your strength and confidence. I think you're a woman who will shine in this world if you really allow yourself to. Don't let them tie you to a tree. This is your final dress from me. You won't hear from me again. Cancer. Find other dresses. Wear them well. The magic is not in the fabric. It is in your body, your bones, your blood. —WB*

Also the daughter of a dodgy billionaire whose source of income no one knew, Wura trusted Ms. Kolawole, because the woman knew what questions not to ask and she did not mistake their silent understanding for friendship. Ms. Kolawole knew that the world was harsh, and so she clung only to her clothes and her jewelry and her Bible. She, too, was a woman who often heard the words "You're so lucky, I'd do anything to be you." She, too, wished she had the energy to ask, "At what cost?" But women like that didn't need to talk too much, didn't need to self-identify; their suffering was encrypted in the dark crescents under their eyes. She had *seen* Wura, and Wura, too, had seen her.

Wura's second favorite client was a man called Mr. Teniola Jones. Wura had sewn more than ten fitted evening dresses for him, complete with tails and veils. They were for his private use, worn only at home, with pearls and silk gloves, and he always sent her photographs. To him, she sent a note saying: *You give me courage. You are legitimate even when you're the only one who knows how to translate yourself onto your body. You are not invisible; you are real. And never alone. I feel you even now. Trust yourself. Take care. —WB*

He called her when he received it, cried hard to her on the phone, asking, "What do I do now? What do I do?"

"You live," she said. "You live, at whatever cost you can bear. That's all you can do." When he asked her what she needed, she said, "Space." Mr. Jones respected this.

Ms. Kolawole was harder to convince. She asked to bring Wura food at the hospital. Yam and owo. Her cook made it best, she said. "I'll be quiet if you want me to be. Just to drop the food and go. It's the least I can do."

Wura agreed and got back to work.

The dress that took the longest was for Rain.

· · ·

When Ms. Kolawole arrived with the food, she also brought a Bible, because if there was anything she knew, it was that Wura Blackson did not deserve to go to hell. After all she'd done on earth, she didn't want her to be thrown into a lake of fire where she would burn forever, over and over, her skin regenerating each time only to slide off the bone again. She felt like she owed it to Wura to tell her about the gospel. She watched Wura as she ate the yam, and then she asked, with steady searching eyes, "Do you believe in Jesus Christ?"

Wura wanted to lie, but she could feel Rain's voice in her ear telling her to flex the word, flex the word. "No," Wura said.

"I will make you one promise," Ms. Kolawole said. "If you just give your life to Christ and pray this scripture I give you—this Psalm 91, every single day—then no matter how far gone this cancer is, God will heal you." She believed herself. There were greater miracles in the Bible. What was a little healing?

Wura considered it. Yes, she had come to terms with dying and yes, she'd released the suffering around it. But she was still in a body, and there were times when the thought of dying still hurt. She'd planned so much. She'd wanted a different future. She wanted more time with Rain.

But Rain's voice again. Like showers on zinc. "So if I don't give my life to Christ, your God can't heal me?"

Ms. Kolawole tried to figure out what to say next. "He can, but you have to surrender first. You have to let him in for him to be able to work on you." Inside, her heart was somersaulting, but she stood her ground even as the concrete of the hospital floor seemed to be shifting. "Know this God and know peace. Don't let all this talent you have go to waste."

Wura realized that she felt sorry for Ms. Kolawole. There was so much desperation in her face, so much effort. But as irritating as the conversation was, Wura understood. Religion helped people cope with death. In its absence, what explanation did people have for all the bodies being lowered into the ground, for all the fell-asleep-and-didn't-wake-up, all the senseless shootings, the disappearances, the bodies being taken by clingy diseases? None. No explanation for how a body could be full of breath and life one minute, then a vacant case of flesh the next. The body you knew and loved, the body you held and hugged or fucked or kissed, now just a vessel with unclaimed organs inside. Just like that.

"Wura," Ms. Kolawole said, her eyes watering. "Please. Just consider it. Just try God and see."

As much as Ms. Kolawole was sure that this was what she wanted Wura to know, that this was the only way to secure eternal life, she was terrified by how calm Wura seemed to be. How immovable. How already at peace. Most sinners she'd told about Jesus Christ were stubborn and argumentative. But Wura was just . . . there.

"What does your God offer you?" Wura asked.

Easy. Ms. Kolawole knew this answer by heart. "An abundant life here on earth. Forgiveness for all sins. A heaven where there's no pain. Don't you want no pain?"

Wura shrugged.

"Can I pray with you?" Ms. Kolawole asked.

Wura needed this to be over. She wanted to smile and say, *Let me think about it*, then tell the nurses not to let Ms. Kolawole in again. But she was too tired now. She was too close to gone for that kind of pretense.

"No," Wura said. "I'm okay. I've heard you, but my answer is still no."

Ms. Kolawole knew she was overstepping now, but she'd gone too far to stop. She loved Wura, she really did. "What do you believe will happen after you die?"

"Well, I'll either return or become nothing. I'm hoping to become nothing."

Wura saw Ms. Kolawole's eyes soften with pity. "Ahhh," she said, a sorriness tiding through her voice. "Ah, Wura."

"You look scared," Wura said, chortling. She sounded like Rain. "Are you afraid of what your God will do to me?"

"Hm. Wura," Ms. Kolawole said, picking up her bag. She wanted to sidestep any possible blasphemy. "Look. It's okay if you don't want to listen to me. I will be praying for you. But please, if you change your mind, shey you know you can call me? Or just invite Jesus into your heart and ask him to take over. Wura, God will ask you about this moment."

"And I will answer," Wura said. "You're the one who's afraid, not me."

"Can I leave this with you?" Ms. Kolawole said, holding out her Bible.

"No," Wura said. "You need it more than I do."

◦ ◦ ◦

The next day, Ms. Kolawole went again, her body both full and empty from praying and fasting—and was told that Wura was already dead. Ms. Kolawole bribed the nurse to tell her more. "She didn't let anybody come inside," the nurse said. "But she didn't seem afraid. She asked for water and music. The next time we went to check in on her, she was gone."

Back at home, Ms. Kolawole's six sons welcomed her at the door. She was too tired to answer them. Now more than ever, she wished she'd had the daughter she'd been trying for, instead of this loud clan of boys, who wouldn't stop bickering about football. She'd given birth to all six in an effort to get that one girl she could talk to, show things to, pass down her dresses to, and yet.

"Mummy needs to sleep," she told them, and locked her door.

Inside her room, she tried on the dress again and cried. On her knees, she repeated Mark 9:24: *I believe, help my unbelief.*

IbelievehelpmyunbeliefIbelievehelpmyunbeliefhelpmyunbeliefhelpmyunbelief.

A presence entered the room, stirring the air. Ms. Kolawole was terrified. She was not ready to see God. "What's your name?" she asked. "Who are you? Who are you?!"

The presence thickened and Ms. Kolawole started backing away. "I rebuke you!" she said to the body in the room, hand over her eyes. "I plead the blood of Jesus, I plead the blood of Jesus! Jesus!"

"Calm down," the presence said back, and Ms. Kolawole lowered her hand, watching it solidify into the shape of a girl. The girl was wearing a black dress embroidered with ruby stones at the neck. Her eyes shone, but Ms. Kolawole knew that face. She had dreamed that face for years.

"My name is Rain," the girl said. "You asked for a daughter. I'm here."

TATAFO

(HALF THE SKY)

At times, you yourself are too guilty to be the narrator. So, you make way. You must make way.

But now I have to say, just to clear my conscience, that sometimes I *was* in charge of the installations—strong technologies made for the insides of boys' heads. Every batch was mass-assembled somewhere in [redacted], and when Èkó had marked them, had storied them in full, we inserted the chips pre-loaded with information on how boys would and *should* be. I watched the new skulls move through the conveyor belt in a cyclical choreography—perfect carbon copies. Some of us messengers were responsible for coding these cultures in the lab; others of us were in charge of delivering them, of fixing them in boys' heads as soon as we were sure they'd at least live long enough to become men.

Their parents knew all about it. In fact, they were the ones who helped their boys acclimatize to the new fittings, and they did so with joy because there was a promise to it: that if their boys grew to be the kind of men Èkó could be proud of, then their inheritances would be longer than the lagoon. They'd inherit more than the water and land.

The sky, the moon, the sun, and even God, could be gifted into their hands and they'd be able to bend the whole world to their will.

In every part of the world, boys are fed a uniform story that they get to spend their lives acting out. Still, every city makes its own unique promise. *It's a man's world*, people say all the time. But even in a man's world, there are men who senior other men, men who steer the ship. And, competitive beast that it is, Èkó always emphasized this hierarchy: *second to none, second to none.*

Have you ever seen a Nigerian excel at something before? They always take it further than they need to, push the wall until it crumbles. You know them before you know them, just by their walks alone. It's in the shoulders, in the neck, the ring around the waist, the legs. It's in the knowing who raised them, knowing what they can get away with, even with nothing in their pockets. Everything has levels. There are animals, you see, and then there are behemoths.

I watched the side effects of this procedure, and each time it jarred me: seeing sweet boys turn into men with iron for bones, men who stuffed their heartvoids with stunning women, women they'd choose and then shrink to the size of a crumb. I saw the way night claimed their heads, how they snuck out of homes in the dark and went hunting corners for young girls who'd either been spat out into the streets or who were trying their anxious bests to get home unharmed.

It's not easy to know when you first start changing. So, of course, everything won't just kpafuka at once. And yes, I'll admit: I was also part of those responsible for installing the muzzle on women's mouths, for seizing the word *no* from their vocabularies, sliding it out of their jaws and then jamming them shut as soon as they were born. Their parents knew this too. None of this is one-sided. We need both parts to play. We need the loudness to contrast the silence, because balance is how all economies work. Shame works, because there are those who we name when we talk power, but not when we talk harm.

Look, I want to say it's not the men's fault that they turn out this way, what with the voice on repeat in their ears telling them, *You're powerful, unstoppable, untouchable; there are no consequences for you.* Because what incentive is there to change if that's the story you inherited—a story of deep power, of inherent godlikeness? It's part of the design. You sef no go accept? It's the way of the road. Because I can tell you that without fear, na me go still tell you this one: they can choose to lose the chip the moment they start knowing themselves. They are told this to their faces when they're configured: you can change if you want. If they wanted to, they could say, *This cruelty is too heavy for my hands, take it back*, and we would.

In fact, we have. There are men who grew up to do that. They are less popular than most—lonelier, too, not as flamboyantly powerful—but they exist. When they come to us to surrender their heads at our head office, they always come quietly, as if keeping clean hands is something to be ashamed of. We always ask them, *Are you sure?* And if they say yes, we take their heads right back, on the spot. Because, wild as it may be, one thing I can say about Èkó is that nobody is forced to carry out its wishes. It sets your default, then shows you the pros and cons—offers a kind of SWOT analysis of every decision. *You're sure?* We always ask. *If you follow through, you will enjoy this. If you don't, you will lose this, this, and this. If you can live with non-compliance, then you know what to do.*

It's hard to choose the harder road, sure. But even me, a common gossip, will tell you that the things men do with their hands are not an inevitable part of the design. Most things are about incentive. Most things are about choice and reward. But there is a difference between a common thing and a compulsory thing. Blood on your hands is not a compulsory thing.

What I will also say is that women are magicians. I don't mean magic like the kind you were warned to avoid. I mean magic as in spinning story as lifeline, as in turning a wound into a star, as in holding an apocalypse in your core and smiling believably. Magic like turning a big burn into a lesson. Magic like a girl generating new selves to stay alive in her body; like *big girl* finally becoming *woman*. Magic like a plot twist, like becoming the opposite of what everything expects, like looking the world in the eye while biting into the word *cannot*. Magic as in, once familiar with its sticky juice, finding strength to discard the half-dead fruit. Magic like looking at one's best and worst selves at the same time and not running, not hiding, not blinking too fast. Like carrying the weight of that seeing while holding one's life. Magic like staying alive despite. Like growing up too fast but also right on time. Magic like being dead for years but staying for the photographs because ghosts don't show well in photos. Magic like goddammit this hurts and where is tomorrow and shit has gotten too fucked up now, but still coming out on the other side; always coming out on the other side. Magic like knowing your lines and reciting them even when you're under. Even then, being a good ghost, haunting nobody. Magic like look at me, I'll be so good at acting you think the statistics are lying; I'll make another body you never touched and it'll look just like the one I lost. Magic as in, watch, I can get so pretty you'll mistake me for alive. Every day, it's happening. We watch rolling miracles so often we forget to thank our stars.

But do you know the skill it takes, to take no time off? Even God rests. I tried to tell Èkó once: You have to be careful with this thing of not letting your best workers rest. You have to let people off stage, because under all their tricks, when the curtains close, even the most impressive magician you know is still a person. Magic is still a job, you know? And every worker must rest. When you refuse this, the whole act implodes.

He told me to shut up. *What do you know about raising anyone?* he shouted. *My sons are powerful. My daughters are the most beautiful. Who have you raised?! Answer me!*

Nobody, I said, shaking. *Nobody*.

Me, what's my own? I said sorry then, because am I not a common servant? I paid for the way my mouth ran then, so I don't need to talk more than this on the issue, or even start to tell you any of the million stories I know, because everywhere you look there are stories telling themselves.

AFTER GOD, FEAR WOMEN

While Mr. Osagie slept, his wife, Maria, lay in chains at the foot of the bed, where he'd kept her for three days now. She'd tried to wrest herself free on the first night, the chains grating and scarring her wrists as he snored away. On the second night, as the moon watched on, full-faced and unblinking, she pulled so hard she feared that by the time she got up, she would have two palms on the floor, facing up in a haunting greeting as the rest of her arms dangled with blood.

But now she lay still. She'd learned in those days, and the fifteen years leading up to them, that when trying to appeal to her husband's soft heart didn't work, she could lean on a reliable second plan. All she needed was to keep being herself—not the dutiful wife or somebody's mother, but her real self, stubbornly content—and soon The Itch inside her husband would begin and he'd punish her for it. *How dare you be so unaffected? Who are you?* Not once, not twice, he'd called her a stone for remaining outwardly unbroken through their shared devastations.

When their third miscarriage happened, he took a hammer to their dining table, then the chair, then the wall, all the while screaming a guttural cry. That evening, it rained wood and foam and concrete. Still, she was the one who held him as his grief ebbed and drained, whispering, "It is well, it is well." Worse things had happened since then by his hand, and each time she kept the ache stored inside, looking blankly at him as he hurt her, which only made him itch harder.

Drained as she was with him and everything, she knew that plan B was her only chance at making him remove the chains himself. Husbands were like that sometimes. All they needed was to remember the power vested in them by godknowswhat, and soon you'd be nothing.

She'd stay this way, then, she decided, until either he or God Themself said *enough.*

Long before all this, when he was still young and clueless, Mr. Osagie's father woke him up to The Itch. "Very soon, you'll start to feel something under your skin," he'd said, sizing up his lean son as they sat on the verandah. Mr. Osagie's father was a man of few words, but when he spoke, he spoke so heavy and so low you had to widen your hearing. "When it comes," he said, his eyes fixed on a tree, focused, as if reeling this wisdom in from somewhere far away, "scratch it. It will feel strange the first few times, then it will not. The more you do it, the more you will become yourself; the more you'll be like your peers and become strong like me." He turned to his son, whose eyes were curious. It was no small thing for a father—the biggest presence in the house—to sit with his son and talk. It was a privilege, the boy knew. "Don't you want to be strong like me?" his father asked. Osagie, who was shorter and weaker than most of his friends, nodded eagerly: *Yes sir, I want to be like you.*

"Then I've showed you the way," his father said, closing the talk.

The first time Mr. Osagie scratched The Itch was after Sunday school, when he pushed his crush, a girl called Mabel, to the ground for talking to another boy. His father was right, it did feel weird, like a seed of badness blooming. But The Itch also deepened, bringing about a sickly sweetness as his friends gathered around him, cheering. (Have you seen the inside of a soursop? The feeling inside his stomach had a texture like that.) The teacher took the girl away as they jeered at her. Inside his body, the sensation breathed and stretched, prickling bittersweetly. He stood, trying to resist it, because back then he wasn't sure he liked the way scratching The Itch sometimes hurt not just him but other people he cared about. He did like the praise that followed, though. He liked that it made him feel like a small god. Mr. Osagie's father was long dead and by now, decades removed from that day at church, Mr. Osagie had a head turning gray and a conscience that had curdled. (You know what age can do.)

"What do you mean you don't *discipline* your wife?" his friends often asked him. Most of them were so used to itching that when it came, they didn't have to think twice before using their wives, daughters, and other lookalikes to scratch it back, until they found that sweet equilibrium that calmed their bodies. "So how do you deal with her when she misbehaves?" they'd add, some of them twitching. "And how do you calm yourself?"

In response, Mr. Osagie always shrugged. He had never hit his wife, Maria, before, no. He had promised her this on their second date, years and years ago, as they sat on the floor in his dusty face-me-I-face-you apartment. "I will never hit a woman. My father used to beat my mother senseless . . . and I could never. I'd never. I'm sorry it ever happened to you." She saw the truth rise in his face like a warm sincere dawn, and she believed him because, back there in that room, something about the way the light fell between them made his love feel like *yes*, like *amen*. And of course, young as she was then, she hadn't been taught that there are far worse ways to be cruel, far more damaging ways to hurt a person without leaving a single mark to prove your guilt.

So far, he hadn't eaten those words. Physical wounds *were* off-brand for him. Instead, he dealt in invisible violences—those ghostlike kinds that dashed around the house and lingered, swimming in and out of furniture and walls so long, so well, that it was impossible to pin them down. He knew what his actions stole from her, but he didn't mind watching her lose it. Try as she might to upset him enough for him to Do Something that would make everything else believable, he wouldn't hit her, though she wished he would for fucking once. She needed marks. For this kind of thing, most people worked by sight, not by faith, because the world was twisted that way. *They had it way worse,* they'd say, *she could never imagine what was happening in their own homes. Didn't she have a mother? A sister? Couldn't she compare? Men needed strong women with strong spines, not wusses who ran back home at the slightest discomfort. Bla bla bla.* She learned the lines by heart.

As life would have it, Mrs. Osagie had long since grown another skin, a stubborn rind that was impossible to cut through. She wore it everywhere, knowing that it could only be peeled with patience and softness. And she was safe, because Mr. Osagie had little of either to give. Recently, noticing the way she'd become—disobedient, defensive, obsessed with those stupid secret meetings she'd started attending—Mr. Osagie knew in his heart of hearts that, if he were *that* kind of man, he'd have beaten the living daylights out of her by now, sending sparks flying above her body as it folded to the ground in a permanent darkness. He didn't need to look far to name friends who would have made sure that she had no eyes to see, no ears to hear, no teeth even, that everything human in her would be gone.

But he wasn't that, he reminded himself. He was Mr. G. Osagie, who kissed his wife as he locked her in the chains he had selected carefully; he was Mr. Osagie, who sang a song from her childhood as he taped her mouth. He was one of the good ones.

Everything he did was only because he didn't want whatever was taking the rest of the women to take her too. He didn't want to lose her or their daughter, Julie, who he'd also tied up before locking her in their largest cupboard. All this was only to protect them because he loved them. He would do anything to keep them together, especially now that times were darkening and God—whichever one was in charge now—was clearly going mad.

*   *   *

After Theresa disappeared, the entire village turned upside down. Maria Osagie and four other women had been on their way back from a neighboring village when they saw Theresa charging toward them. "This world is finished," she said, baring her rotting teeth and laughing. "And now they've also finished me."

The women looked at each other, confused. Theresa hadn't spoken since she'd "lost it" and taken to the road one morning four years earlier. Three times they'd tried to take her to the nearby psychiatric hospital, but each time she stayed for only a week before she resurfaced. Nobody knew how she escaped, but she seemed hellbent on staying in the village and being seen as she went further insane, so what else could they do? They allowed her to stay. What was it to them anyway? People pledged to do their share of the Lord's work, donating food and drink in turns. Together, they'd even built her a shack at the mouth of the village where she could go to dress, use the bathroom, and sleep. Sometimes Theresa didn't come out for days. Other times she roamed the streets all night or slept outside her own door. It went on like that for so long that they didn't even bother greeting her anymore. (Who knew if she could still hear people in this world?) So, listening to her, voice still intact—clear, coherent—jarred them. *Had she been able to talk all this time? Had she been pretending?*

One of the women, Uki, noticed that Theresa's wrapper had been ripped down the middle. "Theresa, did somebody beat you?" she asked with slow condescension. "What happened?" She eyed the madwoman with suspicion, but Theresa just stared on blankly.

"Your husbands are monsters," Theresa said, finally. "These men are monsters. You think they won't do it to you too, abi? But they will."

The five women each felt a matching seedling of unease, which they ignored, because how much of what Theresa was saying could they trust? If her mind had truly left her for all that time, surely it wasn't above lying to her now that it'd returned. Perhaps, some wondered, she wasn't above staging her distress? It must be boring to be mad alone. It was getting late, anyway, and they were already rushing home to cook their husbands dinner, so they made their apologies and scurried home.

They hadn't walked for a full minute before the sky cracked hard and it started to pour. The women picked up their pace, holding hands as they crossed memorized potholes, avoiding the watery mirrors that formed where rain gathered. But there had been a specific fatigue in Theresa's face that stirred an insidious feeling in them. They knew it well. It was close to the bone and an always-horror. Maria wondered what they would do if Theresa decided today was the day she would trail them until she couldn't anymore. Something had clearly happened to break her four-year-old silence open, and it worried Maria not to know. Theresa's sentences had been tired, yes, but Maria could not deny that they were clear and that in all her imagining of how a *real* mad person would sound, Theresa's voice and clarity of speech would never have appeared there.

"What do you think she meant?" she finally asked as they got farther down the road, all of them soaked now.

"Maria, let's go, please! It's late," they responded. "That woman is not well."

Maria turned around again, and that's when she saw it: Theresa in the sky, speeding backward in a gust of wind, waving as she was carried away. Maria tried to call out to her friends, but the rain was getting heavier, the thunder even angrier, so she ran home and decided to wait for morning. When she eventually told them, few of them believed her, and of those who did, not one cared enough to raise any kind of alarm. At least that's what they told themselves, so they could sleep through the night.

"Just wait," they said. "She'll come back. She always does."

. . .

Forty-five more women disappeared. While the village slept, night spread like an amorphous apparition, collecting them. The next morning, those women were no longer in their beds—which made them unavailable for everything, including bathing their children and readying their husbands for work, which in turn meant chaos. Their relatives broke out in cries. Their husbands wilted. The women who remained gravitated toward each other, forming whisper-circles boiling with ideas of where their friends, lovers, sisters, mothers, and daughters could have gone.

The men held meetings in their living rooms over cold beers, debating how exactly they could stop whatever wicked spirit was claiming their wives. Some suggested a lock-in and sundown curfew for every woman and child; others, like Mr. Edosa, suggested appealing to dibias, pastors, and whoever else had muscle in other realms. As evidence, they'd point to how much they'd lost, how unruly their houses and children had become, and all the ways their bodies were falling apart. The men agreed on the first plan and set the curfew.

When they set out during the day, the men locked their doors once, twice, thrice over to make sure their wives and children were secure, not to be seen or even to see outside, except on Sundays, which was the day of mercy. They did the shopping, fetched water for the house, and brought food home for their wives to do the needful. In their husbands' absences, the women slept heavily, attempting to squash years of accumulated fatigue. (But how much catching up can you do in a few hours to quell a lifetime's worth of tired?)

One day, Mrs. Osagie was washing clothes outside when Theresa appeared to her. "I know you're sorry, so I forgive you," she said. "I can teach you how to go too. If you want." Maria blinked twice and pled mercy. Theresa stood unperturbed and calmly slid out her left eye before slipping out a small bead from its socket. "Look," she said, stretching out her palm. A dark pearl rested there, blackly wet. "You have one too. I've always known it. I can show you how to find yours and remove it. It's not even painful. And then you will be free. Don't you want to be free?"

Maria's fear was barking loudly in her, so she picked up her wash-basin and poured both the water and the clothes in Theresa's direction. When she looked again, Theresa was gone.

That night, Theresa appeared to Maria's daughter, Julie, as she was washing her face in the sink. "When they lift the curfew," Theresa said, her voice like something floating, "you'll see that some of your friends have gone. Young girls like you. Gone forever. Just like that." Julie lifted her wet face, soap still in her eyes, and screamed at Theresa in the mirror. *Stay still*, Julie told herself, *don't turn around.* Unlike her mother, she was used to seeing strange things she never discussed; she knew these visions as a side effect of using magic to keep a life.

"If you want to go too, your own is here," Theresa said, pointing to the back of her own ear. "I won't touch you, but I can see it from where I'm standing. If you're scared, then go to Mama Erhun's house. I'm rushing somewhere else." Julie stayed stiff, waiting for Theresa to fizzle. "Don't tell anybody I saw you," Theresa added. "And when you go, try to take your mother too." Then she disappeared.

Julie's heart was pounding. *This could be a way out*, she thought. *This could be a way.*

It was only a matter of weeks before The Itch made the new structure unbearable. Unable to keep up with the details of their own lives, some husbands sent their wives back to work. The women poured back into the streets in tens, and soon the markets filled up again. The Union of Market Women noticed that fourteen women, and girls too, had disappeared in that span, although now their names were hardly mentioned aloud. Julie learned all their names. She was sick of resurrecting herself, sick of the acting, sick of the whole stage and production. One week, two, and no concrete answers. Inside, the husbands of the raptured were thinning, breaking out in hives, looking more sickly. And the other women, of course, continued to talk.

"Why doesn't he answer when we ask about his wife?"

"Look how much smaller they're all becoming."

"What do you think is happening?"

"What if these men start dying?"

"Are we safe?"

"Do you think wherever our friends are going is better than here?"

During work hours—still the only time they were allowed out of home—the women snuck away to meet in groups at one another's houses. The next thirty women disappeared from Mama Erhun's house. She had hosted them there to talk about what she'd seen in a newspaper, a headline stating that women all over the world who had heavy stories about unkind hands were, by some collective magic, finding both the voice and courage to say what happened out loud. Not just that, she stressed, but each time these women gathered to say the truth, a roiling power entered the room and immediately took them elsewhere. It happened gently, too, decidedly—like a sovereign evacuation. She wanted to know: Had anyone else heard or seen it happen?

Most women shook their heads no, though of course some of them were lying. Theresa had appeared to Mama Erhun, too, and she believed her as quickly as Mary believed that angel. She understood their fear and worked to put them at ease. Mama Erhun told them it had happened in other countries, and not just that but in other states and cities in the country too—Ibadan, Calabar, Kano, Lagos, Adamawa, Kaduna, Uyo, Port Harcourt, and so on.

When she asked how they found her, some admitted that a woman, unwashed and unruly, had appeared to them and led them to her. She was frightening, they said, in that she seemed to fear nothing. Mama Erhun knew her by the description alone. "We should have known when they stopped us from watching the news," she said, her voice tight. "I think Theresa came back because there is no other way we would have known. But we know now. Whatever happens here, we will protect each other. We are for each other."

The women watched on, some eager and others reluctant.

"All I'm trying to say," Mama Erhun explained, "is that there's another world already and we can go there. Where we're going, those who hurt us will not be allowed to come." She wasn't wrong. It was a knowing carved into time: repurposed shame—donated by women out of their own bodies, in their own time—was the most powerful foundational ingredient for freedom-making; the necessary raw material for any new world to form.

* * *

Days before the rage and the chains, Maria's lover, Ese, confessed to Maria that she'd been at Mama Erhun's house for the gathering, but that she hadn't meant to end up there, she only went in out of curiosity. Maria knew Ese was lying about the first part, but then so was she. Who wanted to admit to seeing a Gone Woman with directions; a ghost?

A cold breeze swept in from Ese's window as she explained that after Mama Erhun made them feel safe, the women had started recounting their stories one by one, rewinding themselves into gaps. She said that the women all linked arms around each speaker in turn, watching as she faded in color and size, until she was safely Gone, then they closed the space she'd occupied, making the circle smaller and tighter. "There's no way to explain how it felt. Honestly, you had to be there."

"Did it hurt?" Maria wanted to know.

No, Ese said. They looked like they were facing true release, like they were being absorbed by a promising light.

Maria cocked her eyebrow, which was barely an eyebrow since she was in the habit of shaving it off and lining it with black pencil. "Then what did you do?"

"I got up and left."

Maria sat up in bed, letting her wrapper fall softly against her stomach. "So, you didn't tell your own story?"

Ese frowned. "If I did, would I be here? I told them I had no story and I was uncomfortable, so I had to leave." Then, "I was thinking of you."

"And they allowed you go?"

"Of course. It's not a cult naw. . . . If you want to leave, you can leave. But most of them said they'd rather go wherever the rest are."

"So, why did you run?" Maria asked. She felt herself becoming afraid.

"I don't know," Ese said. Then, again, "I was thinking of you."

"What does it mean when you say that?" Maria asked, undoing herself from her lover's grip.

Ese flinched, irritated. "I . . . See, I don't want to talk about this anymore."

"I'm sorry—" Maria said. "I'm just confused about everything." Then, "Wait, what if this is a new God?"

Ese turned to her, wide-eyed.

* * *

It felt that way. There were many holy books and they came in volumes, each focusing on a different God and their priorities. The last one they had was a He who loved to unlook, who pretended not to understand what anyone besides men were going through. People died because of it. Many. (And, of course, whether one survived or not in a world depended on the strength of their God.) One God was written to have slept through a whole century because She was that tired after

creating everything. It would have been chaos if She hadn't also removed the whole notion of free will. In the world that choice created,
people moved like robots. But Ese had shown Maria a small holy book
once about a God-to-return who, fed up with injustice, had once over-
thrown the God who came before Them. They'd laughed about how
they couldn't imagine that, but kept on reading. It was also written
that this same God, long before Maria and Ese were born, had relocated at-risk adults—the Boths and Neithers and In-betweens who
colored outside gender lines—because the world could not hold them
as they deserved, unsaw them violently, insisting they were insulting
approximations of a God whose face they themselves had never seen.
This God was a genderbender, a multiple spirit, an Above and Beyond. The book described this God as the Almightiest of all, the God
taller than life itself, a God the same incalculable size as love, whose
eye no one can reach.

"Imagine a world like that?" Ese had teased, back then. "Things
might actually be . . . fair."

Maria had told her: "If that God was in charge, then this world
wouldn't be this world. It would run on different rules."

They'd let it go then, but was it happening again? Was the world
seeing a new hand in the same lifetime; an old world giving way
for Something Else? What chaos had happened in Heaven? Because
Enough, someone seemed to be saying again, *Enough*. Who could do
this but a huge God? This God could clearly see more than men,
could see all the others—the *othered*—and had a heart for them: no
*but*s, no doors, no locks or fences, nobody left outside.

If that was what was really happening—a hostile takeover of an
inert god's shift—then this God was long overdue.

According to Ese, Mama Erhun planned to host these meetings
every week. She told them they could invite anyone they wanted. Each
session would start with music, food, and palm wine. Did Maria want
to come, just to see?

"No," Maria said, unblinking. "I don't."

"Why? I think it could be good if—"

Maria lay on her side. "I know you want to go back there and that's okay," she told Ese. "But will you go wherever they're going?" She heard the steel in her own voice, the hot pointed edge. What else was she meant to say? She couldn't force Ese to stay.

Ese looked on at her. Sensing the secret hope under Maria's tone, she wondered if lying was a good idea—especially to someone who already knew where her mind was. Ese's daughter, Promise, had been raptured just a month ago from a sleepover at her friend's house. That friend's mother had looked Ese in the eye the next day, her own eyes raw with both fear and fatigue, swearing up and down that she didn't know who or what had taken their children. All the doors were locked, she said, even the windows. The woman clung to Ese's wrapper as she explained, wailing and begging as if that would bring them back. "My own child is gone too," she'd cried. "They also took my own." With Promise gone, Ese frankly had little left to stay for except for Maria, whose own family was still intact. Ese weighed telling Maria as much, but decided she'd rather not argue. "I was just trying to say that I think it's worth seeing for yourself at least once," she said finally. "If I go again, I'll want you there. I don't have to, though."

Maria kissed Ese's forehead, shoulder, nose, mouth. They didn't have much time. They rarely did. Only when her husband traveled, or she managed to lie to him about yet another night vigil. This time it was the latter, but day would soon break and she'd have to leave Ese's bed again. "Well," Maria said. "I wouldn't have any story to share if I go anyway. And besides, I'd rather lie here and listen to you."

Ese leaned against Maria and began to cry, exhaustion scattering her words as they came. "I . . . I'm sorry," she said, forcing her words through sobs. "I'm just . . . I'm just tired."

Maria had never heard her sound like this before. She knew what it meant. "No no no, it's okay," she said. "It's okay. *I'm* sorry. I should have been paying more attention. Let me hold you, my love. Let me hold you. You know nothing matters more to me than you being okay. Nothing matters more than how you feel."

It was true. But for the everlasting obstacle that was her marriage, Maria had done everything to show Ese that she mattered. Ese softened against her body and they pulled their walls down around them. "I can tell you anything?" Ese said. When Maria reassured her, Ese leaned into her ear and said, "I forgot, until I entered that room, that I had a story too. Now I can't forget." Maria listened as Ese went on to tell her a secret with the texture of crumbling concrete. After she was done talking, Maria felt her chest part in two. The air changed, and soon she could feel the exact energy Ese said she felt in Mama Erhun's house as the women spoke: a kind of sticky heaviness.

Maria wanted to cry, to scream, to punch something, to let the already dizzying rage spin her head all the way around, as many times as it would take to snap the whole thing off. She wanted to find and kill the him who unheard Ese's refusal all the times she voiced it. It also made her angry for herself, for her sister, for her mother, her daughter, for everyone she knew who'd been left with phantom flesh and a ghost of an identity in the aftermath of someone else's deaf desire.

Maria felt Ese grow heavier in her arms, as heavy as if she'd been remade in stone. Then, in the space of a few seconds, she felt Ese becoming lighter and lighter, as if she were filled with only air. "Sorry," Ese said again, her voice threadbare.

Maria was crying too. She knew begging would be selfish, she knew. But, god, she couldn't do this, she couldn't. "Ese, please listen to me. Please," Maria begged. "I can't lose you. Tell God or whoever is doing this you want to stop. Please." But Ese only sighed again, her breath frailer than before.

She'd known this would happen; Ese had told her that this was how she'd like to go: in Maria's arms, right there, not at one of those gatherings. But now she could feel the world getting smaller and more pointless as Ese floated out. No matter how close Maria tried to hold her, she only deflated more quickly, until she was just the memory of a hug against Maria's chest. Ese breathed her last in exasperation, a final apology she had no power against.

Losing Ese shattered all of Maria's marbles, sent them clattering into corners. She became snappy, abrasive, and careless. Sometimes she screamed at the neighbors to shut their bratty children up. She stayed in bed all day, refused to eat, lost so much weight that her clavicles shrieked out from behind her skin like frightened things. At night, as Mr. Osagie slept, she sat up writing out the names of the women they'd lost: where they were last seen, who they were last with, connecting dots between them.

It was this strange behavior that made it clear to Mr. Osagie that something was off, and whatever it was, was making his wife sick in the heart. *This is how it starts*, he thought to himself one night, fake-snoring as his wife worked through a whirlwind of newspaper clippings and lists. He decided, then and there, to buy the chains while out.

*   *   *

On the fourth day of Maria Osagie being held by the wrists, her husband's friends visited. After a few minutes, they pinched their noses and asked what the smell was. "What," they asked, laughing uproariously, "are you keeping a corpse in this house?"

"Not that," Mr. Osagie said boastfully. "But close."

He took them to where his wife lay and they watched her, impressed. Soon they started striking her, kicking and hitting her as they pleased. The sight of all this made Mr. Osagie uncomfortable, but not enough to say a thing. Instead he unchained his wife and pushed her through the corridor before letting her out the back of the house.

"Shower," he told her, avoiding her eyes as he returned to his friends.

"I would have asked her to serve us drinks as usual," one of them said as Mr. Osagie resurfaced. "But in that state?" He shrugged. "God forbid."

The Itch spread into Mr. Osagie's underarms and began traveling down his back, but he resisted it. He sat back in his favorite armchair as the worst of them, a childhood friend called Friday, told them what he would've done by now if Maria had been his wife and dared behave all strange like that. The friends all laughed along, interjecting, scratching themselves occasionally. Friday's words were so dark that he had to grit his teeth between sentences, itching wild. Mr. Osagie watched as his friend winced. Friday sat inside his body with an obvious disgusted pride, but they knew that he'd rather die than stop now. What else was there to do, peel his skin off in front of everyone? He didn't even stop smiling. Watching him, Mr. Osagie released his hands from the fists he was hiding them in. He drank what was left of his water, then scratched and scratched while running his mouth, like he was trying to catch up on what he'd missed.

Fifty minutes slithered by and Maria still hadn't returned, so Mr. Osagie went to look for her. He checked outside, then in the closet where he'd kept their daughter. Both places were empty. He rushed back inside and went looking for a piece of paper he'd snatched from her. *This is all their fault*, he thought of his friends as he searched. *This is all their fault. If they hadn't come, this wouldn't have happened.* He wasn't wrong. The Itch was contagious that way.

On the list, Maria had written a list of ten names under the heading The Keepers, with an asterisk by Mama Erhun's name. This was the paper Maria had tried to eat when he caught her with it—it had to be important. Mr. Osagie showed the list to his friends and told them he suspected these women to be the hosts of the secret meetings.

To put an end to this madness, they needed to find them and put the fear of men back in them. They needed to remind the women that even though the men of the village were experiencing a collective wilderness in the wake of these raptures, they were still men, and so, still in charge. "We need to hurry," Mr. Osagie said again. "Please." His whole desperation was showing.

Fifty men gathered near the markets and dragged the few women they found there outside, demanding that they lead them to the addresses. They'd agreed to start off civil, but if that didn't work, they were free to escalate things as they saw fit, because desperate times called for it. When some men started shouting their demands and beating them with sticks, the women agreed to lead the way, praying for no further harm. Mr. Osagie followed the team heading to Mama Erhun's house. He didn't know why. His heart just told him so.

. . .

Inside the house, Mrs. Osagie held her collection of secret stories against her chest, trying to be okay with finally letting them go. She focused her heart on what was ahead, as her daughter watched for reassurance. They'd both decided they didn't want to be a part of a world that allowed these stories to be true in the first place, and Maria knew she'd rather be wherever Ese was anyway. She tried to rehearse the best possible way to present her story, but it all tasted bad at every angle. How should she begin: "When I turned six . . ." or "When I was twelve . . ." or "On our fifth anniversary, my husband . . ."? Which one?

It was then, just as she was imagining the response to her confession—the whole room frozen in attention, loving arms around her as her organs fizzled and her body faded at the edges like a poorly kept drawing—that they heard the loud knock.

Mama Erhun opened the door to screaming men. Maria could hear her husband's voice from the door asking for her, his friends' voices a chorus behind him. "Yes, yes!" they chanted. "Now! Now!" She reached for her daughter's hand and squeezed as Mama Erhun told them they couldn't enter. Mr. Osagie yelled at Mama Erhun, threatening to attack her if she didn't release his wife and daughter.

"Do they want to be with you?" Mama Erhun asked, nonchalance flexing in her voice. Her drabness clawed at his collarbone. "Have you asked yourself that?" She might as well have slapped him then. The men behind Mr. Osagie were scratching his body for him, fanning the flames of his state. "Hit her!" they yelled. "Hit her!" Mama Erhun shut the door and locked it behind her, facing her room full of terrified women.

"Stay calm," she said, including herself. "Are they not just men? God is with us."

The entire herd of men outside seemed to flip at the same time. Some ran around the house, screeching and climbing nearby trees as others poured kerosene on the house. The women they'd dragged from the market scattered, running. Inside, the women were shaking. Maria kissed her daughter's forehead and made her a promise: *Never again.*

"They're going to burn this place down," Mama Erhun said. Her voice did not shake. "But we're going to leave here the way we've always wanted to. On our own terms."

The fire tongued down the roof of the house. As the women wailed around her, Mama Erhun reassured them. "You're free. We're free now. We can go. We can go. Just trust." Soon, the air was crammed with names and crying voices. Mama Erhun's heart pounded in her chest as it occurred to her to fear what would happen if no answer came. But the first woman, pregnant and shaking, faded first. Then more followed.

The men, more confused than ever, quieted down. Mr. Osagie broke the door in half, catching the last of his wife and daughter, now wisps of themselves.

"You know I'd never hurt you guys," he said, sobbing to the emp-
tying room. "You know," he said again, staring around as if their full
forms might still be there, invisible but neatly tucked into the floor or
walls or ceiling. "Just stop this thing and let us walk away. Just come
out, please. I did all this so you can come out and be okay. Just come
out." The fire growled, tearing through the windows and eating the
walls hungrily, like it could live the rest of its life on a diet of just
glass and concrete. Mr. Osagie and his friends retreated back, watching from afar as the house crumbled to the ground in ashes.

The women were really gone. They were *really* alone now. They
pretended, with all their combined might, that there was no reason
to cry.

*   *   *

For days, Mr. Osagie couldn't shake the dread he felt, so one night he
fed his neck to a noose at midnight. A neighbor who came by to check
on him the next morning found him on all fours, rope-end tied to his
bedstand, eyes protruding, body straying far like a stubborn goat.
There was vomit on the floor, which Mr. Osagie had choked on as he
begged for a quick death. Hours had passed since then, though, and
even now, he still wasn't dead. He knew this was no accident.

He cried as the neighbor helped him free and washed his body.
He'd never been touched that gently by a man before, he realized.
Ever.

Later that week, the men gathered to beat a chief, because Mudi, a
prostitute, had disappeared after a night with him, and they were getting fed up. They threw a tire over his neck and attempted to burn
him—not because they cared for her but because he had dared to
shorten their ration. The chief flailed his way out of the fire's insis-
tence. Weeks passed and he still felt the biting sensation all over his
body, unmistakable, though there was no lasting proof of kerosene
meeting match meeting skin. And there were other incidents: two

men who got into a knife fight each felt a screaming pain at the wound sites, though no actual wound was visible. They, too, understood.

They'd made this world intentionally in their image, hadn't they? But now that they'd been left to face it alone, it felt too much like hell. *How hadn't they noticed?* They thought this and thought it well, but because they still couldn't remember the way toward tenderness, the more frustrated they got, the more manically they scratched their itches—which, of course, only meant consequences.

. . .

Ota and Owie were the last two women who remained. They'd lived together for forty years with no children, speaking to each other only in a secret language, so the men believed them to be witches. On one of their usual evening strolls, the men who were out on the streets cleared way for them. As the women walked by hand in hand, a young man started yelling curses. "This is all your fault! This is all your fault, you bloody demons!" He then cursed up at God, who now seemed to look the other way instead of answering back with fire.

The women continued on their way, making him invisible as he tried to charge at them. (What else was there to lose? This was not even their world anymore.) The man was immediately caught in an ambush by the others, who—itching intolerably now—moved toward him, enraged. "Leave them! Leave them!" they yelled at him. "Can't you see they're all we have left?"

As the men tangled their limbs in the fight, the sky began to bruise into a dark violet, the color of a ripely divine rage. Ota and Owie looked on and sighed, fading and fizzing, hand in hand. The men didn't notice as blue-purple matured into a deeper darkness that spread over the village, like the sun had suddenly slipped and fallen away with a most crucial half of the sky.

TATAFO

(FALLEN)

S ince we've known each other for some time now, there's something I need to tell you. Ehehn, don't judge o. Because it's only out of trust I'm telling you. It's only because I know you know how to keep secrets, how to keep a story closed without the whole town hearing about it and running their mouth up and down. I was going to keep it to myself before, but I think that for you to fully understand my vex, to truly see why this story is the way this story is, I have to tell you small small truths here and there. So that you can know, but not only know—so that you can understand.

If I had known then what I now know, I'd have done things differently, that's for sure. But back then, it took me a long time to ask why. I understood the need for Èkó's ruthlessness: you can't climb to where the city is without stepping on some shoulders or snapping some necks. It's not the deaths we caused, or the freedoms we sold that make it hard for me to look at myself. It's how long it took me to start asking questions. Why was Èkó so angry all the time? If anger is fear distilled, then what terror was Èkó running from? Did he keep his face unseeable because even he didn't want to look at himself? How can you make a thing in your image and then ruin it for functioning by your design? Can a person be *disobedient* if the ability to do so is not already built into them? Isn't the power of choice a thing bestowed on a person by their creator? Or does Èkó not know as much as it claims to know? Is He not an Almighty?

I should have known, based on how it gave Èkó a torrid pleasure to watch some of his children break apart, to watch them jump and end everything because they couldn't understand why they were malfunctioning. They thought it was them, that their inadequacies were ungetoverable. They didn't see the city with its hand behind their backs, gently pushing them toward madness, to their knees, toward need. They saw the music, the nightlife, the restaurants, the shops, the cars on the road, the good things, and they thought to themselves: *Why can't I survive this? Is the problem me?*

Èkó always squirmed with glee, watching them get blinder. I didn't mind his wickedness, or his potbelly for cruelty. Me, I'm not a saint, so I can tell you: more than once, I stroked that paunch with want showing through my eyes, and his reaction pleased me in ways I won't say here, lest I spoil you. But let me just put it like this: In the time I worked with him, so many other eyes got plucked out and thrown into the fire, but he kept me. Èkó kept seeing me. Èkó kept me loved. It was for a reason.

Because of that, I saw the most out of all. There is no angel with more stories than I.

Take it from me: hard-walled as it is, there are cracks in power that can be crawled through. And if there's anything vagabonds know how to do, it's to live in the cracks; to grow tall and thick as unfellable trees.

I'm ashamed to say that I believed the veil he put over my eyes all those years when he started coming close to me. I believed it was to protect me from harm, that it was because there was too much power in his face: I mean, the sun rises that far away from us for a reason. He told me I looked beautiful. He told me I had no use for my own eyes, that I should trust him to see for me, because, after all, it was he who made me.

One day though, an itch woke up in me, so I raised the veil and peeped when he wasn't watching. Finally, I saw the city for what it was; I saw Èkó's imperfect body naked. What I thought was a festoon was really just festering. The grounds weren't level at all; all people weren't equal. Some were more necessary than others, some were more useful than others, some were more powerful than others, and none of that was random, but all of it was random. I knew there was an order and disorder to things, but not like this. What was their crime, apart from trying? What was the crime in their loving each other the way Èkó loved me, the way I loved him?

It dawned on me that the ones who needed the city the most were the ones Èkó could not stand. The ones who came to him bare-faced and prideless were the ones who made him itch uncontrollably. They had the most profound effect on him, so he needed to cast them away. I realized how much of a hazard they were, because what would happen if one day, they all refused to move? If one day, they insisted on being seen by force? My heart pounded with a knowing. I didn't need to be told: We'd all be finished. Èkó would fall down fast. Sure, our Excepts, our VIPs, were blessed and highly favored, but even they didn't have as much power as they thought. When I looked closely, I saw that the outsiders, the vagabonds, the ones we were fond of uprooting from the ground were the people the city couldn't do without, the people whose backs Èkó's throne stood on.

But of course, Èkó couldn't say any of this to us. And why would he? He was scared we might worship them instead, that we might see them and love them in full, that we would undivine him by withdrawing our love; that for them, we could gather and peel the beauty off his face. He needed to keep us veiled. But looking is how I realized I was on the losing side. What I struggled with then was how long it took me to see that people punish in others what they hate in themselves. It's the part I'm still forgiving myself for.

* * *

That night, Èkó came out from behind me and dug a concrete hand into my shoulder. It weighed the weight of Carter Bridge. He was breathing on me, so his face was clearly bare. I knew for a fact that if I turned around, I wouldn't be here to tell the story. I already knew, so I stayed still, feeling his glare on the back of my head, and I let him talk.

"How dare you?" Èkó asked, lowly. "How dare you, you ingrate! Am I not the one who gave you your eyes? Am I not the one who crowned you *my* eye? Am I not the one you should be trusting?" He sounded like cement mixing; there were cries and yells trapped inside the crush in his voice. I didn't think this would be the first time I heard it crack like that, that I would be the cause. I turmoiled completely.

I knew what was coming next. There were precedents for these kinds of falls. I'd heard about them before. Think Eden. Think once-naked bodies being pushed out of a garden. Think Heaven. Think a white-clad angel falling from the sky, music tumbling out of his throat, being stripped of a name and given something darker. "I can't believe you didn't trust me!" Èkó said, with the entitlement of a godhead.

I was quivering in my case. "Why did you give me eyes if it would offend you so much for me to use them?" I asked. My voice came out sobbing; my words damp with unearned shame. "I just wanted to see. I just wanted to see what I was doing. If you knew you didn't want me to use them, you had the power to close them. You know you did. Why did you leave them with me?"

"I trusted you!" Èkó said, again, and a door slammed in his throat, his fury a fresh hell. "I can't believe you didn't trust me!" he repeated, pacing the ground. The world beneath us was quaking, but his response answered nothing. Our love had already ruptured—I could feel it. There was hardly anywhere to go from there. My mouth was gone, so I couldn't explain. I couldn't tell him what I needed to. I couldn't tell him that I *did* trust him. I did. I gave myself to him, and I was tender with my hands on him, I was precise, I was useful in all the ways he needed. I saw sides and parts of him that a messenger should not see. I saw his hiding places and I didn't call him ugly. I learned the entire texture and architecture of his body. Even now, I know by heart what parts of him are concrete, what parts of him are cotton or curtained, where his hip dips sweetly, where he melts and spills pure water, where he generates his precious noise. I did what he told me to, went where he wanted me to go, gave him my entire mouth, held him hard against my throat. How could he erase all that just because I was curious? Was that my sin? Using the eye he gave me? Wanting to know?

See, me I have my own skeletons too. I no holy pass. And last last, holiness is not my focus, it is not my dream. When he pushed me, I'm not ashamed to say I fell. I fell majestically from his hands—and it was then that I finally understood what it meant to be outsided, to be where there is nothing but black noise, where you spend every waking second clawing the circumference of the city, trying to get back in.

That is where I talk to you from most times. Imagine. A force like me? When I'm not Lucifer.

It took me long enough to realize: I was them and they were me. I, too, was punishing what I hated in myself. I was punishing what he punished in me.

You can see a lot of things better from the outside, you know? For example, I can see now that, together, vagabonds are the city's power. We're its charge and circuit. It cannot exist without us. It stands on us.

That's why I'm no longer chasing him. It's why I'm on your side. It's why I'm telling you this story.

Now, when I watch him, I flinch. All of his children, pawns in his hand. I see when he remembers me and retreats on a possible move. I recognize it as an act of love. I also see when he remembers me and sets fire to the ground. It flatters me fully.

Even today, he uses them to talk to me still, to say: *I loved you and you hurt me, you love them, so I'll hurt them if it means getting to hurt you.* It's bitter, but it's something. I'll confess that sometimes I wonder if I should have stayed because of how much I miss him. Still, I know I would not have survived that hand on my shoulder, that growing stain on my being. I could never have survived an insanity that vast.

And to think now, that he has only gotten madder since.

THE ONLY WAY OUT
IS THROUGH

My dearest Wura,

Right now, I'm listening to Alice Smith's cover of Nina Simone's "I Put a Spell on You." It's the first time I've been able to play it since the news of you. This song is a door. I've played it three times now, back to back, and it's swelling hope in me; it's pulling me apart with its desperate energy, starfishing me with desire. When she means the words the most, Alice Smith's voice has the power to drag a séance into this room. Something about that bold-faced declaration of want, of desire and longing.

Being a reserved person then, when I first heard that version of the song, I didn't know what to do with it. The song still argues with everything I thought I knew about manners, about being contained, about being passive. Even now, when I play it, it reaches into my body with its ghost-limb and crumbles my shame like old chalk. That song shows me something that matters to me, as someone whose body didn't always feel like it belonged to me; it shows me how to want something without repentance or remorse.

I hear it, and it throws me back to the day of your archive sale. That day, the shop was full of people (Because 40 percent off WB clothes? Everybody knows that's a big deal!), and I couldn't talk to you. I saw grown women trying to pretend they were taking photos of themselves while strategically trying to include you in the frame. You stood with your arms folded across your chest, wearing that asymmetrical dress that danced at the hem like beachwater lapping onto a shore. You were right there, but nobody walked up to you—just hovered—because they saw how there-and-not-there you were. You were the centrifugal force everything else circled around.

People didn't only want to wear your clothes, they wanted to be associated with you, and loudly. You wove story into every fabric, and they were proud to carry it on their bodies. People always wanted to know what you sounded like, what you smelled like, what you did when you weren't spinning magic. But you were just there for the clothes, just there for your work.

All it took was for you to sweep your eyes over me in the space of a blink and already, I thought: *I will love this woman.* I didn't think it calmly, I thought it with panic—in the tone warnings usually take. Before I could exhale, you were looking elsewhere, but I knew I was in soup because my neck stiffened, and that's my body's way of telling me it knows something I don't yet. Even though I wasn't facing you, my body was so alert as it floated between racks, so absurdly awake, that I would have known—felt it somehow—if your eyes had as much as glanced at my shin. But you didn't look back my way; you were busy; you were done and gone.

When our eyes met, that stunning adire dress I'd picked off the rack right before another woman's fingers landed on it was draped over my arm. You smiled approvingly and I felt the fabric grow cold on my skin. I fought for it, you know? Even now, I remember turning to the woman whose hand had almost touched it before I picked it, and smiling condescendingly, my eyes thinning into petty slits. *Ah well*, I was telling her with my whole face, *better luck next time.* Childish, but do I care? Later, I saw her and another woman arguing over who should get the beaded cobalt top. Ha, she wasn't having it oh. I knew she was just one refusal away from bursting out in rage. You'd slinked away by then. You didn't come out again until I left. You had such a nose for trouble.

Sha, me I told your PA to please keep the dress for me. She tried to tell me something about no reservations but me with my sweet mouth, I said one or two things and then she hid it behind the desk. I could have bought it there on the spot, but I lied that I didn't have my card because I wanted a reason to come back.

The next day, when I showed up, there you were. I introduced myself and you said, *What a name.* Then you said a proverb in Yoruba that I don't remember now because I was too busy being swept up in you. What I do remember is you asking: *So, whose Amen are you?* I wasn't startled by your question, even though I'd never heard it phrased like that before. I said, *My mother's, I guess. Well, mostly. In the earlier days at least.*

And then? you asked. *And then I became me*, I said. I laughed; you didn't. Then, as if you could read me under my skin, you said: *That's a lie. You're more than one person's Amen.*

We talked about your taste in music. You told me about Buika and Angélique Kidjo and Brenda Fassie. I told you I'd never been a music person. You told me you could fix that. I told you good luck. When I got back home, there was an email from you. Alice Smith's cover of "I Put a Spell on You." *Listen with your eyes closed*, you wrote. I did. Then I knew for sure.

* * *

Dear Wura,

I remember when you asked me if I'd been in love before. I said, *Yes, a few times.* I jokingly started with the one about my childhood crush, the girl I proposed to with a blade of grass at the back of my primary school. We called each other husband and wife for a whole year and were inseparable. I believed that was love then, so I said that one as a joke. I don't even remember her name. The heartbreaks after her were way more tragic and way less funny on my side and on theirs. They changed me, and so I thought . . . of course I was in love, of course. How could I have felt that much pain if I wasn't? But I was thinking about it again today and I asked myself if I am sure.

I mean, I loved a woman in my early teens, yes. But she was too adult to be "loving" me. She flipped me upside down in my attachment to her. She would be there intensely, then disappear for weeks. Like that, on loop. It ran me noticeably mad. When my parents found out, they didn't confront me. One look at her and they were sure she would destroy my life. They reached out to her behind my back, each with bundles of naira in one hand and a threat in the other. She accepted the payment and moved out of the country. I always believed she upped and left, so she was the first person I ever hated. But I found out the truth by some twisted means when I turned twenty, and everything I thought I knew about my family quaked in that finding. It took me a long, long time to realize that that was a salvation; and that that was a "love" that should never have happened. She should never have turned toward me like that in the first place. She was old enough to know better. And she did.

In my twenties, I dated a woman who was older than me by a decade. Our relationship was intense, to say the least. She was a woman who always *showed*, even when she didn't mean to. It annoyed her that people could take just one look at her and know that she wasn't there for men. We rarely ever went anywhere public together because there was no way to look at both of us, each wearing trousers, and think *just friends*. She hated it so much, that loud visibility, but I don't think I understood how much until she came home one day with a ring on her finger. When I asked her about it, she told me that her boyfriend had proposed. I didn't even know she had a boyfriend.

Neither did I know she was seeing anyone seriously enough to get married. *Where did he come from, who is he, how long has it been, are you really going to marry him?* I rolled all those questions in her direction. *Yes*, she said, *I'm going to, but chill, you're acting crazy, calm down, he's just a man.* It hurt, but it wasn't a dealbreaker for me. It was true: He was just a man, and what did men know? What could a man do better than me? Not much. I could stay as long as she still loved me, I decided. Then her husband found out. Things between us got darkly quiet soon after, in the way secrets of this shade can do. Was that love, or a rest stop?

Then there was my ex-wife, who you know the most about, the one I was too sore to give more details about. The one I was sure of. We were together by date two; quickfire. By the sixth month, while we were traveling together, she said: *Let's get married.* There was no ring involved. We committed to each other in a small court in a "progressive" country, and we went to an all-women's nightclub after. When that holiday was over, we came back to Nigeria. We knew what we were, so it didn't matter if nobody else did, if people looked at us and saw friends, or sometimes even sisters. What did I care? My baby was mine. That's all I needed. I'd done without my family for long enough (you already know that story), so I didn't have to explain a thing when I moved in with her.

But there are parts of the story I left out. Our relationship was about hiding, from the start. You know, for women who come from homes like ours, we have two options. You grew up with money, and you can't fall below your class, so to keep that status you either have to become just as powerful as the men in your field (so that you're just as respected as one) or you have to marry a strong name. You're not supposed to drop the baton. Because both of us knew we would rather die than marry men, we had to compromise somehow; we owed our families that. So we decided to become the sons our fathers never had. Me out of spite, and she out of love.

She faced politics and I faced economics. She had way more practice than I did at that performance: her father's gift to her, for her twenty-first, was her first bodymask. *You are stronger than five men*, he said, grinning. He got a skin sculptor to make it. *It will be believable*, her father said, *if you just follow the script. When you go out, wear the mask; when you come home, what you look like or are is between you and your God. Can you do that for me?* She didn't need to weigh the options. Her father already had his hand deep in the national cake; all she needed to do was show up. He kept his word and took her everywhere, introduced her to all his contacts as his child, his first, his right hand. No one could say shit.

She taught me that you don't have to *be* a man if you can talk, touch, act, or look like one; you just have to masquerade as one. *Anybody can be a powerful Nigerian man*, she told me. *All it takes is believing you deserve a good life and pursuing it relentlessly, even if it means running over everyone else. You need great suits, a large ego, a solid network, a strong voice, and some fuck-you money. Why, because na money be oga, na money be sir. Na money be senior. Na money be man. And men, as thick as they like to pretend to be, know better than to argue with their seniors. With my father on our side, we are everybody's senior.*

She wasn't joking. So: this is how to knot a tie, this is how to talk to women, this is how to enter a room and seize the air in it. She was the father I never had—sliding my business card across cold tables, insisting on my name in strong rooms. To be honest? It was an un-beatable rush. Side by side, we became better at being men than they were. When we showed up to events, powerful men stood up from their seats to greet us. *Oh no*, they used to say, avoiding our eyes. *Please, gentlemen. It's my pleasure.* One day, her father called her with a warning: *Listen, I don't care who you love, I care what you do. I care about the mark you leave. Get the money, make the name, set up your life—and you can move abroad if that's the lifestyle after your heart. But until you reach that goal, know what you're doing. Know who you're allowing into your home so that it doesn't get out. You understand?* She said yes. *All of this is politics*, she used to say, *and in politics, you have to be as ruthless as you can just to get what you want. And I'm so close. I'm so close.*

I didn't mind. I loved that her father didn't hate me or us. I loved that I was the only one who knew her inside out. It swelled my pride. When she came back home, I was the one standing behind her, un-clasping the mask from the neck, unzipping the body down the back, watching it fall to the floor. We took turns washing the body and drying it, every weekend. In my workplace I became just as good as her. The first day I wore a bodymask, it was like a visibility suit: ev-eryone saw me with respect. She got it for me as a gift. Sometimes, when men pissed us off, the power sped to our hearts and we didn't rest until we'd fucked their frustrated wives and given them what their husbands hadn't in years. We'd fist-bump, thump each other's backs in praise like the beautiful bastards we were. Those moments were rehearsals for moments with our peers, our fellow painful rascals. When we got bored of that life, we'd kneel in front of each other in bed, each helping the other unclasp our masks, peeling the sleeves off, unfastening our outside faces, locating each other's mouths. In a mat-ter of minutes, we'd become the tenderest things. We never let those other women see us like this, we never ever let them touch us. We liked that they thought we were stone, and that at home, next to each other, we were soft rock, spilling sweetwater.

It lasted until it didn't. Things moved fast. Elections coming close, her father getting older, her fear about him dying or even worse, him being alive and watching her lose. She went harder, put her back into it. Everything was about winning. I saw her become colder, saw her begin to refuse—more and more—to take the act off when she entered the house. She started sleeping in our bed with her outside body and mouth. Her beard scratched against me when we kissed. But did I care? It was only for a time.

We went on like that, passing time, waiting. She won the election and got her seat. She got us the life, but it crushed us. When they give you the masks, they advise you to take them off when you can, but they don't tell you why. They should, though. They *should* tell you that if you don't take breaks from your acting, the false skin will grow on you; that you might have to sit down and watch the mask chew off your lover's face. It's only right.

After she won, she came home tired and triumphant. Around the time when they were discussing the SSMPA Bill, we talked about it. *You have to stand against it*, I said. She told me it was not that easy. *I can't afford that focus on me*, she said. *Remember what my father said about discretion.* I said, *Okay, babe, but is this still acting? I haven't seen you in so long.* She said, *I'm here.*

God knows how long we spent arguing. I finally convinced her to take it off for that one night. When she turned around and I tried to undo that clasp and we couldn't lift it without it snagging at her, without peeling skin and drawing blood, I knew. She turned to look at me and we didn't need to say anything. We ended it. Her father died soon after. She fled the country, dropped the job and relocated to America. I found out on Facebook that she has a wife and two kids now. In the pictures, she looked like herself, the her before all the masking. She made the right choice moving, reverting, because I know for a fact that it can kill a person to become and remain the exact thing they've always feared.

What I learned from loving her was how to be a partner. How to

ride with somebody completely. How to choose a person with abandon. I learned entitlement too. I learned to think: If they can have it,
I can too. I learned that if you want to live a man's life, you have to be
willing to sacrifice beauty in order to reach for power. When you met
me, I was rage-climbing the corporate ladder. When I succeeded, I
learned that when they told me that the top of that ladder touches
heaven, they lied. I got there to meet only space. She suddenly made
sense.

You asked me once if I was still in love with her. I said an easy no.
You wondered about that. You reminded me that we were together for
years. The truth is, I will always love her, but we were too busy acting,
trying to find heaven, to be *in* love. We were deep in ambition. High
on it. We never stood still. There was hardly time.

And then there you were, all patient and present. With your work
like magic, your jokes like home. I met you and thought: *I've had a life
full of women, a heart and a mind and a body and a world full of them, so
I know that there is nothing inherently gentle about us.* Whoever thinks
women are easier lovers than men has never met a cruel woman, a terrified terror—a woman desperate to save her neck, one who could
burn your world on purpose just so she wouldn't have to go down.
Women can flay you, fray you to unrecognition, turn you outside-in
so quickly you'll forget to remember why you exist. Women will hand
you a bottomless well of pain with tears in their eyes. We can do anything; we can make mistakes; we are not immaculate just because
we've been taught to be docile.

Tenderness is a choice; it's what you choose when you have suffered
enough. You taught me that. When we talked about politics and the
future of this country, with regard to freedom for all, you always shook
your head and said: *Those bastards.* I wanted to tell you it wasn't black
or white. I'd been one with her before, so in some odd way, maybe I
was one of them. I wish I'd been brave enough to look at you and say
yes to the love you were offering, but I've been guilty too.

We've both been terrible before, you and I, without flinching. That was our past, yes, but I was scared of us, I was scared *for* us. In the past, we'd both mishandled women's affections just because we could, watched people cry and felt nothing, broken more hearts than we could count, touched people and made unforgettable moments with them only to wake up and unmake them. We'd both thought we loved a person with our whole lives only to surprise ourselves with how we hurt them. We'd both been people who assumed that if one person must always leave in dynamics like ours, we might as well be the realistic one who leaves first, because the realistic person might be okay in the end. We'd both been destructive and painful on the way to saving ourselves—moving like we had no lives to lose, like we were never even alive in the first place. And we'd both looked in the mirror and forgiven ourselves on behalf of those who suffered at our hands, waving ourselves off as inconsequential injuries, because *how can one cause real harm if they're already not real?*

But look how we broke each other in the end. Who could have killed me better than you?

It's not that I didn't love you enough to stay. It's that I loved you enough to burn all the courts down, to torch the entire country to ash, because you were the first woman I could see a possible life with. But my reason for walking away was always the same: *Can't you see? This is a bubble, a fantasy, an unsustainable fiction. Can't you see the brutal setting of the story we're faking? This is Nigeria. Even if we manage not to kill each other, they might still find us and eat us.* Set up against our brutal histories, what was I supposed to do with us? I wish I'd known that I wasn't irredeemable, that at any point I could stand still, I could stop, I could take responsibility; that we could really just start again. But the fear had entered me. I was so furious at our forbiddenness that I forgot that people can be both pained and painful at the same time. We know a lot about that.

I remember this often: You stripping off your shame in front of me the day I told you I loved you but was afraid. I remember watching you slide it off your shoulders as easily as a silk robe, even though between me and you, we know that shame is tougher fabric than damask. You said: *Choose me over it, choose me over your head screaming no; it's the one who's lying and you know it, the rest of you is yelling yes in the truest languages. Your feet bring you to me before you can think, your hands turn your steering wheel in my direction every single evening after work, your heart won't stop babbling next to me.* You said: *Go with your body; rest, lie your head here, rest; make a home here, rest.* You made it look easy to say a thing like that in a country like ours, with families like ours. I told you I'd need to think about it. I was fucked up already. I had already sinned against us.

I wasn't sure where in my body to move you into, if there was clean enough air there. It would have finished me to hurt you, I already knew, and with all the practice I'd had, I'd become frighteningly good at it. There was only so much surviving a single person could do. I told you I'd been a danger before, that in order to win love back I'd been what we both feared, even though near you I was the softest thing. You should have seen me on the bad days; I was as lovable as that bulldozer we saw tearing down that building on Glover Road. I broke things, I tore walls down, I yelled. I told you some of it and you said: *You and I are both mad and we match each other. Sane or insane, you cannot scare me.* And in saying so, in *meaning* that, you scared me even more.

Next to you, I loved my whole self. I forgot my favorite fake faces. I remembered my whole skin. I felt like grace was an infinite thing and it wouldn't stop giving itself to me. But there was still a world to step out into, there was still life outside your door.

I was so fucking jealous of you, do you know? I couldn't understand how this world hadn't beaten the hope all out of you. You wanted a good love with me? You could see it? A love where tenderness was our shared dialect and it wouldn't matter if we stuttered in it, because we were still learning? You wanted us to peel off our histories, to forget the rot in our blood chasing us? You believed that if it came to it, what we had could beat down every dysfunction in both our families and histories combined, kill them all dead with ease. You saw power, you saw solid strength, you saw our relationship as a gentle and good beast, working in our favor.

But Wura, my eyes were not good then. My eyes were all statistics. How many loves do we know that have survived this country's hate, even when both parties had the best intentions? We tried to count the successful couples we knew when you were still here. I remember that day clearly. Rain was upstairs doing homework. We had four hands between us, but we couldn't even get through one of mine. We only used three of my fingers before we stopped. Even then I joked about how we'd never know what was happening behind closed doors with the couples we thought were happy. You didn't find that funny, I remember.

We could be different, I swear, you said. *I see it. I see it right now. Don't you?* It was the saddest question you ever asked me. While you were waiting for my non-answer, I looked where you were looking—not at me, but at nothing in the air, as you did when you were trying not to cry—and I didn't see what you were seeing. Instead, I saw the seventeen other fingers we didn't count. I counted every reminder I knew, that the wrong kind of love can chew your life and spit, can grind your mind and live.

* * *

Dear Wura,

I'm listening to Lagbaja's "Never Far Away" on repeat. I can only seem to write you with music. This is your song. Our song. I can't see you but I can feel you. There are mushrooms in my body. I'm in bed under a river of cloth, and there is a shifting flame-light dot screaming out of the wall, and she the girl who brought the drugs is busy between her legs and her pleasure is stacking and I'm watching. Earlier there was fear, because she climbed too far too fast and reality slid from her grip, and I wanted her to come back to me but she couldn't because the monsterfarmers took her far away and their hair became tentacles and everyone was fearing and she was facing the wall and then she put two hands on my throat and it pressed me bone down inside out and I pressed hers back, two hands to her throat, bone sliding back under my hands. She pushed her hand against my jaw and I didn't know how to feel and I wanted it to stop, but I heard my mind saying in my head: *No matter what you do, you can't kick me awake, you can't kiss or fuck me alive, I'm dead already.* And I could feel the trying and I could feel her and her cryingscreamkicking in her childcountry. And she wants somebody to hold the world still. And I'm holding my world tight, but she wants to break it open at the thigh because she thinks that's how to get herself held. But there I was, just holding her, and I'm saying, *Please come back and just be with me. Please.* But no. She was trying to fall into nothing, into the roiling deep black, into her own missing. She's lost love too. Often I see grief's voice trapped in her eye, spilling like rich silk. I say, *come back, come back,* but she's stuck in the in-between. She's looking for her person, just as I am looking for you.

The thread between this world and that world is velveteen. I feel gargantuan.

You'll look, I'm telling the girl from inside myself, *but you'll never ever ever find my eyes. Touch me and you'll see I'm a wide and mad almost, no matter how much you try to touch my real. No one can chase the soft pink wide fuzz buzz of me, I am already somebody's. No one can jam my heart open; it swings at the hinge. It's caught in the frame.* She held me square in the jaw and I wept like wax and crying bone. Already somebody's? Already somebody. I think I'm only shouting inside.

Her body heaved open at the waist. I asked her if she could love me and she massaged my throat bone: *enough to kill you.* Metaphor too.

Now my hip is speeding and spinning. She keeps shaking her head, trying to find a world behind my knees. The music slid into me just

now. The music fucked me and then fucked me up. The playlist is
weeping. I'm ironsteel, no wheel. She's spilled out of my arm; she's
gone searching again. Elbow pressed into my breast, crushed it into a
wailing stream of muscle. She's back and trying to find my eye as I try
to find you a good sentence—what a metaphor for my life. I want to
tell her: you can't make a face real by touching it, you can't make a
love real by forcing it. She keeps bending into the crook of her name,
speeding back and forth between worlds.

Her eyes have rolled back, forward, shifted back into place. Thank
goodness, my fear was shivering.

I'll be clear: I'm trying to hallucinate you. I feel my sane sliding
sideways. But that's okay, because what is reality anyway if not a thing
to be played with, stretched and tested—something that echoes out,
multiplying in a sideways stream? Besides, anything is worth bending—
even the facts of my vision, even the truth of my eyes, if it means getting closer to you. What is a little madness? No be only crase? People
go mad all the time. We've both gone there and back for lesser people.
Already, since you've been gone, I've done multiple laps to and from
there and come first place in your name. Hand me my medal, Wura.
You trust me naw, don't you? You know I like competition. I have nothing more to lose; I've already lost you. For you, I can afford it. I have
always been able to afford it.

Right now, I feel like I can never be impossible again. I never knew
life was this large. I want to see it from this angle always. I wish I
could roll you open inside my body so you can feel what I'm feeling
from here. I wish I could unzip myself down the front and lay you inside me, hold you there forever. If it's eternity you were running toward, an everlastingness, shey I can live for you forever. Even when it
starts to hurt. The answer is yes, Wura. You are my in-love.

Oh, wait. On the wall, I see you now. I'm seeing you. Please stay
there, I'm coming. I'm about to go close.

· · ·

Wura,

I'm sure you're laughing at how horribly that went. How at my big age, I'm still trying to suspend my head with drugs, trying to throw my brain skyward and forget it there. You wouldn't recognize this me: I choose girls who know how to choose drugs, who also have wounds to gag, who know how to match medicine to ailment. I'm not sure where all those words came from, but the last thing I remember is blood. Don't worry, they've stitched my forehead now. It doesn't hurt as badly as I feared it would.

Sometimes, I choose a memory with you and I sit with it. I sit in it. Today I'm choosing my birthday, when you showed up to my house at midnight sharp with a cake you'd baked by yourself. It was terrible, but we ate it like wild children, and then I chased you around my estate because you said something stupid. When you got to the end, you waited. Instead of laughing at me as I struggled to get to you after all the mouth I made, you threw your arms wide open and let me collapse against you. And, of course, you could take it. You could hold me, what with all that strength and speed in your legs. I miss your legs, the way you flex them at night when you're trying to concentrate on your dream, when you're trying your hardest not to let your real life interfere with it. I miss you telling me about your dreams in the morning. I miss you waking up bursting with ideas and scattering everywhere for your journal; I miss knowing we wouldn't talk until you were done. I liked knowing that one of us had an outlet. I liked feeling understood by you, like my body was safe near you, like you wouldn't try to take something from me that I couldn't give.

I've started seeing a therapist. I told her about you. She asked if we were ever *intimate*. I said yes, but not in the way she meant the word. She said she finds it beautiful that we were able to give each other as much as we did without ever sleeping together. I told her we *did* sleep together, a lot. That we slept together often, our bodies tangled. She said: *You know what I mean.* Okay. But people should just say *sex* when they mean sex. I told her we never had sex, but that holding you felt like a life well lived; that it was one of our favorite things: sleeping in the afternoons and trying to sync our dreams.

Once, I remember, we even succeeded at it. We ended up in the same garden, as ourselves, and you offered me Blue Bunny. We both woke up at the same time, laughing and already knowing why. I told her that you were the first person I'd ever met as an adult who wasn't ashamed to not want sex. I told her you looked at me and said, *Sex, for me, doesn't mean anything. Even if it did, it wouldn't mean what it does for other people. It wouldn't mean closeness. That's just not how I say I love you.* I told her you were the first person I loved without needing to escape. You didn't do drugs, so I couldn't dump my head in them. We didn't have sex, so I couldn't throw my body at the issue. I had to look at myself, and maybe that was the problem? She said, *Not even once?*, returning to the sex thing with shock. I wanted to slap her, but instead I just said, *No, not once.* She asked me if I regretted that. I told her no, that we knew other ways to communicate, other ways to love, other ways to touch each other. The conversation made me miss you even more. It reminded me that most people think sex is where love goes to graduate, that sex is where love matures. I always forget that we're not the norm. She asked, *Are you a Christian?* I said, *Not that I know of.* She seemed hurt, as if I'd actually hit her or something. Good. Bloody Nigerians. Now I need to find another.

The girl I was seeing is gone. She was twenty-four and quick-witted, fluorescently bright. We tried all sorts of drugs. Acid. Shrooms. Ecstasy. Something unnamed that she got from some mysterious dealer she called Baba. We got high and touched daily, and it made me feel full of helium. We never talked. We didn't use words at all. She would walk in, take off my clothes, and get furious at the world inside my body, then come away with fingers glistening, proud. She made me feel like someone was doing something terrible to me—a terrible thing I liked, a terrible thing that made me feel something. But I realized eventually that we would try to swallow each other, since our understanding of grief was the only thread between us. Her hunger was huge and so was mine, so it was time to stop. I didn't want to vanish into thin air.

Wura, imagine: I wanted to live.

I tried to summon Rain the other day, so I could ask her for advice on how to reach you, but we both know I'm no magician and no god, and even if I were, I doubt there's any entity powerful enough to make Rain do what she doesn't want to. Besides, to my shame, she never got to become *our* daughter. She loved me, yes, but she was all yours. So when I tried, it was as impossible as trying to mold water in my hands.

I hope it's good where you are. Quiet. I hope no one makes you sing hosanna nonstop in a white gown, or I'll have to come fight them—I know how much you hate wearing white, and more than anything, how much you can't even stand congregations. I imagine you'd only ever accept that invitation if they let you make your own outfit, stay quiet and read books all day in your mansion. Actually, I doubt you'd even appreciate a mansion, talk less of roads made out of gold. You hated that kind of excess.

But wait! If you aren't doing any of those things, why aren't you haunting me? Most days, everything in me wishes you were the type of spirit to shatter the plates in my kitchen or break some furniture in my living room as I sleep, just to let me know you'd been there. The type who gets angry, who uses up their allotted five minutes of madness every now and then.

Okay, I don't wish you were angry. I just wish I could feel you. Even me, I'm not angry anymore. My fury is asleep.

Sometimes I wonder: Did you surrender me with everything else? This silence better be because you finally became nothing. That's how I like to think of you: as the nothing that floods my body and follows me everywhere. I'm sure you did fizzle—you always get what you want. I wasn't sure before, but now I know: when my time comes, I'm hoping with all my might to become nothing, too, just like you.

But first, I'll live.

*   *   *

Wura love,

Odunsi (The Engine)'s "Angel" is playing. I just discovered his music. I first heard it on the radio driving to the supermarket and then looked him up when I got home. Young talented guy. You would have loved this song. When the woman comes on—duendita is her name, I like the name—and sings, "and even if I die right now, I'll be your angel," in that big voice of hers that sounds like glory, I cry every time, because I imagine that she's talking to me out of your mouth. It makes me happy to think of you as the angel in charge of me, as an always-present presence directing my footsteps. Sometimes I want to imagine you with wings, but I know you'd resist another body with everything in you, even a heavenly one.

That reminds me: I met someone recently who feels like an angel. You would have loved her. I'm not sure what I do or don't believe about God these days, but she feels like a godsend. She never looks at me like I'm crazy. Ever. She works with me as a housekeeper. She's one of us. She lives on the outside too, in black noise, but she tries to hide it. She loves me and I can feel it. She is holding me and my new home together with her hands. She reminds me of you in that way. With all she knows about me, she could easily tear me apart—as you could have, if you'd had any cruelty in you. She could sell me and all my parts with the kind of access she has in my life. Instead, she's doing what you'd have done, what you did perfectly, until I ran. And even after. She is being my friend.

Oh, wait.

You sent her to me, didn't you?

My sneaky little thing.

OVERHEARD:
HIDE US IN GOD

Y es, because I see my brother all the time," Nkem told Adura, dipping drumsticks into the cackling oil. "The one that follow me, our last born. He appears to me. Sometimes sef, when it's just me at home cooking, he'll come and visit me. He will sit down, and we'll be gisting. Sometimes I'll make food and I'll see that one meat don go. Nobody dey kitchen there, so who chop am? He always comes to see me, especially on my birthdays." Her eyes gleamed in that night-sky way it did when she talked about things like fashion, like her father's abattoir and her mother's tailor shop, like her best friend, Hauwa, like this particular brother. "So that's why I'm asking you," she continued. "Because I know say nobody dey thief pass people wey don cross go. Spirits ehn, no criminal wey fit pass dem."

Adura watched Nkem, eyes steady, trying to keep the skin on her face neutral. She could call Nkem a friend to the few friends she kept, and she could tell Wura the same with ease, but she was still skeptical about showing too much teeth with someone she was paying. She wasn't sure about talking grief with her. Most employees in her past loved to cross the line just when she was showing them that she was willing to hold them close—proving to her that, as her father used to say, too much play-play leads to see-finish. Nkem was still young inside, in that *I want to stay good in this world* way, even though she was way into her twenties. She talked and laughed and joked like a person with a child-self paused on purpose until she could find a home safe enough to rest in. Adura saw that in her and immediately understood it.

"So you think it's a ghost stealing the forks?" she asked. The question made her laugh, even though she felt hope congregating between them like smoke.

Nkem's eyes didn't dim, not even a little. She shook her head and laughed, her mouth slack, belief brightening in it. "Ma . . . Okay, wait, have you ever lost anyone before? Someone you were close to?"

Adura shrugged. She couldn't believe this whole conversation had started because of disappearing forks. But they *were* disappearing. When she first moved in, she had bought a set of cutlery and there had been twenty forks. Now, they had just . . . four? If she followed Nkem's reasoning, she might burst with relief, because truly, Wura ate *everything* with a fork. Even eba. It might make sense. She wanted it to. "Maybe," she said.

Nkem understood that gray. Sure, they had a good relationship, but Adura was still her boss, which meant that the barriers between them remained, even when they were at their thinnest. She couldn't expect straight words from Adura. It was honor enough for Adura to even imply the truth, to cock her head vaguely in its direction.

When Nkem had started looking for work, she'd expected the worst: a madam who would yell, hit her, insist on unreasonable work hours. But Adura was polite. Adura said *please* and *thank you*. Adura was also loudly lonely, even though she thought she tucked it well. Adura was hard not to love past obligation. In another life, Nkem thought, they could be close like sisters, taking long strolls and walking each other home at night. "Na so dem be," she said. "Sometimes they'll take your things so you notice them. You know say nothing dey for this life wey no get destination. Anything wey miss dey enter somewhere."

Adura pressed her back against the fridge's bumpy silver skin, covered with fridge magnets from cities she'd been to, trying to regain her body and her mind: Florence. Barcelona. Lisbon. Havana. Rio. Nice. Monte Carlo . . . "You think so?" she asked. Already, she felt smaller in this boubou she had bought under a tree from some mallams—younger, more naive. But it wasn't the worst thing in the world. Her shoulders were resting.

Nkem nodded without hesitation. She turned to remove the fried chicken and dropped the last two carefully into the used oil. "You just have to open your mind if you want to see the person again. But well sha, na only if you want o. Nobody can force you."

Adura couldn't remember the last time she had prayed. But that night, before she went to sleep, she called God's name and unbolted every one of the doors she'd locked against faith. Nkem had told her to just stretch her arms out, take a deep breath, and clear her head. Adura tried it, waiting, scared out of her mind, until she drifted off to sleep.

She'd been asleep for barely an hour when she found herself at a beach, familiar from a memory tangible as a seashell she could hold to her ear. She sat alone for a few seconds before a body settled beside her. She couldn't look sideways even if she tried; the dream had stiffened her neck. Both bodies stayed watching the water ahead. The body next to hers reached for and held her hand. She didn't need to guess. She would know the warm comfort of Wura's touch anywhere in the world—life or dream.

* * *

Sweet potatoes.

That's what Nkem was going to buy from the market the day Adura first noticed that she wasn't Igbo. Adura had finally sorted out her internet banking after months of putting it off. When Nkem called out her account number, the GTBank app showed a different name.

Adura opened her mouth to ask, pointing at her phone screen. "Is this . . ."

"Yes, ma, that's the one," Nkem answered. "Everything I want to buy will be 4k. I sent the list to your WhatsApp."

Adura saw Nkem realize exactly what she meant, but she couldn't be bothered to ask. The Amitriptyline her doctor had recommended stretched her sleep over eight uninterrupted hours and flattened her anxiety, but it also blunted other things, like her interest in small talk about other people's lives. Besides, she was the kind of boss who didn't care what her staff did in their spare time, as long as they did their work well. Nkem didn't just do her work well, she did it with joy, listening to music in the kitchen as she stirred the jollof rice, talking to her best friend while mopping, and this was the first thing Adura loved about her: that she came to work looking like a BlackBerry Babe, interchanging wigs from black to red to blonde, nails done every other week. Adura liked that Nkem's life didn't stop for work.

Most people preferred to deal with those who referred to themselves as open books—people with nothing to hide. But Adura wasn't like that. Her favorite people were those who knew how to exercise restraint. She liked her people with secrets, something of their own to hold to their chests. So what if Nkem had hers then? Everybody was allowed them.

Adura had confronted Nkem only once before, when she realized it wasn't that Nkem was pretending not to overhear her conversations but that she'd fully drift all the way out of her body on cue.

"Where are you always going?" Adura asked her. "Your mind doesn't stay in one place. Look, you forgot to sweep here."

"Sorry, ma."

"It's not a matter of sorry. Where is your mind?"

"Ma, you were on the phone, so I said I should excuse you. I no dey like to enter person business." She interlocked her fingers shyly as she spoke, as if she was waiting for trouble. Adura had let it go.

Nkem came back from the market with a forehead speckled with sweat. "Ma, I found mango so I bought for you. You haven't been eating enough fruits." Adura didn't know what to do in the face of Nkem's casual generosity. Frankly, it made her want to cry. Kindness always did.

"Thank you so much," she said, her face creasing into a sad smile. "God bless you." She shouldn't have been surprised, but the world was the world, after all. Before Adura hired Nkem, she was one of those people who went around saying, *I don't believe in housegirls*, like they were some type of religion. But she'd heard enough stories for this to make sense. From family friends who kept underage girls in their homes to help them clean and cook and raise their children, to stories about witches, to stories about stealing. And then there was that memory from her childhood, the haunting one involving a pastor and a witch vomiting brown things on the corridor carpet. But she'd found a good one. Sometimes life made sense, she figured.

Nkem served the sweet potatoes with chicken curry sauce. She was by the dispenser getting Adura water when she heard a voice from the television that froze her.

"Is that Senator [redacted]? God, I *hate* this man." Her speech was strangely soft, even when she was talking about hate.

"Yes, it's him o," Adura said, scrolling on her finsta. Of the stubborn belief that she was too old to have a real Instagram account, she used this one to stalk Michelle Obama and hot celebrities. Sometimes she went on the Wura Blackson account and stayed there for hours, even though she'd seen all the outfits before. "Strange guy, abi?"

"Politics, he no sabi. But even in real life, he's not a good person," Nkem said.

"Ah ah. How do you know?"

Nkem leaned against the wall and smiled, crossing her arms across her chest. "I used to work for them. Him and his wife."

"You did?" Adura put the phone down, interested in hearing whatever Nkem wanted to share since she shared so little and not often. "Really? As what?"

"Ma?"

"You said you used to work for them. As what?"

"Oh . . . as their . . . as their houseboy," she said quietly. The silence spread as Nkem held Adura's gaze, her eyes glassing. It was important, Nkem felt, to stay wide awake to the possibility of mockery, of a body lurching across the room with wicked hands, of getting fired. She'd lost enough to know how it worked. There was more than just a dead name, an abattoir, and sewing machines in her past; there was lost blood and billowing ashes.

"Okay," Adura said, communicating her understanding. She wasn't going to probe any further. But it all made sense. Everything was clicking into place now. Nkem's reliability. Her heart for Adura. Her compassion. Her ability to tidy Adura's day with the exact right question. Cornrows for weeks, edges receding: "Ma, can I braid your hair?" Shoes falling apart: "Ma, can I help you to buy new shoes?" In bed for days: "Ma, should we take a stroll?" Not been eating: "Ma, should I cook your favorite soup?" Been smoking: "Ma, should I spray air freshener?" Her vibrator: "Ma, should I charge this thing?" Any time at all: "Ma, what about your medicine?" Nkem knew all the right questions to ask. She knew how to make Adura feel safe even when her life was unraveling and her mind was coming apart at the seams. People didn't grow that much compassion without first suffering tremendously. They got along from inside that void: Nkem needed the big sister, Adura needed the younger one.

Nkem could enter the flat and know—just from the sense and smell of things—whether to flood the place with light or to allow the darkness to keep gathering. In the same way, Adura was able to tell when Nkem was having a hard day. "Don't worry, don't cook today. Next time." "Here, money for transport." "Here, I found this dress. I thought it would fit you." Finding each other was a miracle in that sense: their two worlds colliding in that sweet Venn overlap where everything is possible.

Those parallels shouldn't have aligned, money being the divider that it is, but here they were and what could Adura call it but a miracle? Nkem was an angel and she'd be silly to let her insecurity get in the way of loving her. If the world was clearly going to ash, then it was in their individual best interests, as Adura had read once, to find a way to be very, very tender.

"How's the curry, ma?" Nkem asked, waiting to slink back into the kitchen.

"Too good," Adura said, nearing the bottom of her small bottle of JD all by herself, mouth all sweetbitter. "No be you again? After you, na still you."

- - -

"So why did you choose Nkem?" Adura asked, one random day. Her hair was only halfway done.

Nkem kept her eyes on the attachment she was stretching, pulling strand by strand. She chuckled and then said, "Because it fits me."

"Hm," Adura said, thinking that was a good answer.

"Why do you ask, ma?"

"Nothing. I just thought you were a Christian. Isn't that why you don't come on Sundays? That name on your bank account, is it not a Muslim name? Then again, that day when your mother was sick, you called pastor." A pause. Then, "I guess I'm trying to figure out the story." Adura had been there with her through the breakdown in the kitchen as the man prayed in Jesus' name, rubbing Nkem's back until she calmed down. What Adura *wanted* to ask was, Why did you lie? But that would be the Fat Bastard chardonnay talking, not her. Nkem didn't lie about anything.

At the interview, she hadn't asked a thing about tribe. Instead, she'd asked how well Nkem could clean. "Very well," Nkem replied. "I take my work serious. I also cook. I also go to market. I also braid hair." To which Adura asked, visibly pleased, "So what can't you do?" Nkem replied, "I can't fix toilets." Adura hired her on the spot.

"Well," Nkem said now, "I was born into a Muslim family, but I'm not part of them anymore. Me, I'm a Christian."

"Hm," Adura said. "How come?"

Nkem gisted Adura about her first time in church, when she felt God wrap her entire life with hope. The pastor assured them all that their old lives and all their horrors could be dead at the end of one prayer. "Why I no go choose am?" Adura could see how Jesus would make an attractive God for any person who'd been deserted. Her whole life, she'd been fascinated by religion—by the many routes people took to try to get to God. She'd known Buddhists, Christians, Muslims, atheists. She herself was against choosing a single road and went with her spirit most days. But Jesus knew, more than most, what it felt like to hold the memory of crucifixion in one's body; it made sense that he gave people permission to pass away, to delete old selves and go on living. He knew what it meant to die in one life and come back more yourself than ever. Wasn't it Jesus who Adura also hid in during her earlier years? It was Jesus who first knew, even before she did, that she could love a woman with her whole life. So Adura got it, beneath the surface, when Nkem said, "Na Jesus choose me, so na Jesus get me." Even though Nkem was standing behind her, speeding to the end of a braid, Adura knew exactly what her eyes looked like in that moment.

"I hear you," Adura said. "How did your family take it?"

"Na them know. We don't really talk like that. When I visit home, I still pray five times. E no mean." Nkem said, using the cutting comb to section Adura's hair. "God understands."

Adura realized then that Nkem wasn't a closed person, as she'd concluded before. She was a careful person. There was a difference.

"Two days I can't forget in my life: the day I gave my life to Christ and the day I started speaking in tongues. That day I was baffing, and as the water was pouring down my body, I started singing one gospel song. Before I knew it, I was sitting on the floor and bursting in another language. God was there."

Adura valued this trust. She valued the enthusiasm winging stories out of Nkem's mouth. Already, six months. Already, months removed from when she used to hide her weed and her journals, and Nkem used to flinch whenever she did some small thing wrong, like break a glass. They'd fought only once, when Adura had soft-scolded her, saying, "Please warn yourself so I don't have to warn you." Now, it had been four months since Nkem told Adura that her old madam used to slap her at every opportunity; since Adura saw that Nkem had saved her name as "my nice madam"; since Adura walked in on Nkem eating and Nkem dropped the plate, saying sorry, as if her hunger was a sin. "The house is safe, Nkem," Adura had told her. "This house is safe. Relax."

Nkem *had* relaxed since then. So now she added, "My family don't really know me like that. I haven't seen them in eight years. The only person that knows what I've done is Hauwa. But I still pray for them. And anyway, I have my new family in Christ."

"Who's Hauwa?" Adura asked.

"Ma?" A moment passed. "Oh. One of my friends like that."

• • •

Adura was watching *Blue Is the Warmest Color* and drinking again, as Nkem moved around the house more lightly than she used to. Adura knew something had happened. To open the conversation, she said, "Nkem? Please can you help me pass that remote?"

Nkem leaned over to reach the remote on the center table and handed it to Adura. When she got up, her eyes caught a scene and she looked away sharply. "Na wa. These oyinbo people sef."

Adura looked at her. "Why are you hiding your eyes?"

"See girls kissing themselves. Ha. Ma, this kind of film doesn't used to make you feel somehow?"

"You've never seen people kiss before?"

"I have, but normal kissing."

"What is normal kissing?"

"Man and woman na. Boy and girl."

"You that you have a girlfriend?" Adura felt it was time.

"Me?" Nkem said, her hand flying to her mouth in fake shock. She didn't expect the tackle. "No o. No. Me ke? For where?"

"Uh, look at this one. You can't even keep a straight face. You think I don't know? Dem write mumu for my head?

"Every time I come into the kitchen, you're always on the phone to the same person. And you'll be smiling like say no tomorrow. Say the truth jo. Na police I be? I won't judge you." The wine had loosened her. She looked at Nkem. "Or you people have broken up, abi? That's why you've been squeezing face up and down?"

She knew she wasn't making it up. Even Nkem's ringtone for the girl was different—Fireboy DML's "Jealous" instead of the usual annoying tune she used for most. And Adura *had* noticed the gloom in her face, her new silence, no phone calls as she worked.

Nkem couldn't run now and she didn't want to. No one else had ever asked her with this lightness. "She likes me," she said. "And I like her. But it's not possible. So."

"Where does she live?"

"Kogi State. She has seen somebody that wants to marry her."

"Does she want to marry him?"

"No. She wants something else. She can't find work, and she needs money."

"Do you love her?"

"Ma?"

"Do you love her?"

"She loves me. But as for me o, I can love a woman but I can't marry a woman. I no want make dem go tie us give tree. She say I'm weak because of that, that I'm always hiding. But me sha, I will hide this hide that I'm hiding now, until I die." Typical Nkem. Always ready to mention death.

Adura's skin tightened. She knew this feeling; this *it's love but it's impossible* thing. "Well, fair enough. You know what's best for you," she said, feeling weak behind her teeth. She wanted to end it there but something was moving her differently. "What type of work is she looking for?"

"Any type. Even this work I'm doing now, she doesn't mind. But I don't know anybody. And she dey fear because you know as tins hard. She has been trying her luck since."

"If she finds work, will she leave the man? Is that the only thing that is holding her there?"

"Yes, ma. I swear. It's money. The man has biiiig money."

"Hm," Adura said, making a note in her mind. "I think one of my friends might be looking for someone."

Nkem's eyes shot open and she made to go to her knees. "Ma? God will bless you! God will bless your family. God will bless your home, God will give you good hus—"

"Oya wait wait. I haven't done anything. Let me see what I can do." She knew she was going to take this on. If that was the only obstacle, she was going to find her way around it. She'd been looking for ways to help Nkem. She always was. "And as for your prayer, thank you. Amen to all . . . except that last one sha."

A small silence stretched between them as Nkem tried to remember the last thing she'd said. Then it clicked. "Oooh the one about husband. Ma, how come? You don't wish to marry?"

Adura shrugged. "Not really," she said. "But even if, I can never marry a man."

Nkem was quick this time, spitting the words before she could take them back. "How about a woman?"

"Well," she said, "there's one woman I could have married, but she's not, you know, she's not . . . here anymore. That said, you don't have to marry somebody to be with them. Shey you know?"

"Ahhh," Nkem said, failing to tuck herself back in. "So what happened to her, the woman? Where is she now? Does she have a husband? Did she marry a man?"

Adura was trying to hold herself together. She hadn't expected an answer like that. Sure, men never came to the house and once Nkem had even seen a stack of letters in Adura's room addressed to a person named Wura. But still.

Anyway, whatever. She could go back to being Madam tomorrow, but for now she just needed to be Adura, blurry behind the eyes from drinking too much wine. She just needed to be a person. "No," she said, "she's gone, as in . . . gone. Like your brother. She's the one you caught in the kitchen there, stealing forks." More wine. More. More.

Nkem held her hand to her mouth and her eyes watered. "Ma? I'm so sorry, ma. So sorry. I didn't—"

Adura sat up, fencing herself in again. She wasn't going to sit there and cry over Wura with Nkem. She'd save that for later, when Nkem had closed.

Adura knew what she had done, putting her secret on the table like that; it was a kind of bartering. Nkem saw Adura trying to gift her courage, and she decided to unwrap it. "Well," she said. "Well . . ."

"What's your girlfriend's name?" Adura asked. "My own is called Wura."

Nkem noticed the tense Adura chose to use, how it was so present that the woman might as well be there with them; how at the mention of that name, Adura smiled so softly that it peeled a decade off her face. She fidgeted, turning her phone to face the table. It was the first time she'd reached for it since they started talking. "Ma, you know how to corner somebody ehn? Kai. But well sha . . . hm. If I had a girlfriend, her name would be . . . well, her name would be Hauwa."

"Ehehn," Adura said, satisfied, knowing what she'd done. Sometimes, all people needed was permission. "Next time you speak to your *girlfriend* Hauwa, tell her your madam says hi, okay?"

Nkem nodded. She folded her lips in to avoid blushing. "Thank you, ma," she said.

Adura hissed jokingly. "Oya my friend, sit down, let's watch this film."

THERE IS LOVE AT HOME

The first night Star entered the Upper Room, Divine had long black braids on, hanging down to the backs of her knees, and she was wearing combat boots. Star had just turned fifty that weekend, and funny, it was her sugarbaby F. who'd told her to go upstairs and try to see what else was there. Star told F. about the rejection stories she'd heard in whispers about this room in particular, how stunning women of all ages had been turned away by whoever was behind that door. But the babe was adamant.

"The worst that can happen is that they'll say no, abi?" she asked, nudging Star up the stairs. "That's it. This is a building with endless rooms. The adventures go on for longer than time. If that room rejects us, we'll find another. What's there to lose?"

Star shrugged, knowing F. had a point. "Loosen up jare!" F. teased. "You're alive. Act like it! Life is for the living o!"

What choice did Star have? This was their deal, after all, exactly what she'd signed up for: in exchange for the bright spontaneity that F. brought to the table, Star offered her financial stability and a seat above the law. "If you ever run into any trouble," she promised, "I'm just a

phone call away." She meant it. The one and only time F. used that
privilege, when some Lagos Big Boy slapped her friend outside Silverfox,
a blue Hilux arrived on the scene within minutes with sirens blaring,
MOPOLs hanging out of the sides, guns loaded on their shoulders.
They lifted the man off his feet and treated his fuckup in less than five
minutes and sent him leaping off into the night with a bleeding, beating mouth. Star gave that instruction from the comfort of her bed, a
number dialed calmly from her iPhone. It only cost her a few seconds.

"You're never going there again," Star told F. afterward. "Silverfox
is for commoners anyway. You're with me. Shey na naked babes you
wan see? I know a place."

Star and F. had only been outside the door of the Upper Room for
seconds when a pea-eyed camera winked at them. The photos went
straight to a printer on Divine's desk inside, which groaned softly before releasing them with a proud exhale. The bouncer pressed a finger
against her right ear and nodded, receiving instruction from Divine,
then turned to Star and F., her chest built like a safe. Star imagined
jewels asleep inside it. "She say you shoul' wait," the bouncer said. Her
voice was at least an octave higher than they expected. Star tried not
to fidget. None of her girls had ever seen her take no for an answer.
Just a few nights ago, when Angela was praising her for paying the
tuition for her master's and getting her pregnant sister a three-year
U.S. visa in a matter of days, she'd said, "Mama di mama. What can't
you do? After you, no be you? You fa, you can only ever get two answers in this life: yes and yes, ma!" Angela's excitement rushed straight
to Star's head. She loved the praise even more than the sex they had
that night. *Say yes*, she found herself thinking now. *Say yes*.

Divine had always been able to tell who she'd be able to work and play
well with just by looking at their photo once, so it didn't take long for
a short voice message to come back through to the bouncer. "Just one,"

the bouncer said. "You, on the left." Feeling flushed with confusion, Star held both her arms out to determine where her left and her right were, and immediately registered how stupid this was. It's just that it had been a long time since she'd felt chosen based on her looks alone. F. fidgeted beside her, trying not to feel terrible. Star turned from F. to the bouncer and back again, as if she might find permission on one of their faces. She felt nothing like herself. "No, it's okay," F. said finally— not to Star, but to the awkwardness in the air. "I'll go find something else to do." Star stumbled forward feebly and the door clicked open.

Divine liked her women with age in their legs, with plotlines in their foreheads and cheeks; darkness behind the eyes. All the better if, like Star, they wore their hair short and wore little makeup. She wasn't after beauty, really—which was what most of the women who sought her out got wrong. She was after layers; she was after women who already knew that pain could be a tunnel and pleasure could be the warm light at its end. Women who could understand without too much hand-holding that life was neither flat nor straight, who whimpered at the sight of leather and lace, who moaned at the lick of heat on skin. Women who were open to learning that sometimes shame locked in the body even for decades was not theirs to keep, that it could be submitted, regulated, rewritten into power with just a safe word. Women who could appreciate that scenes like this were about freedom, about honesty, about transcending lockedness. They were about negotiating lust with full intention, about—as she had said to a friend once—"bringing the darkest of one's desires to the surface of the skin." She knew, just from looking at them, which women liked to be gagged or strapped or slapped or choked. Or all. She knew who didn't mind crying if it meant *getting there, getting there, there*. She saw that something in Star: creased curiosity worn well between crow's feet, a subtle exhaustion from carrying a weighty life alone, a low-humming desire to give it all to somebody else—and already, all of it was telling; all of it was story.

"There you are," Divine said as Star entered. She was sorting through a black leather bag, her back to the door. Star noticed her bootlaces undone, her calves sweetly toned. "Wondered if you might leave with your little girlfriend. Some people do that when I don't pick them both." Divine said *little* with the candid curtness of someone Star's age, which made Star chuckle. "What?" Divine asked, turning around for the first time. "It's true." She was wearing lip tar, a black moody lipstick with a decadent nightness to it. Stretching her hand forward, eyes steady on Star's, she said, "Divine."

With Star's name still stuck to the sky of her mouth in awe, Divine added, "You can introduce yourself after. Two minutes. Pick the props that'll make you the wettest." Star fell down some floors inside herself. Who had talked to her like this before? "You heard me," Divine said. The room shuddered as she cocked her head toward the giant shelf.

Star got on her knees to look and thanked her chi that she came in alone. A whip. Hot wax and cold honey. A collar. Clamps. A blindfold of heavy black silk. "Greedy," Divine said. "I like you already." Star knew, too, from that intimidatingly tall energy translating onto her body from the inside, from how at ease Divine was in herself, that she would have to make this a small religion. Divine squatted next to her, calling her close. "Now tell me. What do you *really* really want?" she asked. "It's your show now."

Later that night, when Star made the mistake of looking up at Divine from down where she was kneeling, with a remote-controlled vibrator fitted into her, Divine upped the speed, leaned forward, and said, "Don't be looking at me like I owe you mercy or some shit. I'm not your fucking mummy." Star landed so hard she cried. A belly-falling cry. A worry-drowning cry. An a-whole-me? cry. But there was something about the shape of the resulting shame that did something to her eyes, that stretched them out sideways, broke her sight open, and gave her a new way to see herself.

Now, weekends and weekends later, Star asked for the scene. Stood

in front of Divine in the dark room with her hands clasped in front
of her crotch, she said the go word. The room collapsed outward and
puffed smoke into the air. A cool blue light went under Star's weak
defense and licked between her thighs. It had the coldest tongue she'd
ever felt. Divine watched on. Not far behind Star, a woman yelped
from where she was suspended in the air by ropes woven down from
the ceiling. Her legs were spread-eagle, but it took a red light cutting
through black smoke for Star to see slivers of her, limbs forming perfect planes. Star felt herself shudder. Divine swept her eyes around the
new expanse and Star followed with hers, watching the women who'd
just appeared out of nowhere begin to reach for each other, skin against
skin, hands swallowing space. She'd chosen this: a room with collaps-
ible borders, framed by women who could watch this entire thing
openly with their eyes glassed and thirsty.

One of them, a stud standing alone, caught Star's stare and pinned
her there, then touched herself, two fingers gently sliding. Star would
have been able to catch her breath if Divine's palm hadn't come from
behind and wrapped itself around her neck all sweet like that. Her
mind spun; time melted. It was a new now, and she was sitting down,
Divine's knee working against her. There was a playground-bully mean-
ness in Divine's voice when she said, in front of all the watching eyes:
"Ah ahn, you're excited already? I thought I trained you better. Look at
your mates. No, look." Star could hear small deaths stacking behind
her, tumbling out of moaning mouths, and the thought of it alone—of
being in the same room as other women meeting themselves again for
the first time under trained hands—tightened her skin.

So, her breath cutting quick, the whip against her thigh, the
upside-down and inside-outting, hot wax leaking into her clavicle, a
metal spoon resurrecting on a flame, honey drooling sideways, Divine's
tongue flashing and disappearing, Star's mouth opening quick, her
begging pouring out of it before she could reel it back in, the whole
of her goosebumping, Divine leveling her to her knees, pushing the

chair out of the way, Divine saying, "What, you want to come, you want to come, that's why you're crying? Aren't you a big woman? Don't you run shit out in the world?" Star felt her shame cartwheeling, shape-shifting, reintroducing itself wearing pleasure's mad face and coming closer than close with the rudest mouth; a known beat forming between her legs; wet sliding down the inside of her thighs; Divine's fingers slipping over her torso like an almost-there, then lower, to that soft flesh between her hipbone and trouble. Divine kept her eyes open, focused, stayed on Star's and all their twinkling. Star blinked Divine gone, and then back again. "Someone smells desperate," Divine said, squatting between Star's legs. She never missed this part: this teasing like she just might taste it even knowing she'd never go there. (Her tongue was someone else's; all her clients knew this.) But it didn't stop Star from pleading, pleading. She was here for this pain, for the torture. With a blindfold newly knotted behind her head, a waterfall of black silk tumbling behind her head, Star is all the tenses—future on past on present jamming hard, grinding in a stack.

"Please can I—" Star tried, but Divine shut her up with the flex of her jaw alone. *Focus*, Divine thought to herself as her head attempted to float off. *Keep your mind here.* Divine knew what this kind of sternness could do to Star; where exactly the rejection would flood her. Star shrieked and Divine lifted her by the chin, seeing the fight on her face, that whole wide trying, Divine knew where she was speeding toward, where she was trying to drop to. She was teetering on the edge and trying to stand on it, to wait on it, to listen for permission to freefall all the way, because everything in the whole world felt wetter than wet, slipperier than sane.

"Don't you dare," Divine said. Her voice came out sounding shaded, like a deftly darkened sketch of something sinister. She knew that when she talked like this, words sweetly wrapped in risk, it made her subs want to sit on her voice. "Fine," she said, turning a soft edge. "One for me then. Then one for whoever will be waiting for you at home."

"Who . . . who . . . *who* do you think you are?" Star said, trying with everything in her. It was that fucking smirk, grinding her gears.

Divine scoffed at the dead end in the question. In any life she entered, she landed like a world. Even days into the week, with Star in her glass high-rise office somewhere working, she knew Star would come back and back to this exact second when she let go and her body sang: *Divine, Divine, Divine.*

· · ·

Daisy spread her palms over Divine's back, slick with warm oil. "Ife mi. Mm? Love of my life. Are we dom-dropping over here?" She knew the answer already just from the way Divine's body was lying. Massages were one of the ways Daisy took care of Divine after a long weekend working. Though she almost always came away feeling exhausted herself, she knew that for Divine the crash was different, that after work sometimes, on especially strenuous days, it took her hours to peel that storied world off her body. She needed to wait for it to cool, for the glue to shift so that she could feel her own skin again. "Let me help you with that," Daisy said.

Divine chuckled softly with both her eyes still closed, which usually meant she was still inside-tired, past flesh, past blood and bone, past marrow. During play, when a scene was going the way it ought to, she saw herself the way the women saw her, like a towering force, larger than the building itself. After scenes, she was used to holding her subs' faces and talking them back up, setting their feet back on reality. *It was a scene*, she'd say, *You're okay, here is some water, what do you need?* It was part of her job. But it wasn't easy either to grow that unstoppable adrenaline speeding through you as you stayed attentive to cues. How many times had she reminded clients that they could say the safe word if they wanted to, knowing that they'd swallowed it on purpose? Making it look easy was part of the job, but it was difficult work to stand as custodian and front-rider of someone else's pleasure, to be the one in whose hands another person's desire took form or woke up, only to have all that power crumbling back to flat inside her afterward; to have to bring herself back down to herself.

Daisy's fingers worked Divine's back and then rested under her shoulder blade. Divine moaned and nodded in approval. "Here?" Daisy leaned forward and kissed her neck, her fingers pressing in.

"Mm. Yes, please."

In a matter of days, they'd have been together for three years, and it had always felt like this: soft hands and deliberate care; a love that flowered open and rivered both ways in equal measure—nothing they would have anticipated when they met at a private party in a New Money Honey's beach house. Everybody there was wearing their night lives on top of their real lives, and Divine was walking to the bathroom when she got leashed by a scent.

"Bleu de Chanel?" she asked, walking in its direction. She'd know that scent anywhere, and part of knowing it was obeying it.

Daisy turned around, already smiling. "Correct," she said. Being as visible as she was to anyone with good eyes, she was used to Lagos babes and their thirsty lines. Most of them bored her. But this person standing here, with her burgundy afro and her endless legs, made her want to listen.

"I'm good," Divine said, sensing the invitation and going closer.

"You are. I have to give it to you. Let me too guess. You're wearing, uh . . . Gorgeous, by God." Stroking her invisible beard, she balanced against the wall. They both burst out laughing.

"Wow. So, you're really just . . . Jim Iyke? As you fine reach, you're still dropping dead Nollywood lines on babes."

"That was more like Tony Umez, actually. At least Big Jim had some bars."

It was easy from there. The rest of the party melted into an unreal. "I have a confession," Divine said as the night grew. "I've seen you before."

"For real, or is that another dead pickup line?"

"For real. It was at Afropolitan Vibes."

"Which one?"

"Burna Boy."

"You were *there?*" Daisy covered her face. The night was coming back. It was on brand for her to lose all decorum wherever there was good music. That night, her friend Rose had posted the video of her on stage dancing with three other women—sweat and joy dripping down their backs, crowd going nuts—in her Instagram story. The next day she had twenty new follow requests. "Oh no."

"Yes." Divine laughed. "And yes, I saw."

When Daisy asked, Divine told her her real name—not the one she wore at work or under the harsh sun outside, but the one her mother had named her with love—and Daisy mentioned her true name in return. When a year from then, they decided to take Agbon's offer, they chose each other's names between touches and soft kisses, grip and sweat:

You'll be Divine.

And you'll be Daisy.

But all that was a far future away. "Okay, since we're telling the truth, let me confess," Daisy said, drunk already. "I saw you that night too. You were wearing a *Family Guy* shirt with Stewie on it, and you had locs still. At one point you were at the back where they sell food and drinks, abi? I saw you fighting the woman for your two hundred naira change."

Divine's eyes watered from how hard she was laughing. "I actually remember that outfit. And to be honest, a girl needs her two hundreds, okay? They add up."

"But wait," Daisy said. "If you saw me, why didn't you talk to me? What if you never saw me again?"

"I saw you right after they'd just stolen my phone. You know Nigerians. Plus, I wasn't sure if you were . . . you know?" Daisy did know. Back then, she wasn't visible like Divine. People always assumed she was straight. Even when she was in places with just women, the ones with eyes for just women still couldn't see her. Was it invisibility? Was it opacity? She didn't know, but it broke her heart often. She was constantly editing herself to show more. But it was both too late and too early to start processing that.

"Ah, sorry about your phone," she said instead. "As for the other thing, how does that matter? If I like you, I like you. And I like you." She shrugged. "But I get sha."

Divine backed down the rest of her drink. "Tell you something," she said. "The first thing I thought was *She's so beautiful*. The second thing I thought was *She likes women. Does she know she likes women?*"

Daisy leaned forward and found Divine's mouth. *I know*, she was telling Divine, *I do know*. Before Divine, Daisy had never dated a woman seriously before, although she had kissed more than a few. But it didn't take more than that night to *know*. It was easy from there: dates rolling over into dates, nights into mornings into nights. Not to say it wasn't difficult to work through—with Divine's fear of commitment and Daisy's fear of losing herself in love, they clashed at the heart in the way large lives do when they first meet—but for the first time in both their histories of running and running, of withdrawing their faith in relationships, after just a few weeks they found themselves standing still and facing another someone who wanted to do the same.

"Are you sure?" friends used to ask all the time, at first. "So this is it? Last bus stop tings? You're sure you're not moving too fast?" Their answers were always the same, despite the fear and its mouth packed with teeth: *Yes. Yes. Always yes.* Even now, they still bonded in the same ways: flooding the kitchen with groceries, spending a full day cooking, sharpening each other's tastes. "All that work I grew up doing in the kitchen," Divine said once, standing between Daisy's legs as she sat on the island, "wallahi, she didn't know it then, but my mother was raising me to feed you."

Every weekend they hosted friends, feeding them new dishes they were trying, and the house swelled with a raucous, redeeming noise. The week just gone was a friend's birthday, an Italian night at their request, and they made carbonara and lasagna and drank moscato into the morning. The coming week, Divine planned to make golden puff puffs tossed in brown sugar and the banga jollof she got a recipe for from Kitchen Butterfly's blog. It was a joyful life they'd made, a life with real friends who knew their real given names and the meanings behind them, a circle and a community, a family and a fortress—a home far from old violences, wholly accepting.

When Divine started to feel the ground of her mind again, she rolled over and kissed Daisy thank you. Then her mouth started running again: *How are you feeling? What should we do today? What should I make us for brunch? How's your back?* This was a thing she did when she was worried she was taking too much space, when she was trying to hide something under her tongue.

"Shh," Daisy said. "It's okay, just stay here. What's happening? Tell me. Something's happened."

Divine bit the inside of her cheeks until they stung. "It's my baby brother's birthday today. He turned fifteen. And, well—"

"Oh no, baby. I'm so sorry." Daisy understood the feeling, of having a new and safe life where you were seen, but still missing the one in which you were raised, where love and acceptance were contingent on how good a masquerade you were. In her own home the rejection was ongoing and less overtly violent, but it was still there. She could still go home, sure, but only if she played along at the family dinners and agreed to go on dates with people's sons whom she never planned to see again. There was a tacit agreement under it all: *You can keep being a part of this family, you can keep being your parents' daughter and sister's sister, as long as you never name yourself. Do what you want, but never say it out loud. Or else.*

She knew the subtext: *Love expires the day you say it.* Already, she could approximate how much it would hurt to be cut off like that. Unsure that she could ever survive it, she rotated between her two faces, kept her two lives, even if one was all ash and tall smoke. "I'm here," she told Divine, her voice warm with reassurance. "Ife mi, I'm here."

Divine felt herself tear up. She shook her head and closed her eyes. "Thank you for taking care of me," she said. Three years in and she still cried in surprise sometimes when she realized the solidity of this thing, how well and how often it could catch her weight, how horizonless the kindness was. She still found it hard to wrap her head around it: How she could find a person who wanted to dedicate herself to her in this same world where people had taken and taken and taken from her. This same world she'd tried to jump out of before. She laughed at herself, at the thoughts sliding through her mind. "Hard guy hard guy, ehn?" she said, teasing herself aloud. "But small love now and I'm crying."

Daisy lay down next to her and closed her eyes. She was thinking it too: the sheer luck of it all. Divine being everything she never even dared to wish for: rest outside of work, a good home outside of an office, no barking, no manipulating, no hiding. Just her face, next to another person's face. A normal life and an extraordinary love.

"Should we nap?" Daisy asked.

"I was going to ask. Feelings are a higi right now."

"I know," Daisy said. "Wanna meditate?"

"Yes, please."

Yes, all the things that hurt underneath a good life didn't just go away because you were now loved. But it helped to see each other. And, they did. They saw each other so far past the pain that, no matter how hard their families tried to unsee them, they could never be invisible again.

* * *

Daisy wound down the pole to Dawn Penn's "No, No, No," her eyes on one of the new faces in the booth. There was something about the song that felt prophetic in the moment, like a word uttered right on time. As usual, she was working the Blue Room, a space set up with twenty private booths facing the stage so that none of the customers could see each other. Safety reasons for some, and for others an arrangement that helped them feel special, like this was a show for them alone—VIP behavior. Six out of those twenty booths were wide enough to accommodate couples. All of them were full. In each section there were small card machines, a menu of drinks and drugs, and a digital album of strippers who could be requested to perform private dances as the women watched the stage. A woman sitting alone shifted from Daisy's gaze and blinked multiple times, like this was a dream she was trying not to forget, like that might convince what she had just seen to never dissipate.

In a sense, everything inside was a dream, the club itself a not-quite real. The Secret Place was built into a sixteen-story, neon-lit high-rise that went underground on Friday nights and didn't come back up until Sunday evening. To be in a building where even the buff bouncers— six of them at the entrance, others inside—and the "mallams" changing bundles of naira to dollar bills outside were all women? It changed everything.

Inside, there were glow-in-the-dark body painters, glow-in-the-dark toys and accessories on sale, music pounding through the air, bodies in latex, lethal six-inch heels, a nude silent disco—everything pointing sexward, as if by Monday the club wouldn't go back to acting like one of those random skyscraping apartment buildings with no tenants occupying them. In daylight, the building dulled itself by itself, moonlighting perfectly. But that was the point: these weekend nights were life-transforming, suns rising and setting at the same time in different lives, contrasting worlds eclipsing, a sweet escape. The club was where rich, powerful older women came to relinquish the control they had in their daily lives, and younger women came to gather the power they were used to being stripped of. Money, pain, and pleasure changed hands here: big names on all fours begging for bodies that weren't theirs to have, their fantasies standing at a height, overlooking them with calculated control. All of this done like time was running out and wouldn't wait for anyone. Because it wouldn't.

The working girls never deluded themselves into thinking the club was real. It only took stepping outside to remember that the place was pretty much a shiny hallucination, an experiment in what could be. They knew better than to trust women whose real faces and names they'd never know. They knew to move with caution, because the kind of women who could afford to pay for this service had to be women in top-tier careers or with old money. A good percentage of them were havoc-wreakers during the day, who did and unlooked terrible things in high places. Some of the clients were even hellbent on making freedom like this impossible outside. They wanted it for themselves, in the dark, underground. And why not? Where's the thrill in something that everybody gets to have? Being that untouchable can make you forget your humanity, can monster you out of you. So one of the first things the girls were taught in training was: "You're from the same country, yes. But you're not under the same law. This thing we do here is illegal for you. Not for them. Nothing is illegal for a rich Nigerian. Remember that when they make you promises. Remember: your client is not your friend." Daisy always held that in her mind.

When she got on all fours, arched her back, and swept her eyes across the room, she saw women crossing and uncrossing their legs, trying to resist the damp pooling between. One of them locked eyes with her, stirring some white powder into her whiskey; another was doing a thick line off a stripper's breast with a £100 note. The one who'd looked away earlier was now wolfing down the suya she'd ordered, to avoid watching Daisy. Daisy ran her fingers down her front and watched the woman reach for the menu. She never avoided their eyes; their faces were the most rewarding part. Her favorite kinds were women like this, who fenced their lust with remorse, who shawled their desire with shame. This one, Daisy guessed, was probably thinking of her family, her precious children in their beds and the husband who loved her at odd, unfulfilling angles—always at a half past *no* or quarter to *yes*.

They were all looking for something. Some of them came looking for one of the girls to take care of their child-selves and console them, others for an hour of cuddling. Some queued outside the door for a room with The Priest and confessed all sorts of sins, crawling on small stones, begging for forgiveness. The girl who worked that room had to sign an NDA; Daisy didn't envy her. Some just wanted to talk. Sure, there was also the wild sex one would expect from a place like this: in threes and nines and sixteens, bodies getting tangled in the mix. There was a room for everything. Daisy could give them what they wanted in this one. She knew how to do just enough to make them drool from their mouths and their wallets.

Later, Daisy was smoking a cigarette by the bar, naked save for her latex boots, when someone spilled a drink on her. She turned and it was the woman with the shame-eyes. "Sorry! I'm so sorry!" Daisy, being in the mood she was in, speed-thinking, too far back inside her own head for her own good—what with white lines and small trees and ecstasy talking to each other in her body, all of them making a cacophony, a giant audacity in her—responded by saying, "I only accept my apologies in dollars."

"Sure," the woman said, leaning closer, searching her suit pocket.

"That's your naira pocket," Daisy said, straight-faced. "Put your hand in the dollar one." The woman chuckled.

"My mistake," she said, pressing dollar bills into Daisy's hand. She watched as Daisy tucked the notes into her boots. Behind her jacket, the woman's stomach was falling but what was the harm in asking?

"Now can I please get some time to talk to you?"

Up close, when the woman's mouth was still, Daisy could see that she had three faces overlapping. Daisy wasn't keen, because she already knew how the script went. She didn't show up at the Secret Place to earn anyone's heart; she already had one in her care that she'd guard with her life. Still, most of the patrons couldn't wrap their heads around pariahs with this much power and this little shame, pariahs who weren't searching for a rescuer or a savior. Incorrigible vagabonds. "There is something bright in you," they were fond of saying. "You're not like the other girls. Let me take care of you. You will never have to worry again." Daisy always refused. For months, she'd been dealing with a tough nut called Ruby, who always showed up in a black suit looking like she could be somebody's husband. She could have most things, just based on the landscape of her arms and back alone. She'd had a husband once, she explained, but it didn't last for a reason. *He could not satisfy me. Not because he didn't try oh, but because he's a man.*

Ruby was clear what she was willing to give up for Daisy if Daisy would just give up this life spinning lust. She made a different offer every weekend: *I can pay you more than what you're getting here! We can move to Canada and no one will ever find us. Fine, a car? Okay then, a house!* But for Daisy, all of this was work, and business was business, and money must be made, and leaving this place on Sundays never made her stomach fall the way it did theirs, because there was love where she lived. The thick kind, the staying kind. The patrons were the ones who hated the lives they were towing, and it showed; it wafted off them as they walked.

"May I?" the woman asked again, sensing Daisy's hesitation. Daisy almost pitied her. *No one,* she thought, *resists loneliness as aggressively as a person who's ashamed of their own heart.* Left to her, she'd be at home in bed with Divine already, watching reruns of *Desperate Housewives.* But she was still in work mode, which meant she still had her work mouth on with the fanged wit built into it. She looked down at the money in her boots, the mint notes winking, and nodded her permission.

"Five minutes," Daisy said.

The woman shifted on her feet before starting, looking startled, like she couldn't believe her luck. She was probably going to ask a silly question about nothing, Daisy thought. So before the woman opened her mouth, she let her mind float back to the two IJGB babes she'd seen earlier. She was passing them on the stairs when one said, "My god, I didn't realize Nigeria was so gay. What the fuck?" and her friend, the one with the neck tattoo, said in her American accent, "Oh no. This is all just acting. It's just work. We're the only ones who get to see this—" she lowered her voice "—because we're, like, *rich* rich. But dykes and like . . . queer folk in general aren't allowed in the country. It's against the law. Most of these women you see probably have husbands."

In her head, Daisy played out a different scene she wished had happened instead of her walking past them. In this version, she walked up to them and told them that a thing being forbidden did not make it extinct; that, in fact, bans only created black markets. Besides, desire was itself and could morph anyway. Being in a country where *dykes* were ghosts and shapeshifters for a living, for a life, meant that shit here didn't work like it did abroad. But that didn't mean it didn't work at all, because people still found ways to love each other, even in nervous conditions. "I'm one of them," she said to their stunned faces, lighting up in her mind's eye. "One of *us*. We're ghosts because we have to be, because our lives depend on passing and being passed by. But we're ghosts who see other ghosts often, who hold them and hug them and fuck them, too, in our bedrooms, doors closed. We love them too. Like you. Here, they call us mad. We go again. They strike us down. We choose again. They black off our lights. We learn the dark. We don't die. We never die. We only love harder. We only see sharper. I can appear and disappear in seconds, at will. I can look like a not-sin, a non-outcast. People like us don't need a club full of women to find one who'll go down if we look right. We know our signals, our codes. You're not only real when everybody can see you."

The woman in front of Daisy cleared her throat. "I guess my time is up," she said. Daisy hadn't even heard a word before that. Then the woman said, "Anyway, this is my card. My church is always welcoming new members. Tomorrow, ten a.m." Daisy looked at her watch, as if time was a thing that worked in here. The watch stared back with its round face and frozen hands. She smiled bitingly and said, "You better hurry now. You never know with places like this. Might even be Sunday already."

The woman stood like ice. Daisy waited to see if she might lunge at her, like that one from two weekends ago, who when Daisy said, "Don't touch me!" had responding by screaming back: "I'm old enough to be your mother! I'm not your mate! And I can do as I like. I'm a paying customer!"

Daisy had replied her calmly, "Okay, Mummy, now why are you touching me?" The woman lost it, threatening to relieve Daisy of her job. *Rude little brat!* she said. *She has no home training.* But because power is never really by mouth, when the woman asked for a manager and Agbon showed up, she was the one who got escorted out. Agbon pulled up her details in a matter of minutes. "Mrs. what?" she said to her assistant. "Ehehn. Mrs. Kolawole. Whatever. Now Halima, take her off the system. That woman has issues."

The Secret Place was Agbon's brainchild, and she made it clear who her priorities were. "*You*'re the prize," she told the girls often. "They're here to see *you*. They're paying to see *you*. Anyone who disrespects you can leave."

But this woman seemed different, calmer. She stepped away from Daisy, walking back on herself, her palms in front of her in surrender.

It was this attitude that made Agbon hire both Daisy and Divine on the spot. She had met them having drinks at the Eko Hotel poolside and invited them in as guests for just one night. Agbon pitched her mission to them: something had to come full circle. So many rich women had the desire and the money; they just needed somewhere to spend it. The girls she hired had the bodies and the skill; they just needed somewhere to show it. So Agbon reasoned: Demand meet supply meet Economics 101. Within a year of working in the Secret Place, most of the girls could afford apartments of their own.

"Why did you make this place?" Daisy asked Agbon once at one of their dinners. "What is in it for you? How do we know we're safe?" Agbon explained that she'd started the Secret Place with her partner—a partner she'd had to fight to be with across realms. Even though they existed in the world in a separate way, they knew how hard it was to choose something you were not allowed to choose. "To live freely in this life, you need money. This is our way of making sure you're also able to build the lives you all want too. To choose a woman in this city and keep your life at the same time, you need to be able to afford rent in a safe place. Now, you'll find that most of the women who pay for your services are angry and envious, because at certain levels public scrutiny is a cage. No one is really looking at us that closely, so we can do what we want in our own homes. They don't have that. But they're angry at the wrong people. Don't worry about safety, this land we're on is owned by an Untouchable. The name on the C of O alone will gag the police. Even if some woman who gets banned from here should try to involve them, where would they find the owner to arraign? Where dem go see am? Can they arrest a spirit?"

· · ·

Divine filled their bedroom with music, and the thrum of the speakers rose from their feet to their chests, like a tall bath being drawn. They were standing chest to chest against the wall. Daisy's eyes were closed, and she felt submerged in sound as the beat wrapped them closer. "This is our club," Divine said against her ear as she increased the volume. Her voice moved with such a sturdy assurance that Daisy could stand on it. Always, Divine's voice was this for Daisy: a call back to shore, a safe walk on moody water. "This is the best club in the whole of Lagos. Even the Secret Place no fit. There is for work, here is for pleasure."

It was. They both knew they were going to end up here when Daisy came out in Fenty lingerie. But the private dance in between—Divine tied to the chair and Daisy dancing to Janet Jackson's "Would You Mind" and Beyoncé's "Dance for You"—still flabbergasted them both. When Daisy freed Divine's hands, they unhinged the world from its axes, touch by touch; their bodies harmonizing in shock. Now their hearts were still beating against each other, skin against skin, only seconds removed from that heaven. John Legend's "Made to Love" started playing. Daisy let her hand rest safe inside Divine's. Seconds in and there was a slow dance forming. "This feels so good," Divine whispered, her core still tight from before.

"I know," Daisy said. "I know."

To start the day, Divine made a full English breakfast and served Daisy in bed. They exchanged presents, then took a long bath, talking about what they were thankful for as they shaved each other's legs. Divine helped Daisy wash her hair and condition it after. Daisy shaved Divine's head. Now it was early evening and raining outside like an angerstorm. Three years, and still, every time they held each other, it felt like before the first word, before the first kiss, before the first pinning against the wall, way way before the first *I love you*, when neither had earned the other's trust but wanted to, wanted to.

"Show me why I always go home with you," Daisy said. It was a line they'd picked up from the club, where women so often asked them the inverse: *Show me why I should take you home.* As if it was on them to prove it; as if they would ever even agree. Daisy never corrected them, because what did their fantasies matter when held up against this reality? The truth was, where it mattered, she never had to audition for anything. So Daisy and Divine had made a tradition of *Show me why I always go home with you*: whenever one of them said it, at any time, they both had to hold each other in a hug, cheek against cheek, neither of them performing anything but hereness, but presence. "If they ever ask why I go home with you," Divine told her the first time, "I'll tell them it's because you're you and you're here, alive; because you're my mine, because you tether me to me. That's all you'll ever need to do. Breathe and I'll choose you again. There, see, I choose you again."

In her anniversary card, Daisy wrote: *If they say we don't exist, that they can't see us anywhere except in rotten corners, in perverse bodies, how come I can see you and hold you and you're holy; how come I can love you and home you and you're there, in flesh, in my mind, in my blood; how come I keep waking up in this love and feel rested? What else to do now then, when a love like this finds you? What else but praise? What else but dance?* And now, what else were they to do as rain beat against the window? What else but place a palm on a lover's chest, saying *thank you* to her maker as she says *thank you* to your country, both thanking both for making them into these people with a bold faith in the unseen, for teaching them— by necessity, by difficulty—how to rebel with both faith and sight, how exactly to use their hearts and hands if one day they grew up to be women who risk their lives to stand on the horizon. Women mad enough to see and hold another woman; to love and touch another ghost.

TATAFO

(THE BILL)

—◦<●>◦—

Where were you on the thirteenth of January 2014, when that law was passed?

Me, I was watching, because you know nothing passes my eye.

I can never forget the temperature of the world that day. Things fell apart; people too. Bodies hit the ground; old bones sprouted from concrete. I roamed around after the news broke, testing the air, doing what I do best: gathering stories. Where did I not go? I sped from Island to Mainland and back. I even crossed between cities: Lagos, Abuja, Port Harcourt. Somebody from an old life (*cough*) used to tell me all the time that the ear has no lid. It's true. I didn't even need to press my ear to the road to hear that the reason they passed the bill was to secure the religious vote in the upcoming elections. The air stank of self-righteousness. You know how we are with morality; it's our way! Sure, adults are marrying children legally, and the age of consent is eleven, and people will still go to jail for pissing someone off. But why look at that? Get the sinners!

I'm sure you must know that, even as you speak, breathe, eat, live, love, there are people who—because of the decision made that day—have been outsided for daring to exist, for the perceived volume of their personhood. People who are now alone in madhouses, behind bars, under the ground because of the ripple effect of those signatures. People dropped like flies in Jesus's and Allah's and their own family's names. Relatives imitate the extended arm of a furious God. They call it holy. They call it a sin-purge. They call it the work of the Lord, the work of love, the work of teaching someone else a lesson.

The expected consequences of these violences are that the vaga-bonds will:

    a) disappear
    b) hide
    c) stop existing altogether

They wish it was c, don't they? They do. Or some do.

I heard one crying woman ask: *Why won't they live and let live?* The answer is simple: Because freedom means open air, and open air is a threat because it means that that there's no need for secrets or lies or deceit. It means love who you love and leave the rest be. But do you think those in power know what they love, outside of power?

Look, they will run mad in a world that calls for that, because you can't see some things about others without seeing yourself. And what's the point for them of serving a country without rot eating at its roots, without the bloat under the carpets, without the skeletons in their closets?

Can you imagine a Lagos where vagabonds could love each other in public? That would unmake the city in two heartbeats. That would mean it would have to go around barefaced. There would be no need for swindling, no need for under-the-table business. It would mean fewer masks. (What to hide faces behind?) Can you imagine the city giving people no reason to beg? No reason to die? Have you learned nothing? You don't know by now that blood is an essential ingredient? That the city loses flavor without it? You don't know that bodies falling is what makes the chaos possible and that chaos is the whole makeup?

Ask yourself: if you hated something in yourself and it was up to you to choose between seeing it smiling everywhere you go (a taunting nightmare) and keeping it behind closed doors (a bearable dream), what would you pick? Me, I'll tell you, because I hate lying: I'd pick the dream. I'd pick hiding my secret in the darkest part of my body. I'd insist on the secret nighttime appointments. I'd insist on low light. I'd insist on shadows.

Realizing this, I told myself: It won't be up to these leaders then, this freedom. A free and equal Èkó will be uninhabitable for too many of them. Freedom will have to be *taken*, despite. Freedom will have to be imagined by the shapeshifters, actors, invisibles, ghosts, magicians, vagabonds, outcasts, outsiders.

Always the only hope.

I combed the country for as many as I could find and I watched them, for my own heart, for my own hope, for my own personal goings-on. Because that is my sustenance. I need hope the way people need blood, the way people need food. And *they* need, as all we do, somebody to see them, to bear them witness, to watch over them lovingly. So I did. And I do. I see them and I love them and I'm unashamed of my heart. They are my diamonds in the dust. Life-grabbers, love-hunters. The rogues who do it, despite. The ones who see no point in fearing death, since anybody can go for good at any blessed second. Since eyan le ku at any fucking time, why not live? I'm about to give you another pass, to speed through some more stories. To rest your forehead against some windows. I know you can keep up. I believe in you.

But first, a funny thing I just remembered: Once I saw a girl in the market holding a book with this title: *Why Be Happy When You Could Be Normal?* She was carrying it as one would carry a holy book, pressed to her chest like it had the power to protect her from evil. She herself was clearly not *normal,* so it made me smile.

Why be happy when you could be normal?: That might be our national question, you know?

BUT IF EVERYBODY IS NORMAL,
IS IT THEN GOOD?

The last time Mfon heard her mother's voice, she was a teenager terrified of losing God. But enough time had passed since the day her father decided he didn't want a daughter whose heart could do wild things like love girls—and her mother had stayed silent. Over his dead body was he going to have a child with such a defect, he said, a glitch in the head, clearly not biological, clearly not from his side of the family.

A disownment, then—and why not? He was the adult, no? Adults do what they like because children can't say nothing. So out into the streets. Go! For effect, spit. The father-voice saying, "I don't care where you go, you rotten thing! Find other parents if this is how you'll be." A heap of clothes after Mfon. The father-voice yelling, the mother-silence sirening. All that begging with her tired parent eyes. Unbearable.

It hurt like an ended world. But even through silence, through choice, not every love leaves your body. Mfon's father was a ghost to her the moment he twisted that lock. In order to forget each other though, Mfon and her mother both knew they would need to delete their navels, those everlasting reminders of where it all started. And neither of them could.

Every night, Mfon's mother prayed. She prayed for God to straighten Mfon, to turn every curve into a line. She toiled on that floor and her missing was enormous. She wondered about Mfon often: *Who was this girl anyway? A girl who could look them in the eye and not repent?* Yes, they'd sent her away, but only expecting it to teach her that she had it better than most people, that she should be grateful for the cushion they'd provided her from the harshness of life outside. They wanted her to know that the *least* she owed them for the middle-class bubble they'd raised her in, for all the possible hardships they'd saved her from, was compliance; the *least* she owed them was normalcy. They wanted her to return repentant, a promising prodigal. But a year passed, and they grew scared: A girl who could last this long outside of home and not come crawling back, a girl who might as well slap God by dishonoring her parents and misusing her heart? Whose child was this?

God *was* love, Mfon's father had said before he shut the door, answering the only question Mfon asked with tears in her eyes. *Yes, dear, God is love. But not this kind.* Why wouldn't she listen?

"When she is ready to come back to her senses," Mfon's father told his crying wife, "we will know. She knows what to text me. Or you. She knows what the conditions are. She won't last out in the world before the streets spit her back out. We have to stand as a unit, you know? Stop this crying! Time will cure her of this madness." Time passed, flying flamboyantly between them as they prayed that something—one thing, anything, would break Mfon open and bring her back. *Humble her, God. Break her pride.*

Mfon did break. But when she did—when she *Lost It*, when she was passing out in clubs, when she was coming apart at the seams—she had way more than cruel streets. She had homes opened to her with love, friends with couches, spare bedrooms and free food. She had Kiki, the friend-turned-lover-turned-everything who would crack the world in two to make her okay, to see her be well. Kiki who held her through the crucial highs and comedowns, through the dark coming for her core, Kiki who widened her sense of wonder, who loved her like that quote they'd read: *in a way that let her be free.*

Mfon fell asleep to Kiki reading her Arinze Ifeakandu's story "God's Children Are Little Broken Things." While sleeping, she had a familiar recurring dream in which she was making dinner—always making dinner, jollof rice, because that is the daughter her mother wanted—and opened the door to her mother's smiling face.

Over dinner, in the dream, her mother asks the same question: *So, have you met someone?* Mfon says *yes* with tears in her eyes. The air is often kinder in dreams, so she opens up like a daffodil. *Yes,* she says, *the person is everything. Patient, kind. 1 Corinthians 13. We don't even fight the way you and Daddy always did. This person loves me, sleeps next to me because they want to, doesn't make me feel like a stain. Feels like hope. I can lean against this person and not find myself on the floor. Imagine, we can even have voices at the same time. Isn't this what we wanted?*

Where is he? her mother asks, clearly proud.

Mfon replies: *Mummy,* she.

In every dream before this one, Mfon had dreamed the same heart-saving outcome, where her mother wrapped an arm around her saying: *Okay. Where is she?* That ending was what had helped her hold together this long. It was her hope.

But this ending was different. In this dream, her mother's face is more aged, more stern. She says, *Why do you keep doing this to me? Why won't you just do this* one thing *for your family?*

Even in the dream, Mfon doesn't know how to say: *Because in this fantasy of yours where your daughter gets married to a man she doesn't love to prove that she loves you, my head comes off and I meet the end of my heart. You can't tell the difference from where you're standing, but that's not me you see walking down the aisle in that scenario. That's a corpse.* There's no easy way to explain this, so she keeps quiet instead. Because this is also an answer.

Well, her mother says in her real voice, without the filter of nostalgia, *you have chosen.* Then she carries her bag and gets up. *Take care,* she says. *I'll be praying for you.*

Mfon wakes up just then. Kiki is fast asleep next to her, so she sits up, scanning her body for sadness. There isn't any. Instead, she finds questions: *Can I go on if this dream is the real one? If they never accept? Is this enough for me? A life with this woman asleep next to me? Do I give myself permission to dream other dreams?* And her answer, after careful thinking, is simply: *yes.* Because the dream *was* an echo of reality. Her family *had* chosen and so had she. And look, despite it all, she had made a good life, a new life in which she didn't have to suffer in those old ways. In this second life, she was safe and in love, free from the first and its brutal texture. *Yes,* because she didn't gift herself this second childhood, this new chance, just to have the new one also be violent. *Yes,* she thought again. *Yes. This is my life. This is my life. This is my life.*

And that was what did it.

. . .

Grace jerked out of her nightmare and Glory woke up with her. "Wetin happen?"

Grace was panting with her head in her hands.

"Tell me now?"

"Wetin time dey talk?" Grace asked, her voice shaky.

"Six," Glory said. "We were tired. I no even know before sleep catch me." After doing their work for the day—cleaning the yard, washing the children's clothes, tidying all the six bedrooms in the house, the living room and dining room, making Madam's smoothie and taking Oga's laundry upstairs—they'd both fallen asleep gisting in their room. Six p.m. meant they still had an hour before they had to go and set the dinner table for the family.

They'd come a long way from that day when Glory, who by then had been working in the house for a year, said, "That's not how to sweep. Let me teach you." They'd spent hours after work taking long walks, each hoping the other wouldn't ask to go to bed just yet. They stayed out longer than the drivers and cooks who spent every night drinking Gulder after Gulder and playing betting games.

It was Glory who had led everything, who'd brought them here when she asked Grace to be her valentine. Easy yes.

"Wetin happen?" Glory asked again. "You dream bad dream?"

Grace nodded. "I no even know. I dream say sometin happen for house."

"Let your mind come down," Glory said. "Let your heart come down. I'm here." She put an arm around Grace's shoulder. "Wetin happen inside di dream?"

Grace nodded, trying to hear the calming words. She had nightmares like this from time to time, old stories sneaking up on her. She couldn't always remember them after she woke up. All she knew was how they made her body feel. Glory understood. Always had. "It's okay," she said. "The dream don end. Everything dey okay. You're with me."

"Can we pray?" Grace asked. For as long as they'd known each other, every time Glory prayed for or about anything, God always moved. God *loved* to move at the sound of her voice. This thing they had was going to end one day, because real life was real life and the men in their lives were there for a reason. But it meant the world to Grace to know that she had somebody like this, a love so true she could say to them: *I trust you to take me to God. I trust you to hide me in God.*

"So, of course," Glory said, ever ready.

People didn't go around asking for prayers from someone whose heart they couldn't trust. Every day, they wondered how God had given them the same house to care for, to clean, the same family to grow, to love as their own. It was God that made it possible, Glory was fond of saying. It had to be God.

"Please," Grace said. "You fit jus' pray say make God protect dem. My family."

"Oya," Glory said. She led the women's prayer group at church. Praying was her favorite thing to do. "Let's talk to God now. But before we start, you go fit do one tin for me?"

"Wetin?" Grace asked.

"Hold your chest for me and repeat: *God is here. God dey inside here, with me, inside my heart. God is welcome here.*"

The tears rolled down before Grace could stop them. She tried. When she held her hand to her chest, she could feel a whole city of sad crumbling in there. The words were broken, really, so it took her longer than it would have if her throat wasn't flooded with tears, but she said it and meant it and believed it. "God is here," Grace repeated. "God dey here, with me, in me, inside my heart. God is welcome here."

"In Jesus' name," Glory started.

. . .

Helen took an okada straight from church to her girlfriend B.'s house. Throughout the brief ride, she sped through her memories, rewinding as far back as possible. Even as early as when she was a child, Helen did not like playing with fire. When other kids would steal matches and strike them or play with lighters, Helen always shrieked, afraid. Once, when they were six or so, a classmate had tried to swallow a lit matchstick. She never spoke to him again, just because of that. Years later she realized that it was because he'd shown an untamed appetite for danger, and she could not stomach it. Who could be that young and dream of being a fire-eater when there were safer things to be?

And if you really think about it, that visceral distaste was pointing to a deeper truth stretching through her: *Trouble does not like me, and me, too, I don't like it.* The wind was drying out her eyes as she rolled out that memory over and over again. The world blurred. She was doing this for comfort. Doing it because now, once again, she'd found herself playing with fire.

When Helen and B. first got together, their growing attachment was a sweet heat: close enough to the risk to be thrilling, but not actually inside it. Helen kept on going, inching closer and closer with her eyes closed, testing her own threshold. It took her mother laying hands on her and praying for a good husband for her to realize that she could no longer see a husband. If she was ever going to walk down an aisle, it would have to be because she was going to see B.'s face love-flooded at the end of it. That fantasy, though brief, was the first time Helen felt the flame. It was the first time it occurred to her that if she let herself embrace it, this love would change her life in irreversible ways.

Some people could take that risk. Some people could be themselves without fear. But she wasn't one of them. She wasn't one of them at all.

When the okada stopped outside B.'s house, Helen gave the man a five-hundred-naira note and collected her change. She said thank you, her heart in her stomach now, pounding there. *This has to end today,* she thought as she crossed a puddle and headed up the stairs. *It has to end today.*

The owner of the kiosk nearby called out to her: "Our wife!" Helen gathered herself together, pretending not to hear. Thank God she had earphones. How did she let this happen?

As soon as B. opened the door, Helen started crying.

B. didn't need to guess what had happened because Helen's face was telling it. B. sat down and listened, trying to make sense of what Helen was saying through the stutters. *Can't, can't, can't,* she made out, but most of it was hazy in both their minds. *Can't do this, can't do this anymore.* The pain landed for B. with the lovingsharpness of a new blade.

"Does it feel overwhelming?" B. asked, detached from the situation, doing that disappearing thing she did when something painful was on its way. "This. Us. Does it feel too consuming?"

"It does," Helen said, sobbing. "I love you, I swear. But my . . . my *parents* matter to me. I can't lose my family; they're my life. I've started thinking about you every day, every night, in class, at work, in church, during prayer, in my sleep. I can't. I can't. Please, let's stop. I want you and I love you. But this thing is not good for my heart," she said, crying. "It's not good for my heart."

Even for B., the routine they were building was frightening. Who wouldn't be scared putting all their eggs in a basket that could be stolen at any time? Who wouldn't be scared knowing that the love they were falling in was contraband? B. understood all of this before Helen even explained it, though that didn't make it hurt any less. Helen was scared of becoming the kind of Christian who could enjoy sex with her girlfriend and then get up from bed and go to church. She was scared of cursing God's name.

B. hadn't always been an atheist; she was familiar with a church-goer's guilt. She knew that Helen wanted to *Do Right By God*. And yes, they could do without the sex, sure. But it seemed too far gone already. They'd already *gone there*.

Love was lovely and all, Helen explained, but it was more important to her to be holy.

"So, you're done?" B. asked.

Helen shook her head. "It's just . . ." and then stopped. Nothing she could say now would make any of this better. They looked at each other, knowing there was no coming back from that silence and what it implied. People who know loss know this: there's nothing harder to let go of than an already-gone thing.

So, "I love you," Helen said to B.'s nodding head. "More than this world, more than most things. But I choose simple. I choose normal and stable. I choose the boring script. I choose being my parents' daughter. I choose church and the choir. I choose what I know." Her voice was quaking. "This is too much for me." Helen just wanted her life back. She just wanted to be at peace with God, and she would give anything to make that possible. She'd give everything to correct her heart, to love someone she could take home to her tired parents—not a girl.

B. knew there was no point in fighting. She kept her tongue between her teeth, trying not to cry and scream at everything. They loved each other—that was never in question—but what they had tried to avoid was still happening. They were still ending in shards. Those nights of lying in bed, unable to sleep; of apologizing for reaching out to Helen and trying to cuddle; those nights B. held out so that she wouldn't rob Helen of her right to pray, of her access to God; that one night they even prayed to God together to help them stay pure, stay clean for Him; the times when they begged Him to please see that they were trying their hardest. What did any of that matter now? They had to let it go.

Most people stayed in relationships because they were afraid, scared of their lives falling silent, terrified of the void that comes with a loss. B. knew that kind of staying from experience, having once given six years of her life to a burning building of a relationship. She knew that breaking up, too, was sometimes an act of courage. So, "Okay," B. said, hugging Helen as she cried and cried. She was tired, but wasn't this also love sometimes? Acknowledging when a cost might be too high for someone else and then taking back your hand. Stopping when told to stop, letting the memories rewind themselves to nothing; shrinking your love from the size of a world to the size of a fist, making it safe and sane enough to live with.

"I'm sorry," Helen said again, "it's just . . . I just . . ."

"Shhh," B. said, pulling Helen into a hug. There was hurt in her voice, yes, but no surprise there. Tears streaked down her cheeks in two quiet lines. "It's okay, love, I get it. You're okay. It's okay."

(It wasn't. But at least they started out knowing that God would win in the end. Some people had it worse.)

• • •

"Yo, how fa?" May asked into her iPhone 6s. "Can I help you?"

It was her childhood friend Idris whose voice was slanted, slow and slurred in that way it usually was when he was high and needing a favor. "So, do you know anyone?" he asked.

"For what this time?" May asked. Before he left her three missed calls back to back, she and her flatmates had been playing Concentration Concentration and the game was just getting heated. Already, there were two more babes on their way, so the night could turn any way it pleased. "Talk sharp abeg," May said. "I been dey think say you wan even offer me gig."

"You heard about the bill, abi?" Idris asked. "Pastor asked me to source a few people for tomorrow's service. You know how people are always running mouth about Jade and—" May tried to interrupt, but Idris continued. "No no no, I know say you and Jade dey fight, but I wouldn't be calling if you weren't the last person I could think of for this one. Abeg. It's just a short deliverance. Do you have people? Our people dem. We-we. If you can tell anyone who might be needing money . . ."

Being one of the best DJs in Lagos, May knew the night and most vagabonds on the scene were her friends, so she was the perfect person to call for last-minute things like this. Idris promised to pay her back by putting her name forward when any of the rich church kids wanted to have a messy discreet party.

May would have hung up the phone on anyone else but Idris. She'd passed the stage in life where she needed to be getting involved in messy shit like this; she wasn't bored anymore. Her work was growing and paying. Besides, anything to do with that church made her sore. She and the pastor's daughter Jade had broken off their friendship a whole year ago when Jade showed up to the house after her mother had said, "That your friend is too . . . I don't know. She *shows* too much. Even if you want to date a girl, date a girl that looks like a girl. Somebody they can mistake for your friend." They weren't even in a relationship anymore, but Jade had broken them up in deference.

"Can't you see? They're trying," Jade had said. "Before, they used to tell me to change. They've stopped doing that. Now all she's asking is for me not to flaunt it. Isn't that progress? Isn't that fair enough?"

May wanted to ask if that was all this amounted to: flaunting it. But there was no point. She'd moved on, and as hurt as she was by it, she knew that she didn't envy Jade—the pressure she felt to stay saved, to wear that mask everywhere just because people were watching.

"Hold on," May said, knowing Idris's need was bigger than whatever reservations she had. Being the pastor's assistant and "miracle strategist," he was the one in charge of this big event to come. May put the phone on speaker and then dropped it on the center table. "Oya Idris talk o. Guys . . . he's asking for anyone down to go to church tomorrow? Acting job. Me I no dey go, but you people are free so far Idris involves my cut."

"Ah ah, Mama, I got you," Idris's voice said from the center table. "Good."

Regina backed down her vodka and cranberry juice. "As for me oh, it depends on how much." Her twin, Justina, was next to her eating black seedless grapes.

"Don't worry, it's good cheese, just trust me. Pastor is desperate, so it's a good time. People's eyes will be roving tomorrow and eventually they'll settle somewhere. He wants to give them somewhere to put it. You know church whispers. If we put on a show now, because people are so easily distracted, they won't even notice what she's doing or not doing."

"Fair enough," Regina said.

"Is it really?" her twin asked. "When will they stop all this nonsense? They're ruining people's lives."

"Toh," May interjected. "Dey there dey wait." It always made May laugh when people asked why men became pastors when they know they don't want to truly serve God. Why wouldn't they? That title came with a TOUCH NOT slapped on top of their actions, and power, and security. They could do whatever and people would still worship them.

Plus, it was a good strategy. All great secret-keepers know all about the importance of scapegoats. If people are looking at your child, point at other people's children. Because how wouldn't a *spirit-filled pastor* know if the *spirit of homosexuality* was in his house? And if he knew, why wouldn't he cast it out of his daughter if he could cast it out of other people's children? How to explain that?

Exactly.

"Well," Justina said, crawling closer to the phone, "what does it entail? Are they going to flog us?"

"I can't promise they won't. You know it's as the spirit moves. But I don't think so, sha."

"You mean as the audience reacts. If they cheer more, you people always do more."

"Spirit o, audience o. All join. What's the difference? It sha takes two. No be only the pastor dey act. If you act well enough, if you find somehow to make it interesting for those watching, it won't get to beating. So bring your A game."

"Abeg," Regina said. "How much be di kudi. That's how I'll know if I'm down or not."

"Run us one-fifty k each and we move," Justina interjected. Always restless, now she was shuffling a deck of cards in her hands.

"Well sha, me I don talk my own," Regina said. "If flogging enter, you people should get ready to part with flogging money o. If not, I go blow whistle."

Justina laughed a dark laugh. "So that they will find your body in the street and the pastor will use you to do testimony in church next week and say it was God dealing with his enemies, abi? My dear, if you're saying yes, accept that fuckup fit enter. I'm not ready to lose my twin."

Regina shook her head. "Me sha I'm down."

May lit a joint and watched them out of the corner of her eye, remembering the one year when this was all she did to get money. It happened often enough for her to have half of her rent money in Agungi. She had a collection of masks to choose from. What was it to her? She'd fuck her girlfriend, go to church, and get delivered, only to come back and do it again. It was the same as any job: a performance. At the peak of her church acting career, her cousin—also serving in a Pentecostal church—had hired her to act like a woman who'd had the issue of blood for six years and finally got delivered of it. "You know you studied theater arts. Just for a little money on the side," the cousin had said. Why not? May went and they smeared barbecue sauce down the insides of her thighs, rubbed black eyeshadow into the soft skin under her eyes, and pretended that she had the most rancid smell oozing out of her, but that was pretty much it. She didn't look like herself at all that day, because the makeup did what the makeup did: added years to her face, even altered her complexion. That disguise mattered for her name's sake. Her knees were bruised the next morning from the crawling she did on stage, but it wasn't too bad for the money.

Miracles like this happened all the time: people getting up from their wheelchairs and breaking into a run; people opening their eyes for the first time in their lives and telling you the color of anything. Even comedians joked about it, but it never occurred to people to second-guess, to think of it as an industry, a second Nollywood growing.

The twins were perfect for the job. They didn't even need to adjust anything. With their dreadlocks, half-sleeve tattoos, and Mx-Steal-Your-Girl shoulders, they were just what Idris was looking for. At least this would help with rent.

"Justina, you nko?" Idris asked. "You don confirm?"

Justina looked at her twin and shrugged, "I'm down. But only if you make it two hundred."

"Oya, two hundred k, cash!" Idris said.

"Fine," Justina said. "Una get luck today. Because if not for my church mind ehn?"

*   *   *

"God hates boys who love boys," said the Sunday school teacher, "and God doesn't make mistakes. Boys like that go to hell and burn there, with murderers and people who do bad things with their hands. All of it is sin, and in Godrithmetics, sin equals sin equals sin."

So what am I, then? thinks Junior. *If I'm still like this, then did God not make me? Or did God make me on a day when He was too tired, when He was taking a break from being God? Did He spin me at the wheel like the potter's parable said, but leave an indent, a grain in the clay, something from under His fingernail—does God have fingernails?—that he was too afraid to admit to? Did that fear of being caught, of being pointed at and scapegoated, make Him put the burden on me?*

With his fast mind and slow tongue, Junior can't ask anybody this. And besides, he's learned that people keep their sins to themselves as a matter of etiquette. People didn't go around discussing whatever they did in the dark when they ran into each other in the streets or while eating at the dinner table. For the sake of oneself and others, the true size of the shame one carried had to be between themselves and their God.

So: *Sorrysorrysorrysorrysorrysorrysorry*, a thousand times. A thing called repentance. *Please. Make it go away. Please. I didn't even do anything, I just wanted to hold his hand.*

Junior stays up in bed trying to calculate exactly how much pain Jesus must have endured for this sin in particular. Because Jesus must have trusted that to be enough. "Every time you think of sinning," said the Sunday School teacher, "understand that you're breaking the heart of a God who loved you enough to die for you."

There isn't enough space in Junior's body for the hate he's storing there for himself, not enough mind for him to wrap around how monstrous this makes him. Junior repents. Whenever he dies and gets born again—again—Junior wakes up the next morning feeling bright on the inside, like there are a thousand stars constellating in his organs. Remorse does this; it renews your worthiness.

But it takes as little as one dream to destroy it again.

When Junior dreams that night of his friend lying close enough next to him to generate that odd heat in his sleeping body, of his friend Ade in that bright bright light, his smile like righteousness, Junior wakes up wanting to beat Ade to death—because sin equals sin equals sin. He's as bad as Hitler already. As Hitler as Lucifer. As Lucifer as dirt. As dirt as a gutter. He'd already cleansed himself. Why wouldn't the sin listen to him and leave him? Why won't it leave him to choose God? Why won't God fight for Junior like Junior was fighting for Him?

Under Junior's furious fist, his bathroom mirror explodes. It's not real to him at first, but then it is, because now the mirror is a glistering star, shooting rays and shards. And now this means trouble. But what's trouble to a not-here boy? Junior watches Ade run for cover inside his head, crouching somewhere between his jawline and right ear. *How dare you stain me again*, Junior thinks at a hostile volume. His head is full of voice. Ade shrinks.

Fourteen and too young to race his rage to Ade's house—where the real Ade is probably sound asleep, unaware of this crush—Junior shakes his head until the dark thought slows down.

Outside then: *God, please. If you cannot take this thing away from me, please kill me. Please kill me. Please kill me; I'm tired of fighting you.* There's a whole family asleep inside who don't know what he's becoming, what his heart is singing to him, or about his certain ticket to hell, already in God's pocket, according to church. But if they did know, they would kill him, he's sure of it.

Junior stays there for twenty minutes, cursing and begging the sky, knees sinking in grass—just him and what he thinks is God, arguing. It takes a sliver inside a second for him to look up. First, he watches the moon become fuller, more pronounced. Then he swears he can see all the stars sigh in the sky. It makes no sense how suddenly he's saved. But the message comes cleanly, clearly. *Can't you see it's not us? It's not us hating you.*

Junior—fourteen as he is, confused as he is—understands this finally: God being larger than everything. God saying no. God being bigger than all of this. Big enough, like that song said, to hold his love.

So, a boy stands, then kneels in a pool of moonlight at midnight in his parents' garden, asking God to kill him for being him. Then he looks up and God says a decisive *no* with not just one, but all the beautiful mouths They have. That's it, that's the story. And the lesson, love, is this: If your own god keeps failing you, God can show you another.

• • •

Amenze got out of her car with a screwdriver in hand, all ragedrunk and swollen-shouldered. She was running late for the World Cup and she didn't have a PVR decoder. It had already been a stressful day of stupid drivers—one useless man had even scratched her car—and now she was stuck in Mega Plaza, all because she stopped to get one stupid shawarma. Lai lai, she wasn't going to take it. It had been thirty minutes already.

But just as she stood in front of the car, ready to bend despite her short skirt and high-high heels, Holy Moses—the main guy guarding the area—moved toward her in heavy strides. He'd been smoking a stick of Benson & Hedges across the road when she came down. "Madam wetin dey happen here?" he asked. She looked at him. He was wearing a new bandana this time, thank God.

"I don't know who this stupid person is that came to park like this. I can't understand it. I'm trying to get out and I can't even move. Is it because it's a Range Rover? If I bust his tire now, they'll say I'm wicked."

Holy Moses chuckled. How can? In his presence? Moses was *loyal* to the owner of the Range Rover. He loved her for how generously she showed her hand in his life, always eager to stretch forward where other people would drag theirs back. She hired his eyes to watch her car specifically. The first few times, she'd looked at him and said, "I leave my car for your hand o," and he'd said, "No shaking. Even if dem hijack this whole street, you will still meet your car here." These days, they just exchanged nods. No need for more. She trusted him as she ought to.

So, "Madam, I hear you," Moses told Amenze. "You know say me know your face. I know say you dey vex, but softly softly, sho get? The person wey get this car na my oga. If you wan bust the tire, you go need to bust me first. And how you wan fit?" He laughed from his inside his build and height. He could have been a brick tower. Amenze knew there was no winning this one, because last last no be by mouth oh. If you want people to take good care of you, you have to give them handsome handshakes.

"Oga, if you know who get this car," she started, "abeg call am make e come repark. Abeg."

Holy Moses looked at her then took the final drag of his cigarette. "I no get ein number."

Amenze was irritated, knowing he wouldn't budge. Holy Moses was usually on her side—he'd helped her scare off a creepy man one

time—but now he was picking this unseen person over her so she had
to take down the vex at least a notch. Who knew who it could be,
anyway? Thank God she didn't allow her temper get in the way o.
Before next thing they'll be retweeting Missing Person Alert.

She sighed, trying not to apologize too quickly. "This is just a piss-
take oga. Abeg, next time tell the man to fucking park well, ah!"

Holy Moses lazily corrected her. "She park well. If you look am
well, na the person wey park you for here no get sense at all. If not say
I go ease myself, I for no allow dis kain parking. In fact, which one of
my boys park you? Make you I reprimand am, because na dat person
dey cause all this fuckup for here."

Amenze shook her head and looked away, hoping she could avoid
the question by doing yanga. But Holy Moses was flexing his authority now, because honestly imagine if he was still behind that wall
pissing innocently and this woman had punctured the tire? His whole
rep would've taken a hit. He'd have been begging in the streets because of someone else's foolishness.

"Just show me the guy," he said.

A man passed by selling pirated CDs. "*Avengers*, ma. *One Tree Hill.
How to Get Away with Muhda. Scandal. L Wod.* We get all. You wan
buy? Mama, today na Friday o."

"My friend, shoo!" Holy Moses said, sending him off. And then he
turned to Amenze. "Abi na you park by yourself?"

Amenze nodded sheepishly. She felt stupid. "But na just one minute na. I run inside go pick shawarma come back, now now person
don block me."

Holy Moses laughed. "Oya get patience since na you do yourself.
The person dey come. You dey smoke ciga?"

Amenze shook her head. She wasn't about to start smoking Benson
& Hedges with an agbero in the streets o. What if one of her clients
came out and saw her there? Abeg.

"Okay wetin you dey like? Make I rap for you?" And then he began beatboxing. Amenze burst out laughing. "Ah ah you dey laugh? I senior 50 Cent o. Based on entertainment."

Finally, Tola met them there. Holy Moses hailed her. "My madam! My oga!"

Things moved fast, and Amenze, feeling like she should say something now, said, "It was you that parked this car here? You're so lucky you're beautiful!" *Or what*, Tola wanted to ask, but this wasn't the time to give smartmouth. This was the time to pay attention to the face in front of her, the body, the cue.

"Sorry," she said, laughing. "Did I keep you waiting long?"

"You made me miss the match!"

Holy Moses watched the scene for a few seconds before floating off.

"Hay, I'm sorry," Tola said. "Me I don't know anything about football so I can't talk, but I'm heading out now."

"Thank you," Amenze said, chuckling softly, turning to face her car. "Nice to put a face to all the wahala."

Tola let a moment pass. Then, "Hm . . ." she said. "Can I make it up to you?" She had no idea why she said that. These kind of chance encounters happened to her friends all the time. But not to her. Never to her."

"Well . . ." Amenze said. "I was going to go home."

She'd started it already, so why stop now? "Are you sure? It's Friday o. And it's not like you'll get home on time unless you live close by. Lagos traffic."

Amenze felt herself loosening at Tola's hints." What are you suggesting?"

"Well . . . I was going to offer to take you for a drink sometime. To make up for the match I didn't let you watch. Whenever you want, since you don't seem keen on tonight."

Amenze shrugged, thinking about the match she'd missed, then about the deadline coming for her master's application. None of that compared to this face in front of her—this person, this smile that tilted the balance of everything. Where was the harm in having a little fun? Abeg. It was Friday, true true. Amenze pouted, impressed by how quickly Tola could seize an opportunity. Forget DStv and the World Cup, forget hurrying home just to be there alone.

"I want it tonight," Amenze said.

Tola locked eyes with her, then smirked. "Fine," she said. "It's Friday, why not?" Then, "Drive behind me?"

Tola's car lights flashed and Moses appeared out of thin air. "Mama, you don dey go?"

She shook his hand and filled his fist with notes.

"You see?" Holy Moses said grinning, his right hand all moneyed up, hailing. He looked at Amenze who was now entering her car.

"I for give you something," she told him. "But I no carry cash for hand."

"Leave that side! Una don settle. I tell you. You see? Shey I tell you."

Both laughing to themselves behind their wheels, Tola drove out first and Amenze followed closely behind.

They ended up at a members-only wine bar tucked under a row of trees. Wine does things, so it was at this bar that they kissed for the first time, in the middle of the dance floor as other guests minded their business. Later they ended up at Caliente and danced for hours. After all those shots, they were both so drunk they had to park their cars and take an Uber. They'd think about it tomorrow.

Sure, they weren't going to the same area—Tola was going to Chevron and Amenze to Dolphin Estate—but they needed to get the same car, you know, for, uh . . . safety.

When the driver asked if they wanted to add an extra stop, they turned their drunk faces to each other and raised his question using only their eyebrows.

"No," they both said at the same time. But it was just to make sure, you see. Only to make sure.

* * *

Truly, Feranmi only flew into Lagos for art season. He hadn't set foot in the country in years—not since he left it behind to pursue a love that eventually ended—but he entered Murtala Muhammed International Airport prepared to make a dent in his savings buying some pieces for his collection at home in London. He was here for the art and for the suya. Good Lord, he missed the suya—that soft crunch between his teeth. On the way to his $500-a-night Airbnb penthouse in V.I., he asked the Uber driver to stop at Polo Club which the super-host had recommended. Clearly overexcited, he bought five thousand naira worth of tozo, not caring that the mallams were taking advantage of his foreign tongue. He was just glad to be home.

At the door of the Airbnb, a stunning man with a gray beard was waiting, dressed in clean black trad and simple Gucci slippers. The host, yes. Fela, according to the app. Feranmi knew that, but he hadn't expected him to be so stupidly beautiful in person. Clearly, he'd forgotten what Nigerian men could do with their eyes alone.

An introduction, a tour, and two cabernet sauvignon bottles later, Feranmi found himself saying to the host, "Where are you rushing to? Your wife?" It was 10:00 p.m. but too early, too too early.

And Fela said, "Just say you want me to stay, bro."

Feranmi took a step into the small space between them and said, almost immediately, "I want you to stay." Then he smirked and traced his own jawline with his thumb, unsorry. He was smiling; he knew what he was doing; trying to match Fela where he'd met him. "Stay . . . *bro.*"

Fela was wine-gone and Not His Mate, so instead of flinching, he laughed and said, "Ah, tani bro e? Who's your bro? A whole agbalagba like me? That's daddy to you."

The air coiled around the joke and the tension fizzed, blood racing purposefully, embarrassing them both. Fela cleared his throat, wishing his tailor had left more room in his pants. Feranmi shook his right leg free and reached for a glass of water. "Okay, sir," he said, putting his hands up and stepping away, shyly. "E ma binu."

"Sir works too," Fela said, smiling with his whole perfect mouth. That Lagos man trouble.

Then they were on the floor playing Jenga, using all the concentration they had left to make sure the structure didn't come falling down. Already, they'd swapped secrets playing Never Have I Ever—a childish choice, but a good way to break the ice. *Drink! Drink! Drink!* At some point, Feranmi told Fela about the hypersensitivity of his neck, and how if someone as much as breathed on it, he'd become a mess. They talked threesomes, one-night stands, all the while avoiding pronouns. Then Feranmi asked about Fela's name. Fela told him about the worshipful disposition his father took toward Fela Kuti's music. As soon as the man knew he was having a boy, it was settled! But his father always said, *You will only inherit Fela's good traits, not the other ones.* Fela saw the vision until he didn't, having never laid his hand on a blunt until he turned twenty-nine years old. That was a long way away, but even now, he lived a simple solitary life, reading magazines and novels on his balcony, listening to records from inside the house while he smoked.

"But poor man," Fela continued, "he hoped for a genius musician for a child and got a boring consultant turned real estate investor. That's what you get for being an unconventional Nigerian. God loves playing opposites, clearly. My cousins whose parents wanted doctors and engineers are all artists now."

Feranmi told Fela about his own music collection at home, about how the first time he heard Fela's music he stopped in his tracks and just watched the air as if something magical might sprout from it. He didn't add that he was feeling that way again now, but something about the way his eyes lingered on Fela's shoulders said something. Feranmi had already gone and opened his mouth and said *him* when talking about his ex, even though his ex was really a *her*, as a way of testing something. Fela didn't flinch, he just asked, "How long were you together?"

Why did he lie? He didn't know, but it was too late to reverse it now. So Feranmi said, "Two years, and then one day he said, 'I know you like women.'" The truth was the inverse actually—his girlfriend Stella coming to him with her bleached eyebrows and beautiful septum ring on a cool afternoon in North London and saying calmly: *I think you like him.* Where *him* was a new friend he was on the phone with all the time. Then, *I think you like men, Feranmi.* That was colder. This had happened just two weeks before he showed up in Lagos, so he wanted to try on her accusation/prediction/conclusion/premonition and see how it fit. He wanted to see how it felt coming out of his mouth. He'd been warned, after all, that Lagos was not for honest people, that most people you meet are already wearing a lie. For all he knew, Fela *could* be a married man with two wives and four kids and a wholly different name.

"Do you?" Fela asked.

"Do I what?"

"Like women."

"I mean, I think I do. But . . . you know."

Feranmi couldn't look at Fela when he said this. The man's mouth was unbearable, framed by that graying beard. Plus, somewhere under the influence, Feranmi's entire body was failing.

"Interesting," Fela said, "I've never tried *that* before. Being with a man. I had a crush on a boy once, in secondary school. Everybody wanted him, and I think I thought: Who am I not to join in? Ha ha. He was so beautiful, but I think that was just jealousy that turned into lust. You know how emotions do. One thing can turn to another.

I thought about him often when we were younger. Then he changed schools and I haven't thought about him again since. Not until now. No one made me feel that way again, you know . . ." *Until now.*

The wine was working through Feranmi's body, and he was studying the Jenga tower as he listened and mumbled *mm-hm, mm-hm.* Fela picked up the bottle to pour himself another. "Careful," he said, the last of the wine bleeding out into his glass. "Careful because if you drop it, I'm tickling you until you tap out." And then he swigged the glass back. Fela kept a straight face as he said this, but it was an important thing to say, seeing as their self-control depended on that tower standing. In response, Feranmi looked Fela in the eye and scoffed as he pushed two fingers into the structure, dashing it all to the carpet on purpose.

Fela smirked and then leaned forward, trepidation spreading under his biceps, crawling through his veins. He tickled Feranmi until he was on his back, then reached for him in an awkward hug. They stayed there, breathing and speedthinking, hearts racing. Then Fela kissed him at that softsweet spot where neck speeds off into shoulder. Once. Then again. Then again. Until Feranmi's voice poured from his mouth in pleas.

They saw each other every day until they couldn't. Until Feranmi's flight back. Fela sent flowers that morning. The note read: *Crazy, this. But I couldn't sleep all night. Please . . . stay a few more days? I've got the cost.* Roses. Feranmi's favorite. What was no? The ticket was opened.

That night when they saw each other, the world spun around their mouths meeting. When Fela turned around to grab the chair in front of him for support they were already sweating. Feranmi kissed the width of Fela's bare back as he moved into him. When Fela came, he cried. Feranmi held him there, tongue moving slow over his shoulder blade just where it jutted sharply out—softly, with the lightness of a butterfly landing—with complete trust that this body part, like all the others, would do everything else in the world first, before it ever thought of cutting him.

· · ·

B. woke up to a knock at the door. *Two. One. Two.* At first she ignored it. The half-empty bottle of vodka by her bed was still pulling her under blackwater. She liked the drowning, the feeling of falling to the bottom of herself. Every ache in her body was suspended for as long as it lasted, and each time she came up for air, she'd topped it up just to get back there.

Two. One. Two. Three. Two. That could only be one person. She'd be silly if she didn't know how Julie's knuckles sounded on wood after ten years of bestfriendship. B. held still under the duvet, barely breathing, as if the knock—or she herself—might disappear if not even a single hair on her arm moved.

"I know you're in there!" Julie yelled. "I'm going to wait here until you open the door, so don't think I'm going anywhere."

B. got out of bed, wrapped the duvet around her shoulders like a bulky cape, and went to the door. She had no words when she opened it. Just wet around the eyes.

Julie took one look at her. "Get back in bed," she said. "I figured you're in SOS mode, so I came to clean your apartment."

B. felt shame swirl around her torso. This was one of her flaws—this inability to receive love without feeling indebted. She couldn't see herself having the required energy to pay this kind of thing back. Julie had told her often enough that nothing she did in love had a price tag on it. It was free. It was for her. B. knew it logically. This love wasn't an unsafe love. It was for life. She knew, too, that Julie understood what it was like to not be able to get out of bed, to risk unemployment because your body just wasn't cooperating. Julie knew how depression could fill your whole body with rocks; how loss, a heart shattered to pieces, could multiply the already-there darkness. But now, as B. watched her put things in the bin and head into the toilet to clean, she still couldn't shake the feeling.

"Julie—"

"Shh, just rest. I'll be done in no time. And I'll be out. We don't even need to talk."

The next time B. opened her eyes, Julie was taking out the bin. When she got back in, she opened up the Shoprite bag she'd brought with her when she arrived. Too busy trying not to cry, B. hadn't noticed it before. "I also brought you groceries. Don't worry, I didn't forget your ice cream." Julie flung the white chocolate Magnum on the bed.

"Oh my goddddd. This babe. What are you trying to do to me?" She sighed, turning her lips down. "Thank you!"

"You're welcome. And yes, don't worry, I know you're screaming inside," Julie said, loading the fridge with the groceries. "Should I make you eggs?"

"No, thank you," B. said. That was the answer she thought she should give, since Julie had already gone through all this stress for her. Julie, being Julie, read the hesitation in her voice and said, "Okay, me I want eggs and sausages sha. I'll make you some, too, just in case." She was probably lying about wanting eggs, knowing her. B. felt a strong gratitude she didn't have the mouth for. Her head was definitely pounding; she needed more than ice cream.

Julie got into bed with a full plate of eggs and sausages and toast. "Sit up," she said. "I came to see you; won't you even look at me?" B. turned over and looked at Julie with swollen eyes. "Don't lie," Julie said. "You know the scent of the food is entering your nose. Get up well. Or should I feed you?"

B. laughed and nodded. "Yes, Mummy."

"I mean, I'd say I'm more of a deadbeat dad, but sure. I'll take it." They collapsed laughing. Julie stretched the fork. "Open your mouth jare."

The eggs were delicious.

"Ehehn," Julie said, "May them are hosting a house party at theirs. Want to go?"

"May ke? So I can go and meet another heartbreaker, abi? Another straight babe to crush my heart. No, thank you. That babe's house is the gbese-station."

Julie nudged B., cracking up. "Your heart still dey pain you, abi? Hard guy hard guy, small heartbreak, you no fit get up baff and brush teeth. Na babe dey do you like this?"

B. eyed her aggressively which looked hilarious with her eyes swollen like that. "Ah," Julie joked. "Babe, suffri o. Make your eye no roll commot. You know you've cried enough already."

B. threw a pillow at her. This fool!

"Fine," Julie said. "One-zero. Is that your final answer? No party."

B. nodded. "You can go, though."

Julie eyed her. "Imagine me going when you're not there. Nah fam." Then, "Wow wow wow. Wait . . . wait . . . So, you mean say I no go toast babe this night? Kai. The way I love you ehn."

B. shrugged. "At least people's daughters will rest this night. Nobody will leave the party crying." The food was helping her feel like a person again. Her jokes were coming back.

"Waka," Julie said. "You're a big mumu, shey you know? Now you have mouth now, abi? No P." But she didn't deny it. Wherever Julie entered a party, with those arms, with that handsome neck, that jawline and those dreadlocks, women lost their shit. No matter how often she told them she'd never commit, they still put their hearts in her hands and acted surprised when she curled her hand into a fist, making a bloody mess. It was a running joke: She was Shane from *The L Word*, but black.

"By the way, I know you don't want to talk about that Judas, but it's going to feel better over time, even though you don't feel like that now. It will. She's gone, but you're still here. You still dey." Julie's presence was proof that resurrections didn't have to be dramatic. It wasn't even two hours since B. had been feeling like a corpse, but already some aliveness was returning to her. She reached for Julie's arm and squeezed. They both allowed the silence, and then Julie said, "All right, enough of that. Your internet is working, abi?"

B. laughed until her stomach hurt. This rascal was really her best friend, her longest-standing love. Lovers could come and go, and they did, but Julie? Julie was a fixture. Julie was her paddy, her person through and through.

Julie turned the television on and Netflix made the duh-dum sound. "Perfect," Julie said. "Oya, let's watch *Pose*."

· · ·

May's apartment was high out of its mind; the bodies inside teeming with energy. In the living room, people were yelling the lyrics to Burna Boy's "Heaven's Gate," determined to be heard. They could turn the music down, but why? It was a good night to feel this alive. A great night to feel the beat in your thighs, in your stomach, in your chest, pounding through your veins. You can't breathe, sure, but do you want to? This loud love, the rapid-fire desire, all of it is what resuscitates you after all, what makes you want to love the world again.

This is always what it takes to resave your life: an odd night, some wild body volume, irresistible waists, eyes falling so low you don't even know how the fuck you're getting home. Here, behold your reasons. Take it far enough and you might even want to live forever. The country was going mad outside anyway, raining bodies in furious streams, so they had to move faster and madder than it.

At the door, Jade was giving everyone three shots of tequila and an edible each. Somebody switched to grime and they yelled "SHUT UP" with Stormzy.

"This is the entrance fee," Jade said to a girl she'd never seen before but knew she had to see again. The babe's mouth was blood red and wet with gloss. She looked timid, but she was wearing a choker that read SEX in caps, just in case you dared think you could miss it. Jade took it as a challenge. If Julie was bad, Jade was even worse. "You see the bin to your right there," she said. "Stand in front of it and close your eyes. Any headache or wahala you may be thinking of, catch it and throw it in that bin, then enter. As soon as we go in, nobody is allowed to think of serious things."

"Hm. Omo pastor," someone said walking by, noticing Jade's latex skirt. "Abeg o! Get thee behind us." Jade laughed. Church jokes usually irritated her, but abeg, not tonight.

The babe went where Jade asked her to. Above the bin, there was a poster that read: FUCK RENT. FORGET DISAPPOINTING FAMILY. FORGET HEARTBREAK. FUCK EVERYTHING. GET HAPPY. FUCK NIGERIA. HERE IS OUR OWN COUNTRY. YOU'RE FREE. YOU'RE FREE. YOU'RE FREE. This part had to be May's handiwork. Jade saw her laugh when she noticed it, and she felt thankful that she and May had trashed their differences, that their friendship was reviving itself because imagine not meeting this babe; imagine being elsewhere on a night like this. There was something in the air. Wild electric. The bareskinned risk of knowing that in any other part of the city, even policemen could get arrested for the kind of night they were about to have. This was an untouchable area—Old Ikoyi—and the authorities knew where their power ended. If police entered the wrong house even by mistake, they would have to frog jump their remorse.

Inside, somebody changed the music to Full Crate's "Big Booty Problem" and dimmed the lights. Jade handed the tray of shots to a friend and started moving toward the babe who was now heading for the entrance.

Dirty! the song said. *Nasty! Dirty! Worthy!*

Jade chuckled to herself, hearing it for the first time.

The babe turned around and smiled, her choker gleaming. She let herself speak for the first time. "Don't you just love a DJ who can read a room?"

. . .

All this will fade by morning, but who cares? The two girls look at their client, sound asleep, then at each other. And they know. It's the top floor of Transcorp Hilton; it can handle anything. A whole Head of State had been poisoned by prostitutes with an apple in a suite like this. What was two women still naked, bodies doing what they do, straddling a slippery edge, holding each other close close, going somewhere, putting on a show? Nothing. The walls would survive.

The sleeping woman with the money, the one who made this view possible, was generous. She needed to be up at 4:30 a.m. to shower, eat, and head to the airport, where her husband would be waiting to pick her up. She was going to say *Virgin Atlantic*. She was going to say *The flight was good and the meetings were long, but we thank God.* Her airport guy would have her tags ready, along with a fake boarding pass. He would get her into arrivals so her story looked believable. She'd done this routine often enough times by now. It was foolproof.

Here in the room, the woman's needs were always soft. "Just be touching each other," she liked to say, the same way every time. She didn't need them to do anything to her except tie her up, except make it impossible for her to reach anything. Watching was enough. The torture was the pleasure in full. She liked being teased, being told she couldn't have what she wanted, being made fun of for wanting it at all. Last time, they'd gagged her and poured hot honey over her right thigh. Her senses exploded, gave rise to a small waterfall worth changing the sheets for. After that, she went back to bed. They could order whatever, watch whatever, do whatever and she wouldn't care.

Now one of them looks at the table. The masks are still there and so is the strap. They'd asked earlier if they could borrow her masks—

to see who they could become underneath them, yes, but also, just in case. Like her peers, she went everywhere with a few stacked on her face at all times until they were safely inside, so there was enough for both of them. She shrugged. "They won't fit your face, because they were made for mine. But I have others in that bag over there. Check." The girls looked in the bag and saw an assortment of face coverings. They tried two on and kept them fastened, even inside the room.

"Have you seen how tall this building is?" the woman asked, her face bare. "You don't need masks up here. If you want to wear them, do it because you want to. But you're too close to the sky to be worrying about people who can't afford one night here." When one of the girls said something about the law, she said, "Look. The so-called law couldn't see you all the way up here if it squinted through a telescope. We're above that."

Might as well use the room as she slept.

On the balcony then. Two bodies moving: hard nipples against frosty glass, fingers between thighs, breath against skin. Balaclavas fitting snug over flesh, breathing cutting short. There was something pleasurable about this unnecessary disguise; they felt like true thieves— like *you can't do nothing to us* thieves, like VIPs—the way they were taking the night and holding it down, refusing to return it until they'd done what they pleased with it. Even if they could be seen from down there, they'd be seen as something else, something frightening. And nobody dared look twice at criminals in high places. They couldn't believe it was that simple; all of it a mindfuck.

None of this will be real in the morning, they both think, *but if we're illegal in this country for living and loving, we might as well live and love hard. We might as well hold each other as the speed kicks in behind your eyes, as we fall off the face of the law, of the city, of the world. Where we're going now with our bodies, with our minds, only we can find us there. Nobody can catch us. The door shuts as soon as we both arrive.*

In between rounds they both throw back some neat whiskey, show each other that perfect stretch of throat. That's talking too. One finishes faster than the other, but that's fine; the other goes slow for a reason, which is strapped-on.

Who knows where all of it leads? And who cares? This is how to remember that you're in there somewhere. Can you still cry when your skin stings? Can you tell the difference between what hurts and what feels good? Can you hear your body when it's talking to you?

All of this will fade in the morning, they think, *but who cares? It's not about you or me. None of this will be real in the morning, but if we go hard enough maybe we will* become *real. Maybe we will become deserving too.*

Wherever their fingers are trying to take them, wherever wet grinding against wet is trying to show them, that is where they're trying to go. And fast. That place where bodies go to sing? That is the place that will change it all, they decide. So *give it everything, give it everything. Let's teach this hypocrite of a night something or two. Make it run to its friends crying. Let's make sure that by the time the morning comes, it rises gently and with a humble heart, like it knows what we tried to do to the world tonight, what we changed in the air forever.*

Let it rise like it will never again forget that we were here.

GOLD

Back then, if you'd asked Gold what she wanted the most in life, she'd have started here: As a kid, it was three things: 1) for the frightening chatterscream in her skull to stop every time she looked at the mirror; 2) for her body to make sense; and 3) to keep being her mother's daughter. But now? Just one of those. More than anything, number 3.

She already had 1 and 2 on most days. Imagine. Three, too, to be fair—but anxiety still rolled out of her over it, speeding off like tired thread. A wish is fear becoming hope, you see? And Gold was born with pre-installed fear. She was still learning how to transmute it, so she kept the third wish alive for emergencies, for *just in case my mother turns her back too.* The doubt wasn't personal, because Gold's mother had shown herself faithful over the years. Gold was only still here, alive, because she had a mother who asked, "What do you want for yourself, my child?" and listened when she answered, after all. A mother who saw how un-at-home Gold was in her old body, asked, "What is your real name?" and then believed Gold immediately. Life is different with a mother who listens and believes; a parent who welcomes you when you take yourself home to meet her for the first time; who lets a dead name go quietly into the ground.

Some people want sex. Some people want boyfriends/girlfriends who will hold their hand in public. Some people want to be chosen by someone. Some want to feel anchored in the world. But Gold had no memory of ever caring about being claimed or wanted in that way; she just wanted to remain herself. She wanted to be legible and loved in that reading without being asked for her body or her hand in return. That could be enough for her. It could be sufficient for a life.

Well, she's a genie, that woman—Gold's mother. Sure, Gold was lucky to have been born to someone who'd already sworn up and down never to let her children hold damnation in their bodies if she ever had any; but Gold's mother was more than a good person. She was a fighter—the right kind to take to war with the world. To grant Gold's wishes, she'd sweated out of her pockets, touched her head to the ground and looked up to God in surrender. God took a deep breath at what went unuttered between them and nodded. She made all the calls possible. She found the right everything. After the operation, she stood at the shore of Gold's *finally* body and said, "Welcome, my daughter. How are you?" There was still anesthesia moving through Gold in waves, but she cried so hard on her mother's lap that she had to be warned by the doctor to calm down. It was that word: *daughter*. That word said for the first time, from her mother's mouth, in a hospital. It made her feel born again; born correctly.

Days later, when they were home, Gold tried to say sorry. "For what?" her mother asked, dusting the table by the television. When Gold's mother did not hear anything back, she knew exactly what words were stuck, what questions Gold would ask if she could find the words: *Why didn't you get angry? Why didn't you withdraw your love? Why didn't you act like one of them?* Gold's mother sat down, lifted Gold's feet into her lap and said, "Because you know you more than I know you. You came through me, sure, you were in my body once, yes, but you are not me and I'm not you. Na only you and God get you, shey you get? So it's only you that can tell me who you are. You've told me and I accept."

Gold opened her mouth to say something but just smiled instead.

"Who you are here," her mother said, tapping her own chest with a flat palm, "is who I love."

It wasn't that Gold's mother couldn't see how other parents behaved, it's not that she didn't know she'd be deemed right and righteous if she'd done the opposite, if she had broken Gold's spirit trying to get her to fit in, trying to get her to stand in line. It's not that she couldn't see why people chose that—courage had its costs; there were consequences for standing up or standing out; most people cared more about how they were judged than if they were well. Plus, it was Nigeria after all; people had their necks broken for ruining the aesthetics all the time. Gold's mother didn't tell Gold how, once, an old friend had called her to the side to say, "You can't allow everything, this is going too far, this is not who you gave birth to. Sometimes with these children you have to put your foot down!" Those words had hurt more than a fresh wound in new skin, but Gold's mother had closed that friendship quietly. People put their foot down all the time without first checking if someone is there.

She explained other things to Gold instead: how it was a choice really, how it's the violence (regular as it is in the world) not the love that should be strange, how adults break their own spirits all the time just to do what someone else said is the right thing, yes, but who is anyone to determine who someone else is?

Gold's mother's choices were clear. But Gold still had nightmares of her mother pressing rewind, eating that word whole like a small ripe fruit, refusing to ever utter it again. Not because of her own heart, but because the country was brutal like that; because it could make a bully out of anyone; because not many people could wrestle Nigeria and win; because sometimes your safe life is the odd thing out.

That night, Gold couldn't sleep, so she texted her best friend, F., about it:

> What's wrong with me?
>
> Why am I crying bcos my mum luvs me? Bcos she didn't disown me?
>
> Won't someone normal just be relieved by dis?
>
> Why am I still waiting 4 d other shoe to drop?

It took five minutes for F. to respond:

> Bcuz you're Nigerian bbz.
>
> Bcuz you know a different mother might not be this way.
>
> Bcuz it's rare here.
>
> Bcuz being at home is not the same thing as being safe.

Gold replied:

> !!!
>
> Facts.

But it shouldn't be rare, F. said back. Us being loved shouldn't be rare. What you felt today, is how it should be.

Gold balanced her phone on the edge of the sink and washed her face before looking up at herself in the mirror. *Shouldn't be rare*, she repeated in her mind. *Shouldn't be rare.*

* * *

When people misread Gold on purpose, her mother eyed them to nothing, called them *bloody illiterates*. She meant it too. Because if you looked at her for real, with good eyes, Gold was not hard to read as herself. When they strolled together in the streets hand in hand, running errands, people often commented on how beautiful Gold was. Gold's mother always replied, "Yeso, na me born am," with all the pride in her voice. Sure, the world outside was colorful and bright, but none of it mattered to Gold as much as those moments at home with her mother did, watching M-Net and Africa Magic films together, giving each other Nollywood makeovers. For Mother's Day one year, Gold dressed her mother up like one of the cultists from *Issakaba 2* and her mother gave her Eucharia Anunobi eyebrows. They laughed so hard they both ended up in stitches. "Stop! Stop!" Gold's mother had to say. "No come kill me with laugh."

That day in 2014 was one of those days again. A good day with good air. They were doing each other's nails in the living room when Gold's mother asked Gold to turn to NTA for the evening news. "You know I can't see the remote," she said, reclining in her chair. She had three pink toenails already. "These my eyes, it's like they're getting worse."

Gold did it gladly.

When she reached channel 252, the news didn't wait. It kicked Gold in the chest, pulled the veil down, finding things out. They both froze as the reporter said *illegal*, as he shared the sentence: fourteen years in prison. They heard *UnAfrican*. They heard *Same Sex*. They heard *crossdressers*. Gold saw the country backflip three times and her eyes went insane. Already, she could feel every *bloody illiterate*'s hands in her hair; she could hear their hunger and hunting. She knew a law like this would only make them bolder in the streets. The news was calling them correct; this would be pure vim for their hands. The thought of this—of herself, of her friends being in more danger than usual—closed her whole body. It jammed her in the lock, made her inoperable. She tried to talk but her words were caught in her throat, stuck stuck stuck, and she started to heave, which meant panic, which threw her mother into a rage. When Gold's mother got mad, real life paused and went dead quiet, then a ringing began in her ear, righteous like close-of-church. She moved ghostly toward the TV remote, her daughter an anxious heap on the floor, then she turned off the television. LG, the TV said, obedient, going black. Life Is Good.

Gold's mother didn't know what to feel. She didn't need to see it to know: outside, something was starting. The sun had slipped out and the law was standing in its place in the sky, beating its chest and roaring. What felt like a full minute passed. Gold could see her mother's outline from the floor, moving close, shaking her head; and then she couldn't see a thing. Gold's mother leaned over her.

"They're coming for me," Gold managed, finally. "Mummy, they're coming for me."

"Baby. Look at me, look at me," Gold's mother said, holding Gold's face in her hands. "If they don't call you by your name, don't answer. You're not what they're saying you are. You are Gold."

Her voice was pulling Gold out of the strange water she was stuck in. It was so thick inside there. But Gold's mother had divine hands; their combined strength was infinite. "Baby?"

Gold found her eyes and turned them to her mother. "Mummy," she said. And the words went somewhere again. She didn't know where.

"Keep your eyes open. Look," Gold's mother said, smoothing the back of her hand over Gold's cheek. She sighed and talked to herself first under her breath. God held a curious ear open. "Look. Before they get to you, they'll have to kill your mother first. Do you hear me?" Then, "I hope you understand what I'm telling you. If you will die young because this country is mad, may I die the second before you. Because I will not bury my child, you hear? I will not."

Her voice was a lake of calm. The country shuddered and Gold heaved, finding herself in her mother's sturdy voice.

"This is our country too," she said, helping Gold up and feeding

her water. "That news doesn't apply to you. Nobody can do you any-
thing in this country, do you hear me? Your mother is not a pushover.
Your mother is not a gentlelady. Your mother is an animal, you know?
A lion. Your mother hunts back."

Gold nodded, her brain returning right side up. She felt it then: the
third wish come true. Fear turning into hope into have. It was forever.
Her mother was swearing forever. "Drink more," her mother said. The
mire Gold was stuck in thinned and cleared enough for her to see her
life again. She was looking at a mother who would choose her over the
world without blinking. Without ceremony or need for praise. Wasn't
this what it meant to be blessed? To be loved and seen and accepted?

"Mummy," Gold said, still stabilizing.

"I'm here, Gold. Your mummy is here. Touch me. No be me be dis?
I'm here. Where I dey go? No be only you I get? I'm here. Trust me."

"Mummy," Gold said, her eyes sinking in tears, but back.

Her mother laughed, seeing the thank-you Gold was too tired to
say with her mouth. "Abeg," she said. No ceremony. No need for
praise. "Abeg abeg. Don't mind these hypocrites. Dem no fit."

Gold chuckled, remembering the true thing F. told her another
time: In a place where people threw their kids away all the time just
for existing, a parent who loved you because you were you could sometimes look and feel like God. "But remember," F. had said, "that even
when their love feels divine, they're not God. They're your parent. It's
okay if you still don't know what that means. I don't either, because I
mean, you know how my story goes. We don't have many examples.
But what is life for, if not figuring it out, abi?"

They had been in F.'s bed, lying on their backs, listening to rain
beat the aluminum roof. Gold, not knowing what to say, had reached
for F.'s hand.

F.'s voice shook when she spoke next. "Your mum is showing you
what else is possible. And even me, I'm learning from her. But everything still comes back to us. Whether we will receive that love or not

depends on us; it depends on whether we think we deserve it or not. No one can decide that part for anyone else, d'you get? It has to be you. It has to be us."

Sometimes, a statement is a question, is a chance, is a fork in the road. So, when Gold's mother asked, "Ehehn. Oya tell me jare. What color for your nails?" Gold paused for a moment before she said, with all the voice she could muster, "Red."

TATAFO

(WATER NO GET ENEMY!)

Here is some expo: at the end of this thing I'm telling you now, I will leave you. I just said I should tell you down now, so I won't break your heart when I go. But don't worry, where you are going, I've already put one or two things in place to take care of you. Based on love. Based on: this has been a ride and you have blessed me too. You no go dey lonely without me, you hear?

Don't worry.

Let's go, let's go, I have important things to tell you.

Okay. Now:

- I don't know if you were also raised on this lesson, but any person or thing or city that cannot keep quiet or keep still *no matter what* is hiding something from itself and from others. Constant noise and movement are tools.
- Èkó knows why it needs new bodies cycling through his body, why it/he needs something to *be*, at all times. Why he insists on worship. If people stop acting and doing what people do, the placepersonspirit will fall silent and lose its mind.

- Every new body is a new mask, is permission, is something giving nothing a right to exist. That is to say, the city needs the performance in order to be itself, the spirit needs praise to be himself, every something needs something else in order to be real. For Èkó to stay real, ghosts must continue to pass as people, but people must also continue to fizzle to ghosts.

- The eyes of a chameleon rotate individually so that it can spot threats coming from both ahead and behind at the same time. The eyes are saviors in that way—and I don't say this arrogantly, but Èkó is nothing without his eyes.

- In fact, even if I do sound arrogant, so what? Who will beat me?

- Every body is a body of water. Our organs are our organs for a reason; our survival depends on their cooperation. Will you survive if you try to turn the water in your body into a spare liver or a kidney or a heart? Of course not. Let water be water. Let a kidney be a kidney. Let a heart be a heart. That's how the body works best.

- A city cannot survive without water. If water turns on the city, it will die within minutes. Its masks will rotate so fast its head will roll off completely.

- Water has gotten furious with the city before. But as with everything, we applied a mask. We overwrote its fury. Èkó went to The Water to beg for one more chance. The Water agreed. When The Water from Bar Beach hurled itself into V.I.'s lap, for instance, that was rage, that was water warning the city. When that strange creature landed on the shore and people hacked at it and ate it even before they knew what it was, that was The Water warning Èkó. After that meeting, Èkó negotiated more time, and The Water went back inside.

- People have said they've seen mermaids on that same beach; people have lost their children to the waves on family days out. The story is that the child enters The Water and the most beautiful creature they've seen invites them to a banquet, seduces them with their greatest wish, tells them, *Come with me, I'll give you the best food you've eaten; I'll make your sibling well; I'll give you gold and silver; after you nothing bad will happen to your family for a decade, you won't be lonely anymore.* And the children go, because children go where their hearts go, and their parents suffer the void.

- Life goes on even after people go. So, even after The Water made its rage clear, people still continued to go there to take photos. Couples wait until dark to fuck in the sand a few feet from where some people have stabbed a cross into the ground. The prayers pray their incantations in the distance; twirling as directed by the Holy Ghost, fetching holy water to carry with them, saying under their breath as they walk: *It is well, it is well, it is well.* And it is—it always is, if you don't turn sideways.

- When I said Èkó has only one senior, Money, I lied.

- The people didn't make The Water. Water was here before all people, before Naira, before the country had a name. It was here before the city tried to turn into a megacity, before Èkó lost sight of the hierarchy of spirits, before Èkó forgot that he is not sovereign, that even before the need for currency, there was Water.

- You know about my relationship with him, but Èkó has made worse and more interesting enemies than me. What one wrests out of God's palm must be reclaimed: Bodies. Water. Lives. Bodies of water. That's life.

- Once, after I left, I dreamed that The Water had come back for its things, for her things. The waterkeepers said enough was enough. Throughout the whole dream, Èkó was retching water. And in that water there were millions of girls and boys and vagabonds.

- How Èkó thought of it: Take The Water. If it growls, add more sand. Add more sand. Mask its mouth, cover its face, insist that it forget its fury. Lay a foundation thick enough. Seduce it into keeping quiet. Scrape the sky with all that zinc. Yes. Yes. Yes. Look at our body now; we're getting bigger and thicker and more visible. When they look this way, they won't be able to miss us, even if they try. They'll have to worship us. One look and they'll fall to their knees, they'll have to bow.

I asked him about it once. I said: "Do you know that one day, The Water might get irreversibly furious and you won't be able to return her hand?"

Leave her, he said. *We have a contract. Who of note has she killed? She knows who to take when she gets angry. She knows not to touch my anointed.*

- Sometimes I wonder about the other spirits he made. I know some have left, but others must still be there. I wonder if any of them are thinking what I always wanted to say: You can't be the poverty capital of the world and be a megacity all at once. If 80 percent of your body is suffering/withering/dying, then you are killing your whole self. You cannot afford to ignore that much of you. Sure, there are those who have plenty, but how many are they? What will their money do when you're facing a problem money can't solve? They'll do you like you did your father. They'll carry their things and leave to find new homes. But why say that, even, and risk being thrown out? Èkó knew that already. And he knew that I knew he knew. He reeked of that fear daily.

- Things I wish I'd said: Why are you so obsessed with having? Having everything will not give you a self. You get a self by standing still. By listening. No matter how much you want to tie this world to your chest, you cannot own it. You cannot own a thing that is older than your life.

Sometimes I wonder if it would have made a difference. If he would have listened. But he taught us all—with consequences to match—that there are some things you don't say to your elders, no matter how right you are.

- People will survive every time you try to kill them. But they will also get more beastly.
- Again, you don't say some things to your seniors, no matter how right you are. You tuck your rage in; you hold your insight against the roof of your mouth and you walk away.

I once saw a boy ask a pastor when he thought the world might end. Not what date, but what time of day. Would the world fold in the morning? Would it ride the height of the sun? Would it all unfurl at night?

"Only God knows, my boy," said the pastor. "But you know what? I think it'll be night." I agree. It made sense. Something as drastic and disruptive as a world closing has to sneak up on you. It has to be theatrical. A whole production.

- People say fear the night, because that's when bad things come out. It's not necessarily true. Unmasked things come out at night. True things. But truth is a horror when you're not done hiding. Whatever cannot come out during the day finds a way to show its head at night. People know this. That's why the ones with extra eyes always pray at night. It's a way of bolting the doors between this realm and the other, of sealing the entrance.
- People don't watch the right things. If they did, they'd know that most of us have our own midnight face or name—something we answer to after the day folds, a potential Something Else we could become.
- There's a thing the good book says that Èkó believed in strongly: *Bring up your child in the way they should go, so that when they grow up they will not depart from it.* And you know what has always fascinated me? The parents who say this say it as justification, right after they've broken their children's spirits, when the rage is still hot and the child's face is still wet. The *spare the rod and*

spoil the child types. The *for your own good* types. Èkó is their leader.

- Not everybody will survive their children becoming them from the inside out. What a person wants so desperately to believe about themselves is not the same thing as what is true. When people say they want their children to be *more* than them, they mean better than them, smarter than them, richer than them because they think they can choose what gets passed down. They can't. Some children's only goal is to be crueler than their parents.

- And na from clap dem dey enter dance.

- By now, we're so close that we are almost one. Anything I can see, you can see also. Search your body well and you will feel me when things are clicking inside you. I'm with you always.

- But remember, if anybody asks you where you heard all this, I don't know you. You don't know me. Our lives have never touched. We've never met before.

- If you smell me anywhere or see me out of the corner of your eye, don't even wave. Turn right as I turn left. Find a quiet place to stand.

- Hold your own eye there, my friend. Know its worth and trust it.

WITCHING HOURS/THEY WILL NOT DEPART FROM IT

December 32, 20XX

00:45 a.m.

"Sharp sharp," the devil said, from Brainbox's shoulder as he climbed the ladder. "Make it snappy. You know time is not on your side."

"Boss abeg shift," Brainbox replied. "I need full concentration for this P abeg." The devil almost startled him, and he couldn't afford that. He'd spent months thinking of how to execute this assignment, concentrating harder than he'd ever done in this life. He had to; one of the most important parts of today was in his hands. Everyone was trusting him.

"Ah ah, small play?" the devil asked. "Someone cannot play with you again?"

But this wasn't the time for any of that. They'd all nominated Brainbox, because honestly there was no one in the city, working on anything tech- or engineering-related, who could run this better than him. "Quote me," he used to say, when he was still a young apprentice

in Computer Village. "Anytin coding or anytin electric no fit wise pass
me. I go learn all." But now that he was older and knew to let the work
do its work, he didn't have to say it with his mouth. His mother was
right about that scripture she'd recited over him every day when he
was young: *Your gifts shall make room for you and you will stand before
kings, not before unknown men.* A non-graduate like him, he'd stood in
front of all sorts of people with all sorts of titles. If anybody knew the
workings and wirings of the city, it was him. He had gained that trust.

"Are you sure you don't need help?" the devil asked, already inside
his right ear.

Brainbox almost jerked. "No, Baba abeg. You know me, I ask when
I need help." He could feel his knees shaking. This was the longest
ladder he'd ever been on. If the devil made any sudden moves, he
could fall down disastrously. He wasn't lying about the help thing.
The few times he'd needed to arrange one or two things, he had asked
the devil earnestly. But not today.

"Fine," the devil said reluctantly. In the last two years alone, it had
watched Brainbox execute some of the most complicated projects, from
a vote-hacking system commissioned by some rich citizens tired of
waiting for change, to the largest high-security safe made on the con-
tinent, to ensuring twenty-four-hour uninterrupted power supply in
the outermost part of the city where the money really was, right down
to sex robots. Still, at this point, any fuckup would crush the reputation he'd worked on for a decade. The devil could push for that if it so
pleased, but frankly, it was more interested in seeing what Brainbox
could do.

At the highest rung, Brainbox opened his scissors around the thick
black wire in front of him. "Breathe," the devil said from his collarbone. Brainbox's chest was tight, so he couldn't talk. He just shook his
head.

"Do you want me to go?" the devil asked, one last time.

Brainbox nodded.

"Use your words," the devil said. "So you won't blame me later if it doesn't work the way you want."

"Yes," Brainbox said, stilling himself, his voice weighted. The scissors stayed open in his hand. "I don't need the help today. Please. I want to feel this one for myself." When the devil looked up at his eyes, at how sober they were—more so than he'd ever seen—the devil got the message. That was growth: being able to do damage without needing someone or something to blame it on.

"Oh, by the way," Brainbox said, readying his hand to cut, "if you're bored, go and meet Johnny. He has his own assignment too. He'll probably need you more than I do."

The devil fled, Brainbox cut the first wire, and half the city turned black.

00:50 a.m.

The politician and his boys were swimming at his guesthouse when the phone rang. They were about to start another lap when one of the boys called out after him, "Baby, where are you going again? Don't you stop working?" His voice was always perfect. The second one didn't talk much.

"Fine," the politician said to the boy, who spoke and kissed him. "Fine, I won't take it." The politician had gotten the boys for himself as a sixtieth birthday present—commissioned Brainbox to do it. They came back, made to his exact specifications: *Tall, thin, beautiful fingers, long eyelashes, able to do exercises, waterproof, strong necks, great mouths, and yes, tight. But I don't just want a hole, I want a boy with a voice. Almost real, you know? Almost real.* Brainbox being himself, it was done in no time.

There was no harm in it, right? Since the politician couldn't sleep with real guys—he swears to God it's because he hates real ones who are *like that*, but really he just doesn't want to have to look at them after what he's said on television, in interviews—pretend boys would do. Pretend boys couldn't *turn you into* anything; they're not real so they can't make you *like that*, where *like that* means a common . . . vagabond. Even if they could—and you did a mad thing like fall in love with them—they wouldn't be *able* to tell anyone. That's what robots were: obedient machines.

"What are you thinking about, baby? Give me your attention while I'm still alive," the first boy whined, looking the politician in the eye, a tide of want in his request. There was a red ring moving slowly around his iris. The politician hardened as the boy's hand met him under the water. He looked at the second boy. Both their batteries were low. He looked around, just in case, but it was still mostly dark, the way he liked it. He pulled Boy 2 in for a kiss and sent Boy 1 to his knees. A quickie, then. Both their mouths found him gratefully, and they worked like they were on a cruel clock, as if they, like him, were scared of when they'd have to go. He liked their exhaustibility; it felt almost human. When they touched him like this, their full focus on every inch of skin, he felt loved. Was that insane?

He was trying to focus on what they were doing to him, how good it felt, but he could smell something familiar—wet and metallic— and it kept sending him back into his head.

A lot of his friends had "boys" like these, too, so it had to be okay, right? They were just big man toys that fed off electricity. The total cost of these two was expensive, way expensive, but not enough to put a meaningful dent in his account. It was a rich people thing, he told himself—this thing of following technology with your pocket—not a sexuality thing. When you're rich and bored, you need sophisticated toys. It mattered, too, for him to have many. Even as he was out here swimming, the house was full of his politician friends, testing out the others in rooms. There were real boys there, too, all masked. But he couldn't afford to be seen there, just in case. He considered himself a radical: people shook his hands in the streets every single day for

standing for something, for doing *the right thing*, for insisting that vagabonds be taken down, jailed the moment they were found. There were
people behind bars in his name, bodies in the ground in his name
because they'd fallen on the wrong side of the appropriate. That was
the right thing to do . . . right? That's what God would want.

Ugh—what was he doing thinking?

That smell, that smell again, that distracting smell took him away
briefly, but now he was meeting the back of Boy 1's throat for real,
and *Good heavens*. His mind evaporated, and the next time he blinked,
he felt close, close, close.

"Harder," the politician said to Boy 2, who looked up hungrily
from his nipple. The boy tried to fight his slackening mouth. Boy 1's
eyes were beeping mad, like he might just die right now, but the politician needed his mouth now more than ever, needed to get what he
wanted before that. Obedience was also a rule.

Just as he came, both boys' eyes went dead and their jaws jammed.
He heard it: that crunch, that crunch, before the pain started for real.
The red smell got taller, its babbling more furious and he knew. Even
if he could force their mouths open right this minute, they'd already
bitten in too deep. The pain put a definite image in his mind: his
penis, gone; his nipple, gone. How would he explain? Who would he
blame? He'd signed the contract that warned him about this possibility, this risk. He tried to thrash out of the water, but that stubborn,
accusatory red only insisted on its rage as the mouths on him kept
him locked. Fuck!

He tried to call out for his houseboy James, but no one came. He
cried to himself, begging, realizing that nothing was coming to save
him. All the lights in the house seemed to have gone out. Where was
Musa to turn on the gen?

Who knew?

He went out with pain between his ears and loud screams from the
house like a thousand hyenas cackling.

01:00 a.m.

"Shift," the devil said. It found Johnny squatting over the cemetery ground, shovel in hand, beads of sweat on his forehead, digging ground. There was little resistance on Johnny's part when the devil offered help—he was exhausted already. He'd brought some bodies—bones really—out of the ground already and they stood, lifeless, against the wall where he placed them. That part was only physically hard, but now he didn't know what to do next. Besides, his voice wasn't there, he had nothing to say anything with. But he was the one to choose for this part of the job because he knew where bodies were buried, what with his old job and all. He knew the ropes when it came to discarded flesh. What he didn't have, though, was the devil's ease, the devil's experience in raising the dead.

The devil filled Johnny's body, spread and then flexed Johnny's back while clearing his throat. Letting the shovel fall out of Johnny's right hand, it stood up straight and stretched again.

"Eyss you!" the devil said, using Johnny's voice. The voice cracked like what it was: something unused for years. Livinus jerked to attention at the sound of Johnny's voice. Johnny didn't even know his voice worked. The devil beckoned at Livinus to come close. Livinus hobbled toward Johnny, growing flesh as he moved, knowing also—suddenly—that he had been taken over. He shouldn't be able to move otherwise. Even the way his shoulders sat was different. "I've forgotten your name again," the devil said. "You got a new head?" There was a ring around his new neck to mark the memory on him. He, too, didn't speak, so he nodded. The devil stretched out Johnny's hand and Livinus held it. He nodded at the devil, smiling nervously with his new mouth. The devil went in through his fingers and expanded deftly. This was the widest the devil had been in a while, occupying two bodies at once, but it needed all the hands. When it put weight in all four legs, it felt the sadness under their feet, deep inside the ground.

"Who here wants to live?" the devil asked, projecting both Johnny's and Livinus's voices at once.

The bones against the wall wiggled from side to side and the ground stirred. The devil took the shovel and broke the earth in the restless places so that the bones could rise with ease. It squatted both bodies in different positions, stationed in front of bony bodies now sitting up, whispering something inaudible. Using both bodies, the devil began to breathe on them and their bodies quickened, becoming fleshed out in seconds. By the time the devil stepped away, both Johnny and Livinus's bodies felt dizzy. Too much power had come out of it; it had to let one body go or they'd both fall. The devil slipped out of Johnny through his nostrils, staying in Livinus's body alone. Johnny came back into himself and shook his head, clearing his eyes. He couldn't believe what he was seeing. The ground had crumbled in parts, and now there were full-blown bodies walking toward him, their eyes dead and flat. But they could move. They walked slowly, which was expected after how long they'd been in the ground. But they could move! Johnny's bladder was so full, he was trying not to pee his pants.

"Let's go," the devil said to the risen and their bodies obeyed, moving ahead.

Johnny hesitated, looking at stretches of unmarked ground. His throat was sore for some odd reason. But that was what told him the seal had been broken, that his voice had been used.

"We didn't get everybody," he said. It sounded strange in his ears.

"We did," the devil said with Livinus's broken voice.

"But look," Johnny said, pointing at undisturbed ground.

The devil squinted at him with Livinus's eyes, which were irritated slits. "The rest didn't want to come," the devil said, with Livinus's voice, closing the case.

Johnny lingered quietly beside the body, aware of the devil's presence in him.

"Oh," Johnny said, after some silence. "Thank you, by the way. For the help." Then, "How did you know where to find me?"

"Is it important?" the devil asked. It was so strange to be reunited with his love, knowing it also wasn't him.

"I'm just asking," Johnny said.

"It's not. What matters is that we lead them to where the rest are, that we give them the night they deserve." The devil turned Livinus's new neck to find two bodies lagging behind. "Oya, new-lives, walk ahead of us, we will be behind you, so we don't lose any of you." The two quickened their steps.

They all marched forward without a word, huddling in close to each other, making a small crowd. In the dim light, they looked like heavy shadows. "They're happy," Johnny said.

"Of course," said the devil. "People deserve to be greeted well when they reenter the world. It's love that makes a person; it's love that makes a life. You did well."

Johnny nodded. He didn't have that much history with the devil, but this time felt different: the devil was next to him now, using his lover's body to talk to him instead of just wearing him. He could *see* the way the devil wore a face, how well it could ride a borrowed jawline.

"By the way," the devil said, keeping his eyes on the bodies in front. "Let this be your last warning." Johnny looked at Livinus's face, wondering what was coming. The devil hardened the eyes, making them stern. "Never ever in your life try to dig a body from the ground that you yourself didn't put there. You want to upset Death? Or you want to make the ground open for you? Unlike you, the ground knows how to use its mouth. And unlike me, the ground doesn't always give second chances when it gets angry. What were you thinking?"

Johnny's eyebrows sank. He had been sent to go collect the dead. How else was he to do it?

"No, I'm actually asking," the devil said. Livinus's voice had gained a warning weight. It scared Johnny. The devil saw this and paused. Then he added, in a gentler tone, "Do you know how violent that is? You cannot force a person to want a life. Especially if you don't know how they died."

Johnny hadn't considered this before. He nodded earnestly.

The devil opened Livinus's mouth to talk, but he saw Johnny beg with his eyes. "Good," the devil said and fled, leaving Livinus to his love.

Livinus looked at Johnny, still dazed, then ahead at the bodies walking. "What happened?" he asked, surprised at his own voice. He waited. He was expecting to disappear, maybe to lose a head again. But nothing happened. "I can talk," he said. "I can talk!"

Johnny tried his own voice, just to make sure it was still there. "You can talk," he said, glee filling his body. Even if just for tonight, to be able to hear each other, it saved their hearts.

Livinus moved closer to Johnny and whispered, looking at the new-lives as they marched on. "Wait, but that cannot be all of them, na? That cemetery was huge." Livinus said. "How come some stayed back?"

"Well," Johnny started, remembering the warning on Livinus' face just some minutes prior, when he wasn't the one behind it. "Not everyone is us. Some people want to stay dead, and we have to respect that."

01:20 a.m.

Baba lifted the mirror, trying to get through. He held it in both hands and blinked three times, then began. "Keeper of my head," he said, his voice full of reverence. "You who is wiser than the earth, you who is older than the sun, who will outlast the world, I greet you o. I'm here. It's me your son again. Please, I beg you, let me see you one more time. Please, show me your face." Usually it took her a few seconds to show her face—ripples and waves spreading far and wide. But now she was gone. Where her face should be, he was looking at his own.

Just some days ago, when she'd told him she was leaving the city, that she was taking everything of hers with her, he knew she could do it. She could do anything she wanted, being the lifesource of the world, the one with whom no living thing could make enemies. He'd served her all his life. Now, even at ninety-eight years old, as his business was moving, she was his anchor. She'd taught him how to make drugs from his mind, according to what he felt the city needed; she'd taught him how to make secret potions other dealers couldn't replicate; she'd trained his mind. What his customers didn't know from their dealings with him was that his powers didn't come from him. They came from the deep belly of the water, from the kingdom underneath everything. Yes, he knew he was helping people, but on a night like this, when no business was allowed to go and he couldn't stay distracted, the darkness was frightening for him.

"Where will you go?" he'd asked her the last time they saw each other.

"It doesn't matter. You can't go there." She'd warned all her children about this day, when the lights would go out, when the city would stop moving, when smoke would rise into the air, and in her place there would be a sharp red. "Besides, you are done with your work here. What are you still waiting for?"

When he couldn't answer, she disappeared and dark water turned to glass. Baba was jarred by his own crying face then and put it down. Tonight, more than anything, he could feel the silence of his life. There was nobody scurrying around; all his workers were frozen exactly where he'd paused them. Baba unstacked his four phones from the armchair where he'd left them earlier. None of them had signal. He didn't like to admit it, but even he relied on the city's need, fed off its addiction, this hunger for elsewhereness, this *here but not* feeling they could only get from him. That was his defense against death: the work he had left to do. Ninety-eight whole years alive, and each time the reaper called him he gave the same answer: *Come back later, I'm still working.* His god negotiated on his behalf and who could return her hand? *Everybody knows that without drugs, Lagosians zombie immediately,* she explained. It was one of the core needs of the city, along with water, music, dance, sex. Without those distractions, as she'd told him before, Èkó's masks would rotate faster than the speed of light; the city's neck would snap right off.

The reaper respected Baba's keeper without hesitation. She was everybody's senior. Even Genesis recorded her as being there before God: the face of God moving over her. So, "Leave it," she'd told the reaper about Baba in a clean negotiation. "Èkó's cup will soon be full. And when that day comes, you will know. You'll be free to take those who owe you." The reaper had agreed. Today was that day.

"I'm ready," Baba said into the air, fear and all, surrendering everything.

He knew the reaper had stepped forward when the air raised the hairs on his neck and arms. He closed his eyes and waited for the cold hand on his shoulder. It wasn't a hand at all when it landed: it was a warm high wave, a final reminder from the owner of his head, that as easy as water ebbs and flows, the spirit comes and it goes.

01:35 a.m.

Thomas was coursing through the upside-down when it got dark. He'd seen what looked like a pilgrimage of spirits walking toward Third Mainland Bridge, and he was curious about where they were going, so he planted his feet on the road's shoulder. Under his feet, he felt a pull he hadn't felt in who knows how long. But that pull was unmistakable—it meant he was being called to the downside-up, the other world mirroring his. Thomas tried to resist, but it only pulled his feet down harder. He did what he knew he had to: he spread his legs apart, then folded himself at the waist, his eyes open, watching. A call this strong usually meant a test.

The city flipped then, and Thomas was standing outside a church. He waited for an instruction, but there was nothing but the pastor's voice, drawing sinners in. The church was packed and dark, and there were ushers going around giving people lit candles so that they could see each other. Crickets chirped in chorus outside.

When he got to the mouth of the church, Thomas entered and sat in the back pew. "Welcome," another spirit whispered beside him. "You picked the right seat. This is where they keep the freaks." Thomas didn't want to talk to the spirit, so he looked straight ahead and began reciting stories to himself—the ones he still believed—so he could look as if he were praying.

"Fear not," the pastor said into the microphone, cutting them short. Thomas exhaled with relief. "All the witches are at work," he continued. "You know these are the hours when they operate, when they go about hosting their meetings. They can take the light, they can cause a citywide power cut, but that won't stop us. Our god is the head of all principalities and powers." The church hailed and applauded. "You know why we passed the candles? Because the scripture says the light shineth in darkness and the darkness comprehendeth it not! Now let us go into the spirit." The church cheered, then there was a burst of language in the air, people calling down the fire of God in between strings of words. "Begin to speak, begin to speak," the pastor yelled.

Thomas didn't know what to say, but he sure as hell wasn't going to open his eyes. If he could ask God for one thing, what would it be? He thought hard about it. He didn't know what he would ask God for; he'd never felt entitled to God's answer. In the meantime, he didn't want the rascalspirit listening to his prayers, so he switched his think-

ing to the dead language he'd earned as an inbetweener, as a citizen of
the other side. (Each person had one and could only be understood by
whoever they taught that language to out of trust.)

At first, he said gibberish in his language, because weren't some of
these other people doing that too? But then he started getting terrified by all the violent prayers around him about enemies dying. He
needed to focus on something. Anything true.

Whew, okay. *God is love*, he thought. *Yes, I believe that. Yes.* So he
kept saying it, looping the tail of the last word to the head of the first.
God is love. God is here. God, He is love. God is just. God is love. God is.
And just then, he felt the air change as God entered. Goosebumps sped
up his arm and the back of his neck tightened. Something was breathing on him. *God is love. God is here. God is just. God is*, Thomas kept
saying, his eyes shut tight, his terror growing ceilingscrapingly tall.

Who brought him here? What did they need him here for? *God is
love. God is just. God is.* He let himself go and a new tongue entered
his mouth. The same words over and over again, in that ancient language that had died and come back more times than anyone could
count.

The candle flapped in his hand like a small bird, and Thomas
shifted uncomfortably. He didn't open his eyes, because he'd heard
that people could not see God without being destroyed and he wasn't
ready for that.

A few rows away, Idris was trying to text May: Bitch, I'm bored out
of my mind abeg. People dey here dey catch Holy Ghost and me I'm here
thinking of jollof rice. God safe us.

You fool, May replied. Aren't you in church? Or are you just there to
mark register?

I mean, if pastor can be right in God's eyes after all he's done, then who
am I not to come and chop New Year blessings? If him be pastor, me suppose be Angel Gabriel. In fact call me Gabriel from now, he typed, but the

signal had died. The message didn't send. The woman next to him was falling to her side.

He was trying to restart his phone when a gust of bright heat swept beside his ear, eating his candle flame. It was the color of fury, made of fire and shaped like a bird. The church gasped. To Idris's right, there was an identical firebird flapping on the other side of the church. Idris looked down at his hands and saw darkness. The church fell to a shocked hush as the firebirds seized each flame, growing in size as they moved, swallowing the light and becoming it. They burned like mean suns.

The congregation tried to look away from the birds, at each other, but their necks couldn't turn. This interruption happened while they were in the spirit, the middlespace, and they needed to stay there until God was done unfolding. They had called, after all, and by now they had to know that God could come as anything They pleased: a celestial body, a stick, a bird.

The pastor's mouth creaked ajar, though no word came from it. The firebirds waited on either side of him, illuminating the stage for the church. Trying to block the punishing light the birds were giving off, a second sight was opening inside him. He could see everything and nothing at once. His eyes turned backward in their sockets, and a soft bouquet of optic nerves spilled out. The church's stomach fell. The pastor could see the inside of his body stretching wide. And those in the church could see it with him, because they had grown eyes where it mattered.

The first thing the pastor vomited was the same shade of brown as dead earth: the plea of a girl from the church, still ripe and young. Wet with a should-have-been-heard begging, it rang throughout the church, throughout Christ's apparent body, and leaked into His wounds. The next thing was a gray blob: from an old woman who'd been told not to go back to hospital because she'd been healed. She died because of it. And then quicker: cries and sobs and grunts pouring out of his mouth. The church reeled in shock. Was this their head? Their leader? The person they'd been trusting with their lives?

The firebirds didn't wait for them to answer that. They were from a holy body, here on assignment. They headed straight ahead, straight for his head. And what a hell that meeting was. There were big-boned and insistent pleas pouring out of him, the sound of *something's wrong*, of *someone's wronged*. They hacked at him with their sharp beaks until he met his knees, their fire forming a lake. Nothinging skin, leaving bone.

Thomas thought he might collapse. Idris peed himself. When the firebirds were done, they flew toward the high sill to contemplate their next move. The combined light from them at that height almost boiled the room. The two birds flew out into the sky. Thomas, the only one unfrozen, followed them with his scared eyes. The birds faced each other, their eyes sparkling. They cocked their heads in sync. Too many places to be at once. Then, in a single blink, they split themselves into a thousand furious firebirds, dispersing in the sky.

01:45 a.m.

"So, what, you're building a nightmare? For everyone?" one of the fairy-godgirls asked Bankole, the head dreamweaver in charge. "What about people who don't deserve it?"

The whole bridge was on lockdown, and they were under it as usual—seven people on the loom working on this terror, this night, with the best storytellers, loophole-finders, rescue workers, and tech-heads.

Bankole smiled at her. "Hello, smallie. It's not a nightmare," he said. "It's a dream."

"How?" she asked. Of all the girls, she was the most fascinated by the dreamweaving. While her friends focused on troublemaking and playing rough games, she liked to sit and watch him work or read or recommend books. He'd asked her name before, but she told him she didn't know and she didn't seem to think she needed one.

Bankole itched behind his ear. His fingers looked like they'd been working for hours. They had. "Dreams are . . . intelligent," he said, his voice patient. "Dreams know their way. Dreams know who to latch on to and when. A dream never arrives too early—even when you don't yet understand it—or too late. A dream can appear to a thousand people, and all of them will experience and interpret it differently. All of it boils back down to their mental and biological coding, or where they are in life. We use a technology here, too, which makes sure that this dream, like each individual destiny, is bespoke."

"Oh," she said, "so how come some people on the tapestry look like that? Like they're in pain?"

"Oh, these ones? They are," he said, his hands weaving at a quicker speed. Now he was working on a different scene, one that involved so many people they looked like pencils; working so fast his fingers were a blur. When the whole scene had filled out, he held the loom still and his back straight. "Now, what were you saying?" he asked.

The girl moved her ears back, tightening her forehead. "Hm," she said. Something had changed. "I was asking about the other one, why some people looked like they were in pain there. But these ones don't. They look happy, like they're dancing."

"Yes, because they are. That's a concert happening now at the stadium there. More than two thousand people. It's the biggest scene I've worked on tonight so far. The music they're listening to is okay, but at some point, the Musician will go and take this artist over, and the crowd will go crazy."

The fairygodgirl had always been fascinated by the Musician. It was wild to her that someone dead could live forever if they wanted to, if they had made something vital, something that people loved. Because of his work, he had more flexibility than most of them because he could slide around bodiless as a massive consuming energy and then go back to hovering. He was maybe her favorite thing about being dead. He sang to them for free all the time.

"Wow. Can we go?" she asks.

Bankole let out a small laugh.

Another weaver interjected. He had a whole head of gray. "See your mouth," he said adoringly. "It's not going to last all night. After the Musician gets there, we'll cut their music and then he'll leave the artist whose body he took and come back to us. Shey Guard said we'll have a concert here? Victoria?"

The weaver with the black lipstick nodded. She was busy with her hands.

"Yaaay," the fairygodgirl said. "But wait. So, what's the point of cutting this other concert?"

"So people can get still."

"Why?"

"Because if you want someone to notice something important, you need to take away all their distractions. Music is one of the distractions in the city. Without music, what happens? Like this: What if there was loud music here and you were dancing, and the music stopped. What would you do?"

"Stand still and wonder where it went?"

"Exactly. Now imagine two thousand people wondering that same thing at the same time. What do you think will happen?"

"They'll get angry."

"Exactly so." He beckoned with his head for her to look over his shoulder. She watched from behind him. "Now, see, we've taken the lights out already, but people are still hype because the sound still works. The Musician will probably wear this guy soon, and the crowd will see the transformation.

"The only way for this to work is to make sure it happens at the exact moment when either the musician is getting tired or the crowd is getting restless, when people are shouting the lyrics at the top of their lungs. That's when we cut the sound. Because that's when people have let themselves go, when they're throwing themselves at the song in surrender. At that point, when the sound disappears, everybody freezes. It's like being stuck in a lift, but in open space, of course, with air. You can't run anywhere."

"And then what happens?" another fairygodgirl asks, circling Bankole.

"Then people can't look left or right the way they do. They can't mind other people's business. That's the point of the dream: What will people become if they have to mind their own business instead of other people's business? If they can't find others to hate, to kill, to target? What happens if light, music, drugs, sex, everything all disappears and all you have is you? Do you like you? Can you survive you?"

"So they have to think of what they've done. They have to hear their heads."

"Exactly. They also have to look at who they are."

"And how long will it last?"

"Just until the sun comes up. But once you see yourself, you can't unsee yourself. So that's more than enough time."

The girl was dissociating, with that faraway look in her eye, when the loom started to shake. The energy in the stadium had gone insane. Bankole steadied his hand back on his work, his eyebrows furrowed. The Musician had arrived.

"I need to focus right now. This is a crucial part. And no. If you stand over my shoulder, I'll be distracted. Go there, go and see what *she's* weaving over there."

01:50 a.m.

The fairygodgirl was on her way to the woman Bankole showed her when she walked by one of the weavers, the one who looked most idle of all. Looking over her shoulder, the fairygodgirl staggered back horrified. This woman's whole side of the tapestry was a deafening red. It had a too-familiar texture to it. The girl's eyes shone with shock. "Wait. Excuse me, ma, why is there so much . . . isn't that . . . isn't that *the sea*? Are you turning the sea to . . . blood?"

The woman cackled and there was no kindness to it. She clearly wasn't the type of person who believed children deserved more softness. "Me, I didn't do that oh," she explained, lowering her voice so as not to distract the others. She told the girl she was just an observer, not a weaver, even though her work was just as crucial, if not more so. "I'm just here to watch the consequences and alert the rest if anything looks too wrong."

"Explain it to her," Bankole said without looking up.

The woman cleared her throat and eyed him. "Fine," she said. Only as a favor. She scooted over on the bench, making space for the girl. "All of this is happening because all the water in Èkó has left. When something as essential as water leaves its place, a void is created. And where there is a void—"

"—it must always fill," the fairygodgirl said. She knew this well and she was proud to show that. "A void will always fill because nature abhors a void. And the bigger the void, the bigger the thing that comes to fill it."

"So you're an efiko?" the woman said.

"She's obsessed with books," Bankole said. "She has a book for everything."

The fairygodgirl smiled hard because he was right. She had learned void theory reading Ann Daramola's work, holding the words to her heart like scripture.

If the woman had been a more curious person, she would've asked the question in her heart. But this was a child and she had nothing to prove, so she said, "Do you have any more questions?"

The girl took her time to think, sweeping her tongue across her teeth. "Hm. Okay, so where did the blood come from?"

The woman pinched her nose to keep from laughing out loud. "Oh, child, that wasn't a problem. It's like you said, the void fills. And what fills it? Whatever can, abi. Whatever is the right shape or quantity. As it is, in this Èkó, we've spilled enough blood for it to have been enough to fill the sea."

The girl went closer. The sea *was* full.

"That's like . . . a miracle!"

"Well . . ."

The girl was facing the loom at large. The woman beside her nodded. "But instead of wine, it's enough blood for the bad people to see what they've done."

"Exactly," Bankole said from where he was. He stretched. Clearly, he'd done what he wanted to do successfully. He called her close with his hand. "Now do you understand? We're not *doing* anything to anybody except showing them themselves. Only the people who have too much darkness inside will struggle. Only those who have been privileged enough to be able to ignore blood will flinch at the sight of it. We have to see blood almost every day, don't we. They get to turn their faces every day. But that's between them and the blood they shed. We can't control that part."

"Is it also going to happen to us?" the girl asked.

He held her by the arm and softened his voice. He was going to try to explain this as well as possible. She could understand anything if it was explained properly, with her brilliant spirit and soft moon of a face. "Who looks harder at themselves than people who the world is always hunting?" he asked. "Nobody. We're always watching ourselves because we have to. Tonight, we get a break and they get a few hours in our shoes. They get to feel how painful it is to be a person who can't escape the fact that they're alone or hated or hunted, while we get to have what they have every other day: no fear. Whether this is a dream or nightmare depends on who the person is and what they have to hide, do you get? At the end of the day, people are their own punishment. What is unfair about that?"

"Nothing," the girl said, getting it completely. This was another lesson the Seer taught too: power needed to be *taken*, not begged for. The girl thanked him and made to leave, but then turned back around. "One day," she said, "when I grow up, can I learn how to weave dreams too?"

"You can do whatever, love," Bankole said. The girl could see his eyes water. "You can be *anything* you want when you're free."

02:00 a.m.

The guard could smell the weed from the entrance where he was standing, so he strolled toward the people making the banners. It had to be them. Rascals.

And, of course, smoke poured out of Seun's mouth.

The guard held his hands behind his back. He had a gold walking stick on him for when it got too dark for people to see him coming. "Why are you smoking igbo in front of these children?" he asked. Seun saw only his eyes and teeth, but who else would it be?

Seun hissed. The guard brought out a torch and lifted it to his face. "Are you drunk?" he asked.

"Ah ah. How far now? Na fight? Abeg drop the light abeg." The guard held the torch there, just to remind Seun who he was talking to. Seun laughed, defeated. "Oya boss, you know say we don dey on ground since na. Don dey arrange up and down. I don finish my share. So we suppose begin enjoy na. Based on say the motive for this night na freedom."

The guard turned the torch off and looked at Rosa. "Look at your boyfriend," he said. She was busy sewing the edge of a banner that read WE MULTIPLY. Her new friend Nkem was also there with her girlfriend, Hauwa. The two of them were working on the first part,

which read WE DON'T DIE. She'd met them at the suya joint one public holiday and talked for hours, canceling beer bottle after beer bottle. She knew from that night that she could trust them with anything.
It's why she invited them.

"Boss, you dey mind Seun?" Rosa answered. "You know say Seun
no get sense na. But we're working, we're working." She kept her eyes
on her hands, trying to hide how low her eyes had gotten.

"There are children here," the guard repeated, as if it were possible
for them to have missed all the girls playing ring-a-ring-a-roses.

"Bros," Seun said. "Look. They've seen worse things. I mean, they're
already dead. Wetin I wan do wey do wey worst past death? Is it not
me you should be worried about? With what they've seen they're the
ones that can corrupt me sef, based on say I still dey alive."

Rosa bit the insides of her cheeks and held her breath. This fool!
The guard tried to keep a straight face, he really did, but finally he
laughed. "Fool," he said, strolling by majestically. "If not that I love
you ehn?"

They all waited for him to take enough steps away before they
burst. Mid-laugh, Rosa gestured at Seun to pass them the blunt.

02:20 a.m.

"But isn't revenge demonic?" another of the girls asked. The fairygodgirl who'd started this conversation was explaining what she'd just
learned from Bankole to the rest of them. They'd all gathered around
discussing it, bright-eyed, until this question stopped them cold.

The girl who asked the question was squatting in a corner. She had
a long nose and a thick bush of curls. Small and folded in on herself
like that, her wings fanning out behind her, she looked like she could
be lifted into the air at any moment.

"There's nothing more righteous than a story that insists people
look the truth in the eye," the girl said. "Nothing more frightening to

them than invisible people growing bodies, nothing more terrifying than permanent mask-wearers showing their real faces, their real bodies." She felt like a teacher and she liked it. "For some people—the kinds who believe the world should belong only to them—a dream like this is a worse hell than hell. But that's not on us now, is it? That's their own hate working on them."

"Do you also write dreams?" one of the girls asked her. "Why do you know so much?"

"No, but Bankole let me watch as they were being made, so I know some of the rules."

"Tell us one of them," another girl said. They were enjoying this circle.

"Well," the girl said, cracking her neck on both sides. She loved reciting books. "Lesson one is: What you exclude in the writing of a dream is just as important as what you include. Number two: The effect of a solid dream should last longer than the night it happens in. It should stalk the body, even awake, until a change is made. Number—"

The guard approached them. "Oya oya oya, that's enough talking now. Don't you already have what you're doing?"

The girls all stood up, gathering themselves.

"Where is your head girl?" he asked.

"She went to get something. She's coming back now."

"Oya hurry hurry hurry, time is not on our side."

02:30 a.m.

The guard turned around and clapped loudly to get everyone's attention.

"Everybody should get to the bridge by 3:30 a.m. The Musician will be performing for those interested. There'll be photographers, too, for those who want to take photos. Brainbox has blanked all the billboards and found a way to broadcast photos there. You'll get to see yourselves on the big screen. Never ever say I don't try for you, capiche?"

"Yes, sir," they all yelled back and began chattering again.

"Shhhh, quiet down!" the guard said. "One more thing: you're allowed a plus one if you want. If you know somebody who will need this night but might not know about it, find them. Bring them. No fools, of course. No bigots. No people-eaters. No blood-spillers. We are all trying to have a good but safe night. Now go go go."

And bodies scattered into the night.

02:40 a.m.

Rain was told not to use this spell unless absolutely necessary. *God believes and prioritizes children*, she was told. *So be careful what you ask for.*

She knew exactly what she needed. She stopped by the side of the road, looking at the black stretch ahead of them, and all the other girls stopped too.

"What's happening?" There was no way they could go. Rain thought: *Fire is also light.*

> *Mirror, mirror on the wall,*
> *Who's your dearest of them all?*
> *Mirror, mirror on the wall,*
> *Gather the hands that didn't hear no*
> *and light our way by burning them all.*
> *Mirror, mirror on the wall,*
> *please and thank you,*
> *on behalf of all.*

Eleven torches of fire materialized in the thick dark almost immediately. One for each girl, to light the way forward.

02:50 a.m.

They'd been working tirelessly all night. Rain had dispatched girls in different directions.

Some of them were still deep in the city rescuing underaged house-girls, children raising children on behalf of their neglectful parents. Some of them were posted to various girls who needed a single wish. Men dropped to the ground like flies as those wishes were granted. The rest of the girls were pulling girls out of buildings.

There was no right time, one of the girls decided. "Rain," she said.

"What?" Rain answered, marching forward.

"I was just thinking . . ." she said, her voice low. "Will God be happy with what we just prayed for?"

Rain slowed down to let the girl catch up to her. Calmly, she said, "Whose god? Does your god care more about men than little girls?"

The girl paused at the question. "But some of those men are people's dads," she said.

"Well, they should have thought of that when they were touching other people's daughters."

One of the girls was walking with a weight in her legs, lingering right behind Rain, trying to find the right moment to ask her a question. Rain continued. "Do we not also have parents? Are we not also worth protecting? If my father did something like that, I'd want him to go down too."

The other girls huddled closer, listening.

Rain's steps got more agitated. She had so much to do tonight. The fairygodgirl next to her sensed her fatigue and took over.

"Look," she said. "Rain is right. Let's forget about grown men and their babyish behavior at their big old ages. It's scared girls who shouldn't be alone, and that's why we're doing what we're doing to-night. It's scared kids who need friends fashioned from their own ribs, who deserve helpers like us. Any good God should know that."

Rain looked around. "Are we done now? Or does anyone else want to tell me we're monsters for wanting justice?"

The girls were all quiet, their faces lit by the fires still blazing in their hands. They looked stressed out, anxious about the ice in Rain's conviction.

"Okay, my tone was off," she said. "But I'm not saying this to attack anybody. I'm saying it because where we're going we can't afford to have doubt, or the miracle will not work." She was right and they knew it. To do something as big as what they were about to do, they had to add faith to faith to faith. "So," she asked. "Are we all on the same page?"

"Yes," they all said, in true chorus.

03:20 a.m.

Under the Falomo Bridge, girls stood on the base of the giant pillars that underpinned the span of the bridge. The government had commissioned an artist called Polly Alakija to paint girls under the bridge, in honor of the 276 Chibok girls who were stolen by Boko Haram. It had happened right under everybody's noses. Some were later found, but more than a hundred were still missing. Sometimes the fairygodgirls had storytime there, under the bridge, so that the lost girls could also hear them wherever they were. It was a point of contact. Maybe stories couldn't bring them back from wherever they were being kept, but stories could at least help them sleep at night.

The girls in the paintings under the bridge weren't allowed to sleep. They were painted with eyes open, watching the city, forcing the city to watch them too. What hadn't they seen? They'd seen everything. All sorts of things. In no time, people started standing next to them to take photos for their Instagrams, because the pillars matched their outfits, forgetting what the paintings meant in the first place.

Sometimes the painted girls radiated sadness when the fairygod-girls touched them.

The best part about the paintings was that they still looked alive. Just paused. Just caught. It gave the fairygodgirls hope. Tonight, they couldn't be sad. Tonight, they had to be able to join the party too.

Rain stood in front of the group. She was this project's head girl for one simple reason: There were things she knew to be true; faith could move mountains. Even more important, where most of the fairygod-girls had been flesh and blood before, Rain was made entirely from faith herself, which meant she could move anything that was willing to be moved. So, following her instruction, they recited all 276 names in reverence. Each of the fairygodgirls had been asked to memorize twenty-five by heart.

"If you claim you want friends," the guard had told them. "Then show yourself friendly."

After all the names had been spoken, they allowed a moment of silence. Then Rain asked the paintings, "Who here wants to come with us?" Then she turned around to her posse. "Please, guys, I need you to go around and listen to the pillars. If you hear any movements, or see any of their eyes light up, you can hold them until they come down. If it doesn't work, call me. Okay?"

Being a fairygodgirl meant granting wishes like this. It meant call-ing stolen girls back from their captors' hands. This was one of the most important things they had done together. The girls in the paint-ings started to climb down one by one, hand in their helper's hands. Most of them were out by the time Rain came back around.

Three fairygodgirls called Rain's attention. They each had the same question: "She isn't coming down. What do we do? Does that mean I don't have enough faith?"

Rain touched each of the three pillars. They all felt the same. Neu-tral. No movement, no new light. "Leave them," she said, her voice folding in on itself. "They want to stay." Sensing the girls' sadness at the same time, Rain drew closer and said, "It's okay if you want to stay. I'm so sorry this happened to you."

The girls remained still. The moon was sleepy-eyed above their heads, and here the fairygodgirls were with new giant friends who were eager to know where they were going. They'd slid down the pillars right in front of their eyes, surreal colors swirling all over their arms, materializing in the flesh. Where to go?

Finally, just for the thrill of it, they decided to run down Awolowo Road. You should have seen them: fairygodgirls and lost-but-found girls, their hair haywire against the sky, breeze speeding against the backs of their necks. They looked like angels.

"Wait," three more giants yelled from behind, from inside the paintings, catching up with them.

03:33 a.m.

"Let me tell you people something," the Musician said, slowing his roll after the first song. "All oppression is linked, shey you know? So tonight, we're going to dance like vagabonds. We go troway leg, troway hand, sweat go full all our body. You know why? Because we're alive. You know why? Because we are free. Because we pulled this shit off. Because nobody bad reach us. We will dance the way we're not usually allowed to. You know why?

"Because, like this beautiful couple here, we all deserve love o."

The camera panned to Bimbo and their girlfriend in front. Bimbo was a psychic who dedicated their life to predicting where the Musician might show up next. Ninety-nine percent of the time they were right. Being at the Musician's concert, and being shouted out and blown up on a screen, made them feel ready to burst.

Right before the Musician restarted his set, he took off his shirt and put it straight into Bimbo's hands. The front read VAGABONDS. The back: INCORRIGIBLE VAGABONDS!

"Oya na, let's go, let's go," the Musician said, and the music lashed into the air like a hungry whip.

04:00 a.m.

Junior was singing along to the Musician's song when another boy tapped him and said, "Hey, the V word is a bad word."

"Not to me," Junior said.

"No, it is," the boy said. "It means something bad."

"Not to me," Junior said again. The boy was irritating him. He just wanted the music. He was here at last, with people who were claiming the word, and no one was getting hurt for it.

Gold overheard their conversation and butted in. She had the prettiest eyelashes on. "You're wrong," she said to the boy. "Tonight, vagabond means *free person*. Look around you."

"But I thought . . . waaaait a minute. I thought . . . my mummy said that—"

"Shh, child," Gold said. "I'm one and I'm telling you. So is he. When you get home, teach your mummy that you don't argue with someone about the meaning of their name."

04:10 a.m.

"Me I don dey taya o. I'm ready to go and be dancing," the observer said. They were back under the bridge for the last bit.

"Last one," Bankole said. "Abeg help me watch closely."

The observer was drinking a neat glass of vodka. "Why am I looking at people's wardrobes?" she asked.

"Local babe. That's a closet."

"All join. What are we sha doing here?"

"Didn't you see how many vagabonds came out of these earlier? Oh, you weren't here when Victoria was working on that. She opened them and people crawled out. I almost cried. Imagine that. There's a whole world, and people are being forced to live in closets."

"I know," the woman said. Something about the vodka was making it too hard for her not to feel, which was her usual default. Suddenly, she wanted to cry too. She wanted to be sad. But being flippant was easier. The whole point of dying was so she wouldn't have to feel pain. "Okay, but why are we here now if they already came out?"

"You'll see."

She didn't look convinced.

"What else do people keep in closets? Or rather, what do closets *hide*?"

"Come o," she said, squinting at him. "You be examiner?"

"Just answer."

"Err . . . drugs? Stolen funds? Or, wait, . . . homophobic politicians?"

"Well, close. You're about to see."

She watched him as he straightened his back and began plucking at the loom. His hands were flying fast and his eyes were growing wider.

The closets all burst open and skeletons of all sizes began staggering out.

"What the fuck?" the observer said, dropping her glass on the floor. She became hysterical. It was a laughing shock.

Bankole was smiling, clearly pleased with himself.

"See that large one? That belongs to one of our VIPs. And that one, to the right, is the minister of tourism."

"As in what do you mean? The guy don die?"

"He was sworn in, already dead. You didn't see the list of ministers? Dem full inside."

"Mehn this country dey mad o."

"Na today?"

One of the skeletons shimmied and its hipbone shifted out of its socket. It looked unfazed, like it could gather itself back together if it came to it. "Wetin this one dey do?"

"Oh. He clearly thinks this is a pageant."

"Pageant ke? Wetin concern skeleton with fashion parade?"

"Oh. When politicians from other countries come to Èkó, they host skeleton pageants just for the fun of it. To see whose is taller, bigger, more impressive. Whoever has the ugliest or most unique skeleton will move up in rank."

"*What?*" She looked closer. The loom was shaking furiously. "What the fuck—are they running?"

"Yeah."

"Where are they going?" she asked, afraid now. "I hope not here."

"Nah, we sealed both ends. Anyway, our job on this is done. They'll be on the roads in the morning. Let's go back."

The observer got up and then stumbled. "Careful," Bankole said, holding her. "Don't step on any glass."

"No but guy, I no fit lie. You're a fucking genius. Your brain na weyre brain. Thank God say thunder strike you o. How else would you have this kind talent?"

"Well," he said, "when life shows you pepper, make pepper soup."

04:20 a.m.

"Tell you something funny," Divine said, leaning into Daisy. "As that photographer tried to take my photo just now, I almost hid my face. I thought: What if the photos leak and my family sees me? Then I realized I'm not wearing a mask. My family hasn't seen my real face in years."

A sadness passed between them, which they immediately blanketed with laughter. "Fuck," they said together.

"It is special, though. To see people's faces tonight. Most of us have hidden so much, we don't even remember what we look like under. This is a day to remember."

One of the girls behind them said, "See, I saw my face for the first time in years while I was dressing up to come here. If we can see us and still love us, then we're okay, right?"

"Exactly," Divine said. "This dream was made for us too."

"Yeah, it's for us too."

"What time do we have to leave to be safe?" the girl asked.

"Whenever we're ready," Daisy said. "Tonight is a game changer. We now know we have nothing to be ashamed of. And they know that we know that now. They cannot make us unknow it."

"Anyway, it was so good to meet you guys," Divine said to the girls behind them, and she and Daisy drifted off hand in hand.

"I'm going to go home after the sun comes up," one girl on the left said. "Just to see what it feels like to walk the road without fear of being jumped or killed or dissed. I'd like to feel it."

"Me too," the other replied. She tried to think of how to phrase what she wanted to ask. "We could, um—I don't know, walk together if you want?"

"Hm," the other girl said, catching the hint. "Sure."

Divine and Daisy were moving closer to the stage. Agbon waded through the crowd to get to them. There was a stunning woman on her arm. "Oh," she said. "Guys, meet Toju. Love of my life. Toju, meet Daisy and Divine."

They both squealed. "Finally, we can hear word! My God! She talks about you *all* the time!"

Toju smiled shyly. "Hello. Where were you guys going?"

"Oh, just to the front so we can be closer to the music. I like to feel it here," Daisy said, pointing to her chest.

Agbon looked at Divine and said, "These ones will get along. Oya let's be going."

On their way to the front, the photographer took a photo of Daisy, Divine, Toju, and Agbon smiling in full for the billboard, beaming back at them. The flash caught their faces. On the billboard behind, Toju disappeared but for two stunning red eyes.

Daisy and Divine turned to her. "What the fuck?"

"Sorry," she said. "I just like to do that for fun. Okay, fine, another one."

04:30 a.m.

The fairygodgirls hovered over the party for ten minutes before the guard caught and warned them. "Oya, go to your side of the party jare. This place is for adults." They flew away gleefully. The wingmaker had also dressed the lost-but-found girls.

04:40 a.m.

"Sometimes," Thomas was explaining to a small crowd of people who had overheard him talking to a frightened man, "the problem isn't that you don't have faith. It's that you have too much faith in the story you've been told. What if everything they told you about yourself is not true? What if you're not a sin? What if you're not dirty? What if you're worthy?" People in that small crowd were seen weeping as the Musician's music washed over them. "If anybody here feels like they don't have any doubt of their own," he continued, "let's all close our eyes. Just raise your hand for me and I'll come to you."

He tapped the people who had raised their hands and they formed a circle together, holding hands, repeating the same words. "What they have told me about me is not true. I put my doubt in that and my faith in what I am. What I am is worthy. Worthy."

Thomas had learned his lesson fully now. Being doubtful was not a sin, he realized. One just had to doubt the right things.

5:00 a.m.

The sun was starting to rise, and Adura didn't want to be out when it did. She leaned forward to try to find Nkem and Hauwa, but the crowd was too wild.

Just then, a man appeared beside her. "I'd know a Wura Blackson any day," he said near her ear.

"Oh my . . ." Adura said, flustered. He'd scared her.

"So sorry," he said.

"No, it's okay. I just . . . Hello. You're, uh—you're correct." She'd been thinking of Wura at just that moment. She could often be found imagining exactly what Wura would be doing at any given moment, but she hadn't expected to hear her name spoken aloud. It was Wura she was running home to write to.

Then his own attire caught her eye. "That's her, too, isn't it?" she said, knowing it from just the neckline, which dipped down his sternum. His dress was mostly sheer.

"Accurate," he said. "Teniola is my name. Teniola Jones. You?"

"Adura," she said.

"Can I say my name too?" a voice said, cheekily. Adura's eyes bulged in shock. She'd know that voice anywhere.

"Sure," Mr. Jones said, looking down in the direction of the voice.

Adura tried to turn to catch that voice.

"Mama!" Rain said, coming around Adura's body to face her.

The man looked up at Adura after noticing Rain's dress. "Ah ah, is this a WB party?"

"Isn't it always?" Adura said, still trying to gather herself from seeing Rain. Her heart was thumping.

"I knew I'd see you here." Rain's new face was Wura and Adura combined, like they had made this baby together after all. Rain threw her arms around Adura, who leaned down and sobbed into her neck.

"My baby," she said.

Behind them, the last billboard came on and fireworks exploded across the city. The Musician played an unreleased single, "Don't You Know You Love You?"

By the end, all three of them were crying.

"That was everything," Mr. Jones said. "Everything."

Adura still hadn't found her voice. All she could do was nod and smile feebly. "I've never showed anyone this, but look," Mr. Jones said, nudging Adura.

"What does that say?" Adura asked. He put his wrist in her hand and Rain leaned closer. On the inside sleeve of his boubou, Wura had embroidered a message by hand:

If anybody deserves to live, it read in the coming light, *it is us. It is us, after all this dying we have done.*

ACKNOWLEDGMENTS

I'm thankful, always, to my first readers and community, the people who deepened my belief in this book, who remind me why I wrote *this* work in the first place: Akwaeke Emezi, Fadekemi Abiru, OluTimehin Adegbeye, Nwando Ebeledike, Mercedes Onyemenam, Joshua Segun-Lean, Kaisan Rei, Keside Anosike. To Cal Morgan and Kish Widyaratna for your incisive editing, patience, and brilliance—line after line after line. I'm so grateful for how clearly you both saw this work and how seamlessly you worked together to get it to where it is. To Keaven and IIIrd for holding my hand on the mountains and in the valleys. To The One Who Owns My Head, for teaching me the texture of tenderness, for never scolding me through what You could hold me through. To my brothers, the miracles, for being themselves. To Silvia Anie-Akwetey and Dolapo Igboin for being my sisters. To my parents, for the lessons. To Lagos, for the bridge behind me. To the entire Riverhead and Fourth Estate teams, for everything. To my agents Jacqueline Ko, Kristi Murray, and Alba Ziegler-Bailey and the entire team at the Wylie Agency for championing this book and being forever ready to push it where it needed to go. To the journals and publications that published stories that appear here: *The Paris Review, The Georgia Review, Berlin Quarterly, Guernica, Gulf Coast, Somesuch Stories, Catapult*, etc. This work got tighter and became more itself under all your hands. To vagabonds everywhere for being impossible things living impossible lives. Finally, to the young who (have) want(ed) to die, for believing, for hoping, for reading, for staying.